"People change,"

Annie said defensively.

Trace's laugh was harsh. "They sure do, Annie. Look at us. Everyone expected me to be in prison by now, or six feet under. And you were supposed to be destined for greatness. Who would have thought I'd make more money than a hundred people could spend in a lifetime, and you'd end up here?"

She met his gaze. "Trace, I wouldn't trade what I have now for anything in the world."

"Is that so? And what exactly do you have?"

Annie swallowed convulsively. "I have work that I love. I'm making a difference to the girls I help."

"All spiritually fulfilling, I know. But aren't you forgetting to mention one other tiny thing you have that I don't?"

"What's that?"

His eyes narrowed, and Annie felt a sinking sensation.

"You have our daughter." Trace's voice was jagged with hate. "And I want her."

Dear Reader,

The weather's hot, and here at Intimate Moments, so is the reading. Our leadoff title this month is a surefire winner: Judith Duncan's *That Same Old Feeling*. It's the second of her Wide Open Spaces trilogy, featuring the McCall family of Western Canada. It's also an American Hero title. After all, Canada is part of North America—and you'll be glad of that, once you fall in love with Chase McCall!

Our Romantic Traditions miniseries continues with *Desert Man*, by Barbara Faith, an Intimate Moments-style take on the ever-popular sheikh story line. And the rest of the month features irresistible reading from Alexandra Sellers, Kim Cates (with a sequel to *Uncertain Angels*, her first book for the line) and two new authors: Anita Meyer and Lauren Shelley.

In months to come, look for more fabulous reading from authors like Marilyn Pappano (starting a new miniseries called Southern Knights), Dallas Schulze and Kathleen Eagle—to name only a few. Whatever you do, don't miss these and all the Intimate Moments titles coming your way throughout the year.

Yours,

Leslie J. Wainger
Senior Editor and Editorial Coordinator

Please address questions and book requests to:
Silhouette Reader Service
U.S.: 3010 Walden Ave., P.O. Box 1325, Buffalo, NY 14269
Canadian: P.O. Box 609, Fort Erie, Ont. L2A 5X3

A FATHER'S CLAIM

Kim Cates

Published by Silhouette Books

America's Publisher of Contemporary Romance

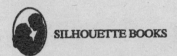 SILHOUETTE BOOKS

ISBN 0-373-07580-4

A FATHER'S CLAIM

Copyright © 1994 by Kim Ostrom Bush

All rights reserved. Except for use in any review, the reproduction or utilization of this work in whole or in part in any form by any electronic, mechanical or other means, now known or hereafter invented, including xerography, photocopying and recording, or in any information storage or retrieval system, is forbidden without the written permission of the editorial office, Silhouette Books, 300 East 42nd Street, New York, NY 10017 U.S.A.

All characters in this book have no existence outside the imagination of the author and have no relation whatsoever to anyone bearing the same name or names. They are not even distantly inspired by any individual known or unknown to the author, and all incidents are pure invention.

This edition published by arrangement with Harlequin Enterprises B. V.

® and TM are trademarks of Harlequin Enterprises B. V., used under license. Trademarks indicated with ® are registered in the United States Patent and Trademark Office, the Canadian Trade Marks Office and in other countries.

Printed in U.S.A.

KIM CATES

is an incurable fanatic, addicted to classic tearjerker movies, Chicago Cubs baseball, and reading and writing romances—both contemporary and historical. Married to her high school sweetheart, she divides her time between her writing career and enjoying her daughter, Kate, from whom, Kim insists, she learned everything she knows about the temperament of royalty.

For Aunt Peg,
with love

Prologue

Annie...

Just the echo of her name shouldn't hurt so much after nine years. The barest whisper of her voice shouldn't rake open a hundred old wounds, make them fresh again, bleeding.

Trace McKenna fought against waves of darkness, pain reverberating through every fiber of his body. But he would have endured any torture to escape the sounds that taunted him, tormented him.

God, Annie, it hurts, he moaned inside. *Make it stop hurting.*

But Annie wasn't there for him. She never really had been.

Trace gritted his teeth, dragging one shaking hand across his face. He had to hold on to the truth. The ugly, jagged truth that still ripped at the emptiness inside him.

Annie had betrayed him.

Nine years ago she had walked away—from Arizona, from countless scholarship offers, from her parents, and from the seventeen-year-old boy who had gotten her pregnant.

Trace twisted, a guttural moan tearing from his throat as a white-hot poker seemed to shoot up his right leg, his arm slamming into something cold and cylindrical at his side. His fingers closed around it, and he identified it by touch, the way some men would the steering wheel of their sports car or the breast of their lover.

A hospital bed rail.

Trace cursed. How the hell had he ended up in a hospital bed again so soon? He strained to remember, images flashing through his mind. A Texas oil well spouting flames—someone yelling that a tanker of God-knew-what kind of flammable stuff was about to go. The world disappearing in a blinding flash. Trace remembered the sensation of being hurled through the air, then darkness.

How many times had he awakened this way before, gingerly feeling arms, legs, trying to see if they could still move? Did it matter? He'd always ended up the same way—in a hospital. Alone.

That was the way Trace liked it. Granted, he'd had more than his share of hospital roommates with adoring wives and children, but Trace had long ago learned to block them out. He'd given up his right to children with cookie-crumb-dusted smiles and bandages decorated with cartoon characters. He'd refused the comfort of a wife fussing over him, loving him.

He'd decided to pay that price long ago. Penance for the child that would never be. Bitterness over the woman who had betrayed him.

Trace muttered an oath. Hospitals were the one place the emptiness closed in on him, where the solitude—not loneliness—of his life was drawn into irrefutable focus. He hated the damn places with the smell of antiseptic and sickness, with the lowered voices and frigid linoleum.

Trace grimaced. If this hospital was as rotten as the one in Kuwait, he'd get the hell up and walk out the minute he could open his eyes. Stupid doctor telling him one more injury, one more blow to the head, and FireStorm Enterprises could be looking for a new executive trouble-shooter.

Trace grimaced. As if anyone would give a damn if he'd been vaporized in the last oil-well fire he'd fought or if his parachute had drifted him right into the heart of the forest fire that had struck Canada last year. Hell, his old man would make a conference call to Trace's sisters, and they'd all dismiss the whole matter, saying they always knew Trace would end up in a body bag someday, if he didn't wind up in prison. They'd forget their hard-case brother in time.

And then Trace could forget, too. Death would wipe out the sensation of Annie's butternut-colored hair slipping between his fingers, the feel of her hands on his skin, her mouth searching for his, driving away the darkness inside him and giving him light.

He could forget that Annie had given him a glimpse of heaven, then ripped it away. Maybe he could even forgive her.

But not as long as her voice reached out to him from the dark places of his mind, giving him no peace. Not as long as he clung to the sound of it, like life-giving water pouring down his parched throat after an eternity of battling hellish flames.

That voice had whispered to him a thousand times in the darkness. But this time was different, somehow.

So real . . .

A sudden sharp burst of static pounded against Trace's ears, Annie's words were lost as a nasal voice suddenly began discussing "hemorrhoids, that painful, private ailment." Trace struggled to get his mental bearings. What the devil? A television?

Trace swiped one hand across his gritty eyes and forced them open. Mustering all his will, he levered himself up on one elbow.

A hospital room swam into focus, pastel walls, art prints that seemed designed especially to induce nausea, a black television set dangling from a brace near the ceiling. And some jerk in the next bed flicking channels.

"Turn it back, damn it," Trace croaked out.

His roommate leaned to peer around the curtain that separated their beds, and smiled.

"So you finally woke up. The nurse said you were hurt in an oil-well explosion near Dallas. You're some kind of hotshot—"

"Turn the goddamn television back to the station you had it on." Trace had made Third World warlords back off with that tone of voice. This guy looked ready to dive into a bedpan for cover.

He fumbled with the remote. "It was just some stupid news thing. One of those bleeding-heart docudramas about some place near Chicago—"

The television screen filled with jagged lines for a heartbeat, then suddenly switched into focus. Trace stared at the screen, where the picture was divided into a montage of images: a teenager was frozen midair as he tried to dunk a lay-up; another bent over a computer while a blond woman gave instruction—although dressed in jeans and a gauzy peasant blouse, she had obviously been raised on champagne and caviar. The third picture looked like a wall covered with graffiti, while in the last one, a girl of about seventeen lay on her back in lush green grass, dangling a laughing baby above her.

Trace's heart squeezed tight as he searched the girl's features. No. It wasn't Annie. Annie's hair was tawny gold. She wasn't a teenager anymore. She'd be a woman now. Probably a professor of music or something at some highbrow college. The teachers had all been fighting over her, even in her junior year of high school. Besides, the thought was acid bitterness in Trace's gut. There was no baby. Annie had made sure of that.

He sagged back, ready to tell his roommate to put the channel on the blasted Home Shopping Network if he wanted. But at that instant, the montage shifted away to reveal a playroom with a half-dozen baby swings, plastic jungle gyms and slides.

"You have already met nationally known child-advocate, J. T. James, the force behind HomePlace, one of the most celebrated shelters for runaways in the world. Now we wander into the playroom of BabyPlace, a home for expectant mothers. Here we will talk to Ms. Annalise Brown."

It *had* been her voice that had pulled him from his sleep! Trace froze, his eyes locked on the screen as the camera panned in on a slender figure in a big rocking chair, a baby nestled in her arms. The baby's chubby fist was clenched in her shoulder-length hair, and it was drooling on her blouse. Trace felt a stab of anger at the sight of her, cradling someone else's child.

What the devil was Annie doing in such a place, anyway? Volunteering between concerts? Indulging in some kind of weird guilt-induced backlash to what had happened years ago?

As Annie noticed the camera, she smiled with a confidence that surprised Trace. That dizzy sensation Trace had felt every time he looked at Annie shivered to life inside him as she climbed gracefully from the chair and approached the reporter. Hell, Annie hadn't even been able to give an oral presentation in front of a class without throwing up the hour before. This Annie looked as blasé as if she gave nationally televised interviews every Tuesday.

Annie dropped a kiss on the baby's café-au-lait-colored cheek, then tucked the child into one of the motorized swings.

The kid gurgled contentedly.

"Ms. Brown, is this one of BabyPlace's clients?"

"Please, call me Annie," she said with that heart-melting smile, then stroked the baby's soft black curls. "This is Tasha. Her mother is at class right now."

"Finishing her GED?"

"Actually, Natalie is training in computer science. You might have heard of Addison Computers? They are helping to finance her education. They'll be lucky to get her."

The newsman looked genuinely perplexed. "Then what is Natalie doing in a shelter? No offense, Ms.—Annie," he corrected himself. "But I would think she'd have other options."

Annie got that look in her eyes Trace remembered far too well—a little stubborn, a little hot, like her temper was simmering under the surface. She wouldn't yell, or let all that anger out. But by the time she was done, she'd make that reporter feel like he'd just kicked a puppy.

"We're Natalie's family now, Mr. Banes. I'm sure that someday Natalie will be ready for her own place. But for now, she has a dozen adopted aunts and cousins who love her and help her balance building a future career with being a good mother. This is home."

"As it is for you, Annie?"

Trace scowled. This was the last place he'd suspected Annie would be. She'd always tried to fix anything injured—birds, baby rabbits, Kennedy High's star pitcher, a hard case whose life was going to hell with far greater speed than his fastball could get across the plate. But music was her life. Her piano had been so important to her that she had...

A commotion off screen shook Trace from his thoughts, and he stared as another kid barreled into view—this one on her own two feet. Flyaway mahogany pigtails were caught at the end with clips the shape of baseballs. A White Sox jersey skimmed inches above knees that sported two monster-sized bandages.

Trace expected the cameraman to cut to black, or Annie to send the kid scurrying with a wave of her hand. Instead, she opened her arms to the little girl and scooped her into a hug—no small feat since the kid was about eight years old.

The girl's back was to the camera as she twined her legs around Annie's slim waist and held on like a baby chimpanzee. Even the newsman seemed enchanted with the girl's antics.

"Do you belong to someone here at BabyPlace?" he asked.

"Yep. I just totally trashed my bike. We've got this awesome ramp J.T. built in the back. I came down off the hill an' tried to stand on my seat to jump it, but—"

"Don't tell me," Annie groaned. "Your right elbow? It was the only one left without a scab."

"Just broke open the old ones. Do I need disinfectant on 'em before I go back out? Moms are real weird about that stuff, you know."

Moms? Trace's heart stumbled.

"I know how mothers can be." The announcer chuckled. "What's your name, honey?" Even stunned as he was, nothing prepared Trace for the instant the child turned toward the camera. Gray-blue eyes the unique shade of Trace's own danced in a face that might have been a miniature, more feminine version, of Trace's rugged features.

There was the same stubborn jut in the chin, the same straight, dark brows. The grin she flashed could have been lifted out of his own third-grade picture. He felt like he'd slammed into concrete after a forty-foot drop.

"I'm April Brown," the girl said.

April.

The month Trace had made love to Annie.

The month he'd believed in miracles, for just the briefest moment in time.

Trace stared into the face of his daughter, the depth of Annie's betrayal, the reality of her lies, cutting deeper than he could ever have dreamed.

Even after everything that had happened, he had never truly hated Annie.

Until now.

Chapter 1

Sarah was crying again.

Annie hesitated outside the door to the teenager's room. The knees of her rumpled jeans were wet from kneeling in a puddle to drive in a loose tent stake, and one hand was still clutching the wrappers of the new flashlight batteries she'd just taken to April and the three James kids who were sleeping in the backyard.

Annie wanted nothing more than to take a hot shower and bury her head under her own pillow after a day of dealing with hostile parents from Albuquerque, a girl in her seventh month who had been battered by her boyfriend, and one young mother struggling with a baby still filtering crack out of his system.

Instead of heading for the stairs that led up to her private apartment, she raked back the tousled strands of her butterscotch gold hair and rapped softly on the door.

There was a ragged catch in the sobbing, then a small voice. "I'm sorry. I'll be—be quiet now, I promise."

"You're fine, Sarah. I was just passing by. April called me on her walkie-talkie to tell me they ran out of batteries in the tent. And you can't tell ghost stories without a flashlight."

Sarah gave a watery laugh.

"Sarah, I don't want to intrude, but if you want some company, someone to listen, I'm here."

Annie could hear the shuddery sound of another choked sob. "I'm so scared!"

At those words, Annie opened the door to see Sarah curled up in one of the beds. The girl looked barely older than April in her pink, nubby robe and tousled curls. Annie's heart twisted at the sight of Sarah's arms, clutching the teddy bear J. T. James had bought for Sarah's baby, Timmy, the day he came home from the hospital.

If it hadn't been for the bassinet at the side of the bed, Sarah would have looked more at home in the tent with the smaller kids, sneaking candy and holding seances.

I'm so scared, Sarah had choked out. Annie knew the sensation far too well. She crossed to the bed and sat down beside the girl.

"It's okay to be scared," she whispered. "You've been through a lot, and there are a whole bunch of decisions to make about little Timothy—"

"I'm not scared about the baby," Sarah said. "Timothy's great. I'm scared that I'll never forget Johnnie. I love him so much."

"I know." Annie cuddled the teenager in her arms. Sarah's face seemed all eyes—pain-filled, frightened.

"Johnnie said he would take care of me. He promised. But when I told him about—about the baby, he was so angry. I know that I should hate him for deserting Timmy and me. But I keep thinking about him, all the time. I keep—

keep hoping that he'll try to find me. That everything will be all right.''

Annie stared into the darkness, feeling as if she were holding a mirror image of herself. A terrified, rain-soaked, heartsick girl who had stumbled through HomePlace's door seven years ago, April a fever-stricken little bundle in her arms.

"It hurts to keep hoping, doesn't it?" Annie asked softly. "You keep watching the doorway, jump whenever the phone rings. You keep thinking you hear his voice."

"Natalie and the other girls say Johnnie's scum, that I'll meet another boy who will take care of Timmy and me, and I won't even be able to remember Johnnie's face after a while."

It sounded so reasonable, so logical. But there was nothing logical about love. Annie stroked back Sarah's hair, listening.

"Annie," the girl said timidly, "do you . . . do you ever think about April's father?"

Think about Trace? Only every time I look into my little girl's face. Only every time I see the boys at HomePlace playing baseball or hear a song by the Moody Blues. Only late at night, when I'm alone in bed, listening to the night all around me. . . .

How many times had girls asked her that same question? Why was it always so hard to answer? Annie sucked in a deep breath.

"I wish I could tell you that time is a miracle cure that will swipe away the memory of the boy who fathered your child," she said slowly. "But sometimes it doesn't work that way in real life. It gets easier, but no. I've never forgotten April's father."

"What was he like?"

Annie winced. Her memories of Trace were already far too vivid. To take them out and show them to someone else...to put Trace McKenna into words...was it possible? He was a comet, blazing out of control, so beautiful she had wanted to cling to him and fly, ignore the fact that he was burning up with anger and rage and rebellion, destroying himself. She just hadn't realized that her love for him would bring her so close to destroying herself.

"Half the girls at Kennedy High would have traded all their daddy's charge cards to date him. He was tall and lean and his hair always looked like it needed to be cut, and when he smiled..." Annie fought for words to describe that dazzlingly beautiful grin. "Everyone said he was trouble in cowboy boots. But they didn't know him like I did. I knew...he never meant to hurt me."

"But he got you pregnant."

"Yes. He got me pregnant, but it wasn't really his fault. It just...happened."

"Did he feed you some line about loving you?" Sarah asked, swiping at teary eyes.

Annie looked away. "No. He never said he loved me."

"Then why did you—you know, have sex? Because all the other girls wanted him? Bet he was putting the pressure on."

"No. He was hurting. I'd been tutoring him in English. He had to pass the midterm he'd flunked or he wouldn't be able to play baseball. A scout from the Atlanta Braves was coming to see him pitch."

"You mean he played professional baseball? He must be rolling in money."

"Trace didn't ever get to play ball."

"Oh," Sarah said, crestfallen. "Flunked the test again, huh?"

"No. He aced it. He knew it all. He'd worked so hard...." Annie's voice trailed off, the memory of that last tutoring session rippling through her. Trace slamming his literature book closed, then banging it down atop scrawled notes.

I bet I know more about Shakespeare than his mama does, Brown-Eyes. Miss Twigg is gonna have heart failure when she grades this test!

"But if he passed the test, why didn't he get to play?"

"Because the teacher found crib notes under Trace's desk."

"They could've been anyone's."

Annie shrugged. "The rest of the students had taken the test a month ago. Trace was the only one repeating it."

"Do you think someone else could have put the notes there? But then, why would anyone do that?"

"I don't know for sure. Maybe one of the other players did it out of jealousy, or in hopes that if Trace was out of the lineup, the scout might notice someone else. Maybe one of Trace's enemies planted the notes out of spite. However the notes got there, Trace was devastated. Especially when his father sided with the school. I remember Trace demanding that they let him prove himself—take the test over with one of them watching his every move. His father said he'd blown two chances. He didn't deserve another. A month later, the scout called, offered him a private tryout, but by then it was too late."

"Wow. Trace must've been real mad."

"He was so broken up inside that I would have done anything to help him. But sometimes people have to help themselves, you know? Sometimes, no matter how much you want to fix what's broken inside them, you can't do it."

Sometimes they break your heart.

Sarah sighed, quieted. "When I was little and it was storming, I got real afraid. My mom would come in and hold me and tell me stories and everything bad would go away. I miss that more than anything since she died. Can you stay with me for a while? Until I go to sleep?"

"Of course I'll stay." Annie stroked Sarah's hair, her eyes going again to the window. But it was as if Sarah's questions had stirred up old ghosts, set them wandering the night.

Annie stared into the darkness, but all she could see was Trace McKenna's face, anguished, filled with hurt and betrayal. Blaming her for rejecting him. No, Annie thought. She had done what she had to do, for Trace, for herself, for her child.

She just didn't know how it could still hurt so much after nine long years.

Needles of sunlight were pricking beneath Annie's eyelids when a hand gently shook her awake. Every joint in her body felt fused together, every muscle aching as if she'd just run the Boston Marathon—in a way she had. An emotional marathon that was all too frequent. She opened one eye to see the familiar clutter of her own bedroom. Her mind filled with hazy memories of staggering upstairs at four in the morning, to fall, fully dressed, onto the bed.

She expected to see April looming above her, demanding doughnuts and pop or something equally insane for breakfast, but it was nineteen-year-old Natalie leaning over the bed. Just the sight of the girl—one of BabyPlace's success stories—lifted Annie's sagging spirits.

"Sorry to wake you," the girl said, "but there's someone downstairs demanding to see you."

Annie struggled upright, dragging her hand through the tangled masses of her hair.

"Who is it?"

"Don't know. But there's something about him that made me nervous. Like he's real mad, or…I don't know."

Annie groaned. "I thought we'd met our weekly quota of irate parents and pond-scum boyfriends yesterday."

"Sorry, chief. I could tell him you're taking a cruise in Tahiti or something," Natalie offered. "What can he do? Yell at me? My dad did that all the time."

Much as Natalie's offer tempted her, Annie shook her head. "I'll take care of this." She forced a smile. "I eat guys with attitudes for breakfast!"

Natalie laughed. But Annie's sense of humor was definitely diminished when she caught a glimpse of herself in the mirror behind the dresser. She grimaced. One look at her and this mysterious visitor would run screaming the other way.

Her face was pasty, her clothes crumpled beyond imagining. Huge circles ringed her eyes like bruises. She knew she should change, but she couldn't bear the thought of putting on clean clothes until after her long-overdue shower. She grabbed a brush and dragged it through her hair a couple of times, then made her way down to her office.

The door was open. The visitor stood at the window peering down at some abused African violets Annie had been nursing back to health. Fists were shoved deep in the pockets of obviously pricey black pants. Broad shoulders were encased in a dress shirt the color of cream, the cuffs rolled up muscular forearms. He was tall and lean, with a body that would have made a confirmed spinster's mouth water. But Annie's gaze locked on the dark hair tumbling below his collar…mahogany waves that needed to be cut—

Her heart slammed to her toes and she fought the urge to turn and run, to scoop April out of the tent, to hide.…

From what? She was being ridiculous. It wasn't Trace. It couldn't be.

He turned around to face her. Annie couldn't breathe. Every nerve in her body sizzled with awareness, and an answering heat fired deep in his storm-blue eyes. She stared into features rugged and dangerous as a sea-swept cliff, her gaze skimming down to a mouth that was sulky and sexy as any hunk on the big screen.

She'd imagined this meeting a hundred times during the years since she'd left Arizona, with only a few cherished belongings tucked in her backpack. She had listened for the sound of Trace's footsteps, watched for him to come walking toward her with that animal, athletic grace. There were times she would have sold her soul just to see one more of his smiles.

But even in her wildest fantasies, she had never imagined Trace McKenna as he was now. The features that had been so dazzling on the boy were now devastating, hardened into those of a man. His body had filled out with sinewy strength. His hips were impossibly narrow, his legs long and strong, the shoulders she had leaned on as a sixteen-year-old were broad and thick with sculpted muscle.

The rebellious, angry boy was gone. This Trace McKenna reeked of power and danger and success.

Annie thought of April and prayed that the child was still sleeping in the tent. She hastily shut the door, as if she could keep Trace from discovering ... discovering what? That he had a daughter? A daughter who threw a fastball better than any boy on the block? A daughter who didn't even know his name?

No, Annie thought fiercely. Just because Trace showed up on her doorstep didn't mean he knew about April. But it was obvious Trace McKenna had come here for a reason. What was it? Nothing good, Annie was certain. She had to be careful, so careful.

Her heart was thundering in her ears as she struggled to find her voice, battled to think of something vaguely coherent to say. "Trace."

Just his name, quavering faintly from her lips.

"It's been a long time, Annie. I wondered if you'd even remember me."

Remember him? God, she had tried so hard to forget.

"What are you doing here?" she blurted out. Her nape prickled with a sense of menace, something so subtle, so guarded, she hoped, prayed, she was imagining it.

His gaze skimmed from her hastily brushed curls, down her crumpled blouse to the patch of dried mud on her knee. There was a shuttered quality to his eyes, a frightening restraint in that slow smile. "Nice way to greet an old friend, Brown-Eyes."

Brown-Eyes. Annie shivered with the memory of the first time he had called her that, teasing her, always teasing. She had looked up at him so solemnly and told him her eyes were green.

Trace paced over to her desk, picking up one of the awards lined across its front, and Annie was terrified he'd catch sight of the pictures of April she kept under the sheet of glass that covered her desktop. But Trace seemed oblivious, worlds different from the hot-tempered, fiery Trace McKenna she had known.

Annie clung to that hope, but felt as if she were crossing a raging river on paper-thin ice, waiting with each step to fall through, plunge into the torrent.

"I asked what you're doing here," she repeated.

"FireStorm Enterprises just gave me a hell of a bonus and I'm looking for some tax write-offs. You know, toss a little loose change to the downtrodden and stiff Uncle Sam."

Loose change? Annie had seen enough info on Trace McKenna's multimillion-dollar company to wonder exactly what he considered "loose change."

As if he could read her mind, Trace shrugged. "Guess I figured I might as well throw that loose change toward an old friend."

Annie swallowed hard. "That's very generous, Trace, but we're independently funded here. I can suggest some other shelters that would be grateful for your help."

She crossed to the desk, making a great show of scrawling down some notes. The pictures of April were buried beneath mounds of paperwork. Annie silently thanked the Albuquerque parents who had kept her so late that she'd been unable to clear off her desk last night.

"That's one of the great things about being filthy rich, Annie," Trace said with low mockery. "See, I'm used to doing whatever I want, *getting* whatever I want."

A sick, sinking sensation racked Annie's stomach.

"You might as well not bother writing those other places down. I consider my bequest nonnegotiable. It's important to me that the money be used here. Think of it as my way of making peace with what happened between us in Halloran's abandoned stable."

Halloran's stable. Why did the words sound a little ragged on Trace's tongue? Why did they conjure images of that long-ago night with such intensity that Annie could feel the hungry brush of his hands, hear the gritty desperation that had been in his voice?

I've gotta get away from here, Annie. It's killing me, being trapped in this awful town, my father hating my guts, the teachers... I've got nothing here, Annie... nothing. Nobody.

She'd done everything in her power to show him that he was somebody. She'd opened herself to Trace's loving, tried to take his pain inside her, heal him in those few hours when she'd lain in his arms.

Annie looked up at the man, so different from that shattered, anguished boy. She tried to keep the terror from her eyes. "What happened between us was a long time ago. It's forgotten."

"Is it?" Low, rough, his query set Annie's hands trembling. She knotted them together in an effort to keep them from betraying her.

"Absolutely."

"I'm amazed. You were always so damned hard on yourself. Saint Brown-Eyes, never allowed to make a mistake. You really screwed up with me, didn't you?" A shadow of bitterness twisted his lips. "And I don't mean that literally." He sank into her chair and started riffling the papers there.

Annie slammed her flattened palms against the scattered sheets to keep him from brushing them aside. She wished she could shove him out of the door, out of her life. She wished she wasn't so damned scared. "Blast it, Trace, what do you want?"

Trace's fingers stilled, and he looked up at her. A thrill of tension sizzled through Annie. "Maybe I wanted to make sure you were all right."

"After nine years you were suddenly stricken with a need to make sure I was all right?" Annie couldn't keep an edge out of her voice. "I'm fine. Feel free to get the blazes out of my office and get back to the important things in life, like jumping out of airplanes and diving into fires."

Trace rocked the chair back on its rear legs, his brow arching, just the way April's did when she was surprised. "Don't tell me you've kept track of my adventures?"

Her cheeks burned, and she feared he would know how she'd grasped any snippet of news about Trace McKenna and FireStorm, that he'd suspect she'd tried to catch glimpses of his face, sooty and smoke-blackened, exhausted and triumphant, while reporters marveled at the crazy stunts he pulled. They called him a hero. Annie knew he was still trying to destroy himself, only now he was doing it in a way that got him national news coverage.

"Adventures?" Annie said archly. "Don't you mean your stupidity? It's been splashed across the television and newspapers often enough. Feel free to go off and try to kill yourself. You're absolved of any guilt or responsibility on my account."

"Am I?" His voice was so soft, the rustle of leaves beneath a predator's feet. "This place isn't exactly what I pictured when I thought about you these past years. Some dump of a shelter, you playing the Madonna to a bunch of kids in trouble. I guess your gig at Carnegie Hall fell through, huh?"

Annie stiffened. The girl who had spun all those dreams, who had worked so hard over the piano keys, was still hidden away inside her, fragile, vulnerable. Trace's words struck that girl and hurt. "People change."

Trace's laugh was a little ugly. "They sure as hell do. Look at us. Everyone expected me to be in prison by now, or buried six feet under. And you were supposed to be the golden girl destined for greatness. Who would'a thought I'd make more money than a hundred people could spend in a lifetime, and you'd end up here?"

Annie gritted her teeth against the subtle mockery. Even in high school, Trace had been able to level people with verbal blows. He'd had an instinct for finding the raw places in people's souls, maybe because he had so many of his own.

There was a time Annie would have been crushed by his attitude. She was a lot tougher now.

She met his gaze, defiant. "Trace, I wouldn't trade what I have now for all your money or all the concert stages in the world."

Something flickered in his expression. "Is that so, Brown-Eyes? And just exactly what is it that you have?"

Annie swallowed convulsively. "I have work that I love. I'm making a difference to the girls I help."

"All very spiritually fulfilling, I know. But aren't you forgetting to mention one other tiny thing that you have that I don't?"

"What's that?" Annie asked faintly.

His eyes narrowed to slits, and Annie felt the sensation a felon on a gallows must know when the trapdoor drops beneath his feet.

"You have my daughter." Trace's voice was jagged with hate. "I want her."

Annie groped for the back of a chair, trying to shore up legs that were suddenly weak. "Wh—What are you talking about?"

Trace's hands shot out, manacling her arms, his face inches from hers. There was a savagery in his eyes, the look of a man on the edge, just begging for someone to push him over. "What are you going to do, Annie? Lie to me again? You let me believe that you aborted our baby, then you ran away. You made certain I didn't know she even existed."

"Don't you dare act so blasted superior! You didn't want me. You didn't want any kind of responsibility at all!"

"I want the girl now."

Panic clotted Annie's throat. "You can't have her!"

"Is that so? I wonder what the courts would say to that. It's simple enough to prove paternity—hell, they wouldn't even have to do the blood test, just look at her, look at me."

"You've seen her? Oh, God, Trace, how—?"

"I watch the news, too, Annie. I was laid up in the hospital, saw the program on this place. April came charging on camera. What? You think I was too stupid to figure it out?"

"Trace, you can't—can't want to disrupt April's life this way. If you have any feelings for her at all—"

Trace cursed with such fury Annie staggered back a step, truly frightened. "Don't you *dare* start pontificating at me that way. You never gave April and me a chance to have feelings for each other. But that's going to change. She's my child, goddamn you! Does she even know my name?"

Annie swallowed hard. "No."

"What did you tell her about her father?"

"I thought it was better if...I didn't want her to think that...that her father..."

"What? Deserted her? That he didn't give a damn about her?" Those blue eyes blazed with so much pain Annie had to clutch tight to her own terror, her fierce protectiveness of her daughter.

Annie sucked in a shuddering breath. "I told April her father was dead."

Trace's features were bone-white, his body stiff. "Wasn't that convenient for you."

"Trace, I know you want to see April or you wouldn't have come all this way. You wouldn't be so upset—"

"Upset? Lady, that's the understatement of the century."

"Still, I can't believe that you'd want to do anything to hurt April. Children are so fragile. She's happy, Trace. Loved. She has people here who are like family."

He was stalking her, moving toward her with measured steps. "What, Brown-Eyes? You got some other man to play daddy to my little girl? Some bastard who keeps your bed all hot and bothered? Hell, we didn't even have a bed, did we?'' There was cruelty in his voice, harsh, deliberate.

Dangerous. A thousand times she had heard Trace labeled thus. But he'd never turned that blade-edged anger on her until now.

''That's enough,'' she said. ''My private life is none of your business.''

''Yeah, I'm nobody to you. Nobody to my daughter.''

Annie couldn't keep herself from taking a step back. She slammed into a bookcase. Trace moved with dizzying speed, flattening his hands on either side of her, imprisoning her.

He was close—so close she could see the tiny scar at his temple, she could smell the wind-swept scent of him. His breath was hot on her face, his mouth curved with acid mockery.

''Hell,'' he said with an ugly laugh, ''according to you I don't even exist. Maybe I should do something to prove otherwise.''

Annie read his intent in that heartbeat. Wild panic bolted through her. She made a tight sound of protest, but Trace shoved it back into her mouth with his lips, kissing her in savage possession. For a moment, she stood as if in a trance, aware of the fire-hot movement of his lips on hers, the rasp of his breath, the frenzied pounding of his heart and hers. It was worlds different from the kisses she had shared with the boy in the stable. Worlds different from kisses she had experienced with what few men she'd managed to date in the years since then.

Elemental. Primitive. Soul-searing. Trace took things she didn't want to give him, stripped her down to raw vulnerabilities she'd battled to overcome, poured acid regret into the empty place that had been in her heart since the day she'd run away from Arizona and from the unbearable knowledge that Trace McKenna could never be hers.

For an instant there was a pulsing, yearning sense of reunion, but as his tongue drove past the moist-silk crease of her lips into her mouth, Annie remembered the other time Trace had kissed her with this desperate hunger, the repercussions of which had changed her life forever. She was chilled with the certainty that the backlash of this meeting could be even more perilous.

Mustering all her strength, she flattened her hands against his chest and shoved, but Trace hadn't taken his fill of her. His big hands drove through her hair, holding her mouth for his plundering.

"No!" Annie choked out, terrified of her own physical response. "Trace, stop it!"

"Stop what?" He raked hot kisses across her cheek. "I'm not here, Annie, remember? I don't exist. Or can you feel me now? Taste me?"

Tears burned Annie's eyes, and she was torn by the poignant memory of Trace's other kisses, driven by pain and need instead of fury and hate. *"Let me go!"*

"Not this time, lady. Made that mistake before— umph!" A guttural cry of pain ripped from Trace. Annie could feel the impact of something smacking into his back, hard.

Annie froze in horror as she glimpsed a baseball bouncing crazily across the floor. She barely heard Trace's savage curse as he wheeled to face his attacker, both their gazes locking at the same instant on the small figure framed in the doorway.

April stood there in her White Sox pajamas, outraged, defiant as she glared at Trace McKenna with storm-blue eyes.

Chapter 2

The first time Trace had jumped from a plane, some smart aleck had rigged his parachute so it wouldn't open until he pulled the emergency cord. As Trace stared into his daughter's face, he felt the same indescribable rush—bone-numbing panic, rib-crushing terror and an exhilaration that screamed through every nerve ending in his body.

He stared at the child as she dove for the baseball, scooping it up with small fingers. Her eyes sparked with a temper that was all too familiar. "I fire this next one at you, mister, and you'll be looking for your teeth in the next county!" she promised.

If the girl had followed through on her threat, Trace couldn't have been more dazed. His daughter. A part of him he hadn't even known existed until a few weeks ago.

Time seemed to freeze as his eyes roved over soft cheeks framed by bedraggled pigtails. Her coltish legs were spangled with scabs—mosquito bites scratched until had they bled. There was a bandage on her chin, but it didn't disguise the fact that it was a miniature of his own—stubborn as hell, like she was daring someone to take a swing at it. Trace eyed the bandage and wondered if someone had. If so, he had a feeling the other kid looked a helluva lot worse.

He'd never seen anything so beautiful.

He couldn't stop himself from stepping toward her. He reached out a shaking hand, intending to touch her cheek, make certain she was real.

The girl smacked his fingers away from her, but she didn't retreat. "Watch it, mister. Try touching me or my mom again and you'll pull back a bloody stump!"

She was afraid of him.

The knowledge hit Trace like a fist in the gut. He was her father, dammit, and she was afraid of him.

At that moment, Annie snapped out of whatever trance had held her still. She swept by, scooping the child into the protective circle of her arms, as if she expected Trace to— to what? Drag the kid, kicking and screaming, into his car? Blurt out the truth—that her mother was a damned liar who had kept April apart from her father all these years?

Trace clamped his mouth shut, his hands knotting into fists. "I'm not going to hurt you." The words were meant to soothe. But they were roughened by anger, pain and the soul-deep jolt of being in the same room with the child for the first time.

The kid frowned and said, "Yeah, right—you won't hurt me, and a lion wouldn't bite down if I stuck my head in its mouth."

"It's all right, sweetheart," Annie said, holding the girl tight.

"No it's not. You're crying. You never cry. And he wouldn't let you go." If the kid had been a queen, Trace would be on his way to the headsman's block by now. Hell, he hadn't been in the same room with the child five minutes, and she already hated his guts.

"I was just surprised to see him," Annie said lamely. "Mr. McKenna and I were friends. For a little while. A long time ago." Trace knew what Annie was doing. With each added phrase, she was putting as much distance as possible between them. It might even have worked, except that he could still taste her on his lips.

"April," Trace tried again, "I didn't mean to—" To kiss the hell out of your mother? To let my blasted temper run amok? To let you see me this way? Angry? Out of control? "I didn't mean to frighten you," he said at last.

Great move, ace. The instant April's brows crashed into a thunderous line, Trace realized he couldn't have found a better way to alienate the kid further if he'd had a week to think about it.

"I'm not scared of you," April said. "I just think you're a creep. Major pond scum."

"April!" Annie said with that maternal warning tone as old as time.

"It's okay," Trace said. "She's not the first one to come up with that assessment of my character, is she, Brown-Eyes?"

"My mom's eyes are green!" April snapped.

For some reason, Trace's throat tightened. "I know."

"April, Mr. McKenna and I have some things we need to talk about. Why don't you run out and find the other kids?"

April eyed Trace as if to say, I've got your name, mister, and it's mud. She went and cozied herself up in a chair, tossing the ball up and catching it in a lazy rhythm. "I think I'll just stay here. Talk all you want. Don't mind me."

"April, we have private things to talk about. I need you to leave for a little while."

"But, Mom, he—"

"Out, April. Now."

The girl positively reeked of mutiny, but in the end, she stalked out of the room, shutting the door with sage defiance—enough oomph to make a satisfactory bang without overstepping the limits and making her mother angry.

Trace stared at the chipped panel of oak April had disappeared behind. When he had anticipated this reunion in the past few weeks he hadn't expected any kind of fairy tale—Annie in rags, waiting for him to rescue her. April, flinging herself into his arms. He'd figured there would be a certain stiffness among the three of them, an aura of discomfort, unease. But he hadn't imagined anything like the scenario that had just played out in this cramped office.

Rejection. Major-league.

Just like old times, Trace, he jeered inwardly at himself. Considering the fact that Annie didn't want a damn thing to do with him, she must be thrilled by April's reaction. No doubt Annie figured he'd just cut his losses, flip the world off and go back on his suicide quest. But it wasn't that easy now that he had seen April. Touched her. *Now that he'd kissed Annie again,* a voice inside him whispered.

No, he swiped away the thought ruthlessly. It wasn't like that. It had been an impulse, a mistake. . . .

"Trace," Annie's voice broke through his musing. "You can see how upset she is already. Surely you understand now that telling her about you can only hurt her."

He rounded on Annie, his temper a conflagration. "Why will it hurt her, Annie? Not because of me. Because of you, dammit. Because you were so ticked off at me, you decided to wipe me out of my kid's life. She's scared to death of me. But I haven't done a damn thing to her."

"You're a stranger."

"Not by my own choice! You lied to her. You lied to me. You set everything up real cozy, Annie. Just the way you wanted it. And you didn't give a damn about what anyone else might need."

Annie bristled. "I've given April everything she needs!"

"Yeah. Except her father."

He could see her flinch. He hoped it hurt her half as much as he was hurting.

"I did what I thought best," she said evenly.

"Best for whom? For April? For me, Annie? Or did you do what was easiest for yourself?"

"That's not fair."

He swore, a dark, biting oath. "Let's get honest, shall we? Ugly honest. Brutally honest. You didn't tell me about April because it was easier for you to forget I ever existed. Because you hated yourself for that night in Halloran's stable when you let me bury myself inside you."

She was shaking, her slender throat constricting. Trace was tempted to put his hand around it, just to scare her. Scare her the way she had scared him when he was a kid terrified of leaving himself open to anyone emotionally. Scare her the way it had scared him nine years ago when those hands of hers, so shy, so deceptively gentle, peeled away every protective layer that had guarded his soul.

Left him vulnerable, raw, exposed in a way he never had been before, only to fling his fragile sense of trust back in his face and run away.

"You didn't tell April about me because then she'd ask you questions—what I looked like, talked like, whether or not I could throw a goddamned curve ball...."

"I told her about you when she asked—"

"You didn't tell her about *me*, Brown-Eyes. You told her about a ghost. Only you couldn't forget about me, could you? Because every time you looked into her eyes, it was *my* face you saw. Hell, she's even got my arm, doesn't she? Can throw a ball like a blasted bomb—''

"Don't flatter yourself, Trace," Annie said. "If you think I've been spending the last nine years mooning over you, you're wrong. I was a child in that stable—naive, lonely, trying desperately to make believe I was in love. I made a mistake. I forgave myself for it a long time ago. I put it behind me."

God, who could ever have guessed that Annie's melting honey voice could be so cold it would send slivers of ice through Trace's veins? But it didn't matter, Trace told himself ruthlessly. He couldn't let it matter.

"When I found out I was pregnant, I didn't ask anything of you. Now I'm asking something. Leave April alone. Leave me alone. I think you owe me that much."

"Maybe I do." A muscle in his jaw ticked, his temples throbbing with barely restrained fury. He stepped toward her, his eyes narrow. He could only pray she didn't have a clue how close he was to going over the edge.

"But no matter what I owe you, I owe April a helluva lot more. She's my daughter. Someday, when she's older, she's going to know the truth. When that happens, I'm already going to be a part of her life. She's going to know that her father loves her. That he wanted her."

Trace fought back the tightness in his chest, held on to the lump of betrayal, the hard core of hate. "I'll take whatever steps I deem necessary to build a relationship with my daughter, Annie. If you try to cross me, I'll make damn sure you never have the guts to try it again."

Trace turned and stalked to the door. He faced Annie one last time. "I have a place in the Colorado mountains. I want three weeks there with April. Time to get to know her. Time for her to know me. You can either let her go with me easy, or we can make this as ugly as you want."

"Trace, you have to listen to reason—"

"No, babe. *You* have to listen. Either call to make arrangements with me by midnight tomorrow or I phone my lawyer and we can get mean and nasty real fast. I'm in suite 2732 at the Beaumaris Hotel."

"Please, Trace, don't do this." Her voice broke. He felt it in his gut.

He jammed his hands in his pockets, and for an instant, just an instant, he was seventeen again, looking into the meadow-green eyes of a girl he had suddenly discovered could break his heart.

"Don't do this?" he echoed her words as he opened the door. "Annie, you haven't given me any other choice."

With those words, Trace turned and walked away.

The next day, Annie paced the confines of J. T. and Allison Jameses' living room, feeling as if the familiar walls were caving in on her. It had been agony fulfilling the myriad obligations of the workday, then making idle conversation until April fell asleep with the Jameses brood of three. But now, with the toy-littered room quiet, empty of raucous, high-pitched voices, the tension coiling inside Annie seemed to fill the silence with the same inexorably building pressure as the storm threatening outside.

J. T. James braced his chin on his fists, watching her with wolf-gray eyes, while his wife, Allison, picked at a loose button on a stuffed elephant named Ellie-Pants, two-year-old Beth James's favorite toy.

From the moment Annie had straggled into HomePlace with fever-stricken, two-year-old April in her arms, J. T. and Allison had been her family, her staunchest defenders, her most trusted friends. They had praised her for her resourcefulness in finding the hundred and one odd jobs that had meant Annie and April's survival. They had comforted her with the certainty that the only thing April would remember from those years was her mother's love. They had showed her that her life wasn't over. That this was just a new beginning. And Annie had always been certain J. T. would walk through fire to shield her and her child.

She had expected anger on her behalf and on April's. She'd longed for a little of that notorious J. T. James fury, that instinct that had always driven HomePlace's founder to fling himself into the fray for the kids he cared about.

She hadn't expected this crushing silence, the watchful light in those gray eyes, the flush on Allison's cheeks.

Annie jumped as a crack of thunder split the sky, then she raked trembling fingers through her hair. "You might as well just say what you're thinking, both of you."

J.T. turned his chair around and straddled it, leaning his arms across the back. "You sure you want to hear it?"

"I wouldn't be here if I didn't. I value your opinions. You know that." She waved her hands in helpless frustration. "I still can't believe that Trace expects to waltz into April's life after all these years. That he expects to—to—"

"Have a chance to know his daughter?" J.T. finished levelly.

The words stung. Annie wheeled on him. "How can you suggest such a thing? I know you love April!"

"I do. That's why I'm giving it to you straight. Lies never work, Annie. Nobody knows that better than I do. My mother laid out a whole raft of sugar-coated lies when I was a kid. They fell apart. Lies always do. I almost drowned in the anger and the pain. The betrayal."

"I'm only trying to save April from being hurt!" Annie's chest felt brittle as glass, as if the next crack of thunder would shatter her.

She felt Allison James's soft hand against her shoulder. "I know you believe you're protecting April. The question is, what are you protecting her *from?*"

"From Trace! From a man who—who... He jumps out of airplanes, for God's sake. Plunges right into the middle of the worst fires imaginable."

"Is he a physical danger to you or April?" J.T. probed.

"Of course not! The only person Trace has ever tried to hurt was himself."

"Then I think you need to be real careful, Annie. Think this through all the way to the end. The bitter end. Because if you aren't careful, bitter is just what it's going to be."

"J.T., I thought you'd help me. That you would find some way to get Trace to leave April and me alone."

"Suppose I do," J.T. offered. "Suppose I get Trace McKenna out of April's life. Suppose you manage to close the book on him. For how long? Until April is eighteen? Nineteen? Until she's married and has kids of her own? Then, all of a sudden, April finds out that her father is alive. What are you going to tell April ten years from now when Trace McKenna walks back into her life and she knows that he tried to contact her, wanted a relationship with her, but you kept them apart? How is she going to react when she finds out that you—the person she trusts and loves above anyone in the world—lied to her? Told her that her father was dead. And then, when he tried to contact April, you sent him away."

Annie closed her eyes, not wanting to deal with the images J.T. was invoking. "The only thing Trace McKenna ever wanted was to get as far away from Arizona as he could. Trace didn't want me. He didn't want the baby."

"He obviously wants a relationship with April now. I guess you have to decide whether or not you have the right to bar him from April's life. Do you want to be responsible for the fact that she never gets to see her father in the stands when she's pitching a game? That she never gets to hold his hand or listen to him tell about...hell, about anything? His favorite bike when he was a kid, his dreams?"

"Trace never had any dreams," Annie said, but even as she spoke the words, she was remembering that brief window of time when Trace's life had seemed to be falling together. He had told her a dozen times he didn't give a damn about baseball—that the only reason he even went out for the sport was because the coach, Frank Riley, was McKenna's DJT, or Designated Jerk Teacher of the year. For some reason, Trace had found it hilarious that he was an ace on the pitcher's mound and old Riley had to play him. Even though Riley hated Trace, the coach had told him he was a natural, a kid with an arm like a rocket launcher, who could fire a fastball at the major league level if he just applied himself a little.

Of course, Trace hadn't. He'd told Annie that it was a hell of a lot more fun frustrating the devil out of the coach. But something had changed that spring. Annie had watched with quiet joy as the notorious rebel of Kennedy High had channeled almost super-human energy into his pitching, and his schoolwork, pulling his act together in a way that had elated the idealistic teachers at the high school, while it made the more cynical ones tiptoe around Trace, as if waiting for a bomb to explode.

And it had, Annie thought, raising her fingers to stinging eyes. It had exploded with a vengeance the night April had been conceived.

He had aced that test. But instead of congratulations he'd been confronted with suspicion. Suspicion that had hardened into accusations of cheating when the batch of crib notes were discovered beneath Trace's desk. When confronted with such evidence, even Trace's few teacher allies had worn pained, sorrowful expressions. Only Annie had believed he hadn't cheated. She had rushed off to find him, comfort him, tell him she believed . . .

She shoved back the thoughts, ruthless, desperate. No, she didn't dare think about Trace that night, didn't dare remember what had happened. She couldn't risk the crushing sense of sympathy that had driven her to find him that night in the tumbledown stable.

The Trace McKenna she had loved was gone. The man who had kissed her in her office was a hard-eyed stranger. A stranger whose very presence was threatening her daughter, threatening Annie's own hard-won peace.

She turned back to J.T., focusing on her anger. "You're suggesting that I should just hand my daughter over to a maniac with a death wish? Let her love him, knowing that any moment he could jump off a cliff or be fried in some oil-well fire? Do you have any idea what you're asking me to do?"

J.T. rubbed his fingertips across his tense forehead. "I'm asking you to think about this from April's point of view. You've given her everything in your power, Annie. She's a terrific, healthy, well-adjusted little girl. No one is more tuned into the rights of kids than you are. If you trash everything that happened between you and this Trace McKenna, all the anger and betrayal, all you have left is a little girl who has a right to know her father."

"Are you saying that if I don't let Trace see April, I'm cheating her somehow?"

"I'm saying that if you don't let April know her father, she might never forgive you. I love the two of you too much to stand back and watch that happen without saying a word."

"Allison?" Annie turned to the slender blond woman, whose eyes were shimmering with sympathy. "You're a mother. Tell me you don't agree with him. Please."

"I can't," Allison said softly. "Hard as this is for you, Annie, I can't help but be glad for April. April follows J.T. around like a puppy sometimes, looking lost. A little sad. Much as I love you, I can't help being glad that she's getting this chance to have a daddy of her own."

Annie's eyes burned, her voice quaking as she gave voice to her darkest fear. "What if Trace tries to take her away from me? April is all I have."

"He can't take her away from you, Annie," J.T. said. "You can only lose April if you hold on too tight."

The suite of rooms at the Beaumaris Hotel was a study in sophistication and elegance, but there was nothing cool or restrained about the man who paced in front of the huge stretch of window that looked out across the storm-tossed expanse of Lake Michigan. Every muscle in Trace's body was pulled taut in a fever of anger and frustration, impatience and anticipation, a relentless stress that even the scalding, blasting shower he'd taken a half hour before had failed to ease.

Hair still wet, a towel anchored low around his lean hips, Trace prowled the room, holding on to the memory of the little girl he had seen so briefly. In the single instant his gaze had locked on April's impish face, his life had been changed forever.

And Annie—Annie had done it again. She had turned him inside out, left him stinging and raw and uncertain in ways he couldn't even begin to explain.

He'd done his damnedest to intimidate her, force her hand. And God knew, the past nine years he'd had plenty of practice being a card-carrying bastard. But she was so much different now. There had been a strength, a self-assurance, a kind of serenity in her face that hadn't been present in the shy girl he had made love to. Just by walking into that cluttered office, Trace had chipped away at Annie's tranquillity, leaving her drowning in a thousand questions, fearful for April's welfare.

He'd left her life in shambles again, just the way he had in high school. But didn't the philosophers claim that turnabout was fair play? She had turned his life upside down, had given him hope for the first time in his life. Then she had shattered that hope and left him to scrape up the shattered pieces of his life. She hadn't told him about the baby, hadn't breathed a word during those tense weeks when she must have suspected she was carrying his child. And when he had been told, when he'd wanted to fix things, make things right for her, she'd turned away from him, she hadn't believed in him, trusted him, the way she'd made him believe she would. That had been a blow far more devastating than anything Coach Riley, Miss Twigg or even his father could have made him suffer.

She'd laid him out but good, with that kick to what little belief in himself had remained. God knew, he owed his daughter the last drop of blood in his heart. But as for Annie Brown—he didn't owe her a damned thing except anger, contempt.

Then why did he feel like the worst kind of bastard for bringing the uncertainty back into her eyes? For bullying her so shamelessly? Why had he charged back into her life and into April's with all the subtlety and forethought of a shark in a feeding frenzy?

Because he was weak where Annie Brown was concerned. He always had been. If he hadn't been able to hold on to his anger, he might have let Annie push him back out of April's life. He might have listened to her just a little. . . .

If you care for April at all . . . you must see you can only hurt her. . . . Annie's words echoed in his mind.

God, he didn't want to hurt his little girl. He just wanted April to know that he loved her. And he did love her, Trace realized with a jolt. Immediate, blinding love that rocketed through every part of him, leaving a desperate eagerness to get to know her—every mood that changed her pixie face, every hurt that had made her sad, every triumph that had made her whoop with pleasure.

He wanted to pore over pictures of April as an infant, devour every printed image of the child, so he could make believe he hadn't lost so many precious, irretrievable years.

No, not lost, Trace corrected himself with brutal honesty. Years that Annie had stolen from him. And from April.

No matter how deeply Annie still stirred him, no matter how those beautiful green eyes had pleaded with him, Trace could not, would not, allow her to sway him from what he knew he had to do. He wouldn't let April suffer the way he had, certain her father didn't give a damn about her.

But April didn't think of her father that way, Trace thought with a grim twist of his lips. April believed he was dead. Hell, if he'd been five yards closer to that explosion when it ignited, he might well have been. He'd heard more than one person say it was a miracle he was still alive—that he had a cat's nine lives, but that even with that kind of longevity, Trace must have used up his share of luck. His partner, Paul Malley, heir to the FireStorm empire, had been half crazed with worry during the last phone call Trace had taken before he walked out of the hospital.

Malley. Trace grimaced at the swift jab of guilt that nudged his conscience. The guy had been shaken up, bad, over the accident, as if cracked ribs, a concussion and some pretty spectacular bruises weren't everyday fare for Trace. Malley had called the hospital five times a day to check on Trace's condition, and sent enough flowers to fill a medium-sized funeral parlor. A special delivery of the imported candies Trace loved had followed. Malley had gone so far as to threaten to fly in to make sure Trace was following doctor's orders, even though it was Malley's youngest kid's birthday. Trace had skipped out of the hospital before he could follow through.

Trace's mouth curled in a half grin. When the nurses had come to give him his ten o'clock hypodermic full of painkiller, all they'd found was his cast-off hospital gown and a scrawled letter to be faxed to Paul. Trace could imagine Malley's reaction when he received it; the guy would not be amused.

He hadn't told Malley anything—hadn't wanted to give the guy a chance to try to talk him into staying at the hospital or out of going to Chicago. But Trace supposed it was time to put the guy out of his misery. If—no, *when* Trace took off for Colorado with April, he should at least let Malley know not to expect him at work for the next three weeks.

Shaking the long, damp strands of his hair back over bare shoulders, Trace scooped up the phone receiver and punched the number. "Malley residence," a sweet little voice piped up through the phone. "This is Tina speaking. Who are you speaking back?"

Trace had always studiously ignored Malley's daughters. Ignored all kids in the years since he'd left Arizona. Other people's children had only been a reminder of the one child he thought would never laugh or smile or throw a baseball on a perfect summer afternoon. Because of that shadow child, Trace had been certain he didn't deserve another chance at a wife, a family.

Now Trace found himself wondering how April had answered the phone at that age. "This is Trace McKenna. Is your father home?"

"He's berry busy and berry crabby right now and doesn't want to have a damned tea party, even though I put the whole bowl of sugar into the lemonade. He doesn't mean to be bad, but he's berry worried and going to wring your neck when he gets a hold of you. Are you sure you want to talk to him, Mr. McKenna?"

"McKenna?" Trace heard Malley's muffled curse in the background, then a child's cry of indignation. Evidently, Malley had snatched the phone away from Tina because the next thing Trace heard was Paul's voice.

"McKenna? You crazy bastard! Where the hell are you! Are you all right? I've been going insane, figuring you were dead in a ditch somewhere!"

"Yeah, yeah, yeah. I never write. I never call. You sound like my mama," Trace said wryly. "To answer your first question, I'm in a hotel room. But you know how they all look alike. Maybe I've got amnesia or something."

"You're a damn comedian! The hospital staff went crazy when you disappeared! The nurse said you could barely sit up without passing out and that bump to your head was dangerous, man. Then I get that blasted letter saying you were taking up that damned plane of yours—hell, I expected to hear you were splattered all over a cornfield somewhere! When you crashed and burned six months ago, the doctor warned you—"

"Well, the doctor was wrong as usual. I hit my head again, and I'm still here."

"Maybe, but I've had no way of knowing that the past three days. Blast it, McKenna, we're partners. I care about you."

Trace winced inwardly. He'd been at FireStorm eight months, just one more firefighter on the line, when the company's owner, Brock Malley had sent his son Paul out into the field for a little hands-on experience. Old Brock's ruling maxim was that no one could really understand FireStorm without getting their eyebrows singed off in a blaze a time or two. When Paul had gotten trapped behind a wall of flame, Trace had pulled him to safety. Brock had claimed to know a born fire-eater when he saw one, promoting Trace with a rapidity that would've made the other men resentful as hell if Trace hadn't had the skill and daring to back up the old man's confidence in him.

The approval of Brock Malley had been gratifying—especially to a kid whose own father had written him off long ago.

But even Brock's gruff affection had been pale in comparison to Paul Malley's almost hero-worship of him. Paul's open adoration had always made Trace a little edgy. Trace had always attributed it to his own emotional garbage—psycho-babble would have translated it into a fear of intimacy caused by rejection in his relationship with his parents, no doubt. Trace just figured he was a selfish son of a bitch who didn't want the added baggage of getting tangled up in other people's lives.

There had been times Malley had been almost wistful in his attempts to get closer to Trace. Trace had always shut the guy down with a joke or a determined ability to change the subject back to business. All in all, though, they had made a great team since the old man had died. Paul dealt with the business end of FireStorm and Trace made the dangerous plays that kept his adrenaline rushing at warp speed.

"Yeah." Trace threw up his old defenses with a laugh. "You care about me, all right. Hell, if I get fried, Paul, you might have to go diving into forty-foot flames."

Trace could sense the hurt, the edginess in his partner.

"Don't say that," Malley snapped. "Damn, I don't know why I even try—" He swore. "Fine, then. I don't give a damn about you. Back to business. That's the way you like it. The insurance adjusters have the usual questions."

"Tell 'em the well exploded. Accidents happen."

"McKenna, you *are* an accident just waiting to happen. That's the problem. Damn it, man, I was afraid you'd finally pushed the limit. That you were dead!"

"You know where my will is, Malley. Check out the prices on cut-rate funerals."

"I don't think I deserve that," Malley said quietly.

"No." Trace sighed, tightening the fold of terry cloth that held the towel in place. "I suppose you don't. You want to know the truth, Malley? At the moment, I don't give a damn. About the explosion or FireStorm. I don't even give a damn about your ulcer, man."

"So tell me something I don't know."

"How about this one. I've decided to take the doctor's advice for once in my life. I'm taking some time off. Three weeks to rest and recoup and take care of some personal business. I just called to let you know."

"Three weeks?" Malley echoed, incredulous.

"The mess'll still be there when I get back. They always are."

Malley chuckled. "You're right about that. Okay, just tell me where you are so I can get in touch with you if I need to."

"That's the great thing about being so good. FireStorm can't get along without me. I don't have to do a damned thing I don't want to. And at the moment, I don't want to be disturbed by anything. I'll check in with you next month."

"You sure you're all right?"

"Would it make you feel better to know that there's a lady involved."

"A lady?"

"Actually, there are two. One hates my guts and the other is dangerous as hell."

"Anybody I know?"

"Just someone I knew back in high school. Annie Brown."

Silence fell on the phone, and Malley's voice was a little unsteady. "*The* Annie? The one you kept calling for when you had that nightmare in Saudi Arabia last year?"

Trace felt his cheeks heat. He said nothing.

Malley hesitated for a moment. "She messed you up pretty bad, man. You sure it's a good idea to tangle with the woman again?"

"What would you do for Tina, Malley?" Trace asked quietly.

Malley's voice dropped low. "I'd do anything for her. But what does that have to do with this Annie woman?"

"I've got a daughter, Malley. A little girl by Annie."

"My God." Malley sounded as shaken up as Trace had been at the discovery of his daughter. "Why would she surface now? After all this time?"

"She didn't surface. I found her by accident. And Annie doesn't want anything to do with me, and neither does April. I'm the one forcing this. I'm the one who wants it."

"Why, man? Some things are better forgotten. She turned you inside out before."

"It won't happen this time," Trace said, regretting like hell that he'd slipped up after the nightmare and confided even a little bit in Malley. "This time Annie and I play by my rules."

"You above anyone should know that there *are* no rules. Not the way you play. Let 'em go, man."

"Can't do it."

A knock on the door made Trace turn and scowl. He checked the digital clock on the bedside table. Twelve o'clock? What the blazes?

"Trace?" Malley said. "Trace, what is it?"

"Someone at the door. I don't remember calling for room service. I'll be in touch."

"Trace, no! Don't hang up!"

Trace grimaced as he placed the receiver back in its cradle and stalked to the door of his suite. Instinctively, his fingers grasped the knotted towel to hold it in place. He opened the door wide enough to glare out into the dimly lit hallway.

"Whoever you are, you've got the wrong damn room—"

His stomach did a flip as a slender figure melted out of the shadows. Her arms were crossed over her chest, her green eyes hostile, wary, holding the same bravado a kid might have, trying to pretend she wasn't scared of a hellish storm.

If a bomb had exploded in Trace's face, he couldn't have been more stunned.

"Annie?" he breathed in disbelief. "What the devil are you doing here?"

Chapter 3

Annie stared into Trace's smoke blue eyes and felt a primal urge to make a dash for the nearest bank of elevators. Survival instinct, Annie thought. She'd felt the same desperate need to flee the first time seventeen-year-old Trace McKenna had swaggered into the study hall for a tutoring session. He'd been a little dangerous, a lot sexy, and totally unattainable with those sulky rebel's eyes and that mouth that seemed molded to make feminine hearts melt. Annie had taken one look at him and wanted to dive under the table.

She'd been too naive to listen to her instincts the last time Trace McKenna had barged into her world, and he had left her life in chaos, her heart in tatters. Left her with his child growing inside her. But nearly three years of living on the streets, trying to provide for herself and a baby, had ingrained in Annie's consciousness exactly how perilous an encounter with Trace McKenna could be. Unfortunately, this time, she had no choice but to confront him.

She clutched her arms tighter around her ribs, trying not to shiver as those predatory eyes swept over her.

"Annie," he repeated, "I said what the hell are you doing here? It's after midnight."

It took all her willpower to keep from shivering as rivulets of rain dripped from her soaked hair to creep beneath her collar and drizzle down the path of her spine.

"I know what time it is," Annie said with all the disdain she could muster. "As I remember, you're the one who gave me a deadline. You threatened to call your lawyer. You made it perfectly clear that you're rich and powerful now, and that you do what you want. I can't imagine you'd be overly concerned about waking up your lawyer after midnight if the spirit moved you."

Trace's eyes narrowed, and for a heartbeat Annie thought hurt flashed in his eyes. "You figured that right. My lawyer is used to me being an inconsiderate jerk."

Annie ground her teeth. "Do you want to settle this, or was that whole performance in my office just your twisted idea of revenge? Now that I've jumped through your hoop are you going to leave April and me alone? Disappear to wherever you came from?"

Trace's lips whitened. "Disappear? No, Annie. That's *your* trick. Come in, by all means. Let's settle this."

He pulled open the door, the panel all but concealing his tall frame. Annie swallowed hard and stepped into the room.

It was so elegant she almost choked, the opulence of the room in comparison to her own tiny apartment over BabyPlace a ruthless reminder of how different their circumstances were.

She'd read all about the FireStorm empire Trace had helped the Malley family build. But somehow, this room made his wealth real, and his power. Enough power to get away with almost anything, Annie thought with a flutter of panic, even forcing his way into a little girl's life.

Annie's fingers trembled. Despite J.T.'s assurances to the contrary, was it possible that Trace could take April away altogether if he chose? She had heard of rare cases where that had happened, odd loopholes in the law discovered by expensive lawyers, judges who could be bought and paid for.

Annie smoothed back the sodden lengths of her hair. Steeling herself, she turned to face her nemesis. "Let's just get everything out in the open," she began, but the rest of the words snagged in her throat as her gaze locked on a broad expanse of naked masculine chest. Bronze skin was stippled with a dark mat of hair; a smattering of scars and faint bruises crisscrossed the well-defined ridges of muscle that had been hardened by dangerous physical exertion, not by tame workouts curling barbells at a gym.

He looked as if he'd just stepped from the shower. Annie was excruciatingly aware of every sinew of his body—his long legs, stretching far beneath the skimpy shielding of the towel, his narrow bare feet half buried in thick pewter-colored carpet. His shoulders were broad, wisps of damp, dark hair clinging to the strong cords of his throat. A few drops of water still pooled in the shadowy hollows above his collarbone.

Trace arched one dark brow, the corner of his mouth lifting with biting sarcasm. "I'm about as 'out in the open' as I can get, Brown-Eyes. That is, unless I get rid of the towel."

"No!" Annie cried a little too forcefully, unable to keep heat from flooding her cheeks.

"It still doesn't take much to get you to turn red after all these years," Trace observed. "C'mon, Annie, no need to get all flustered.'' He brushed a hand over the towel. ''You've seen all of me before.''

''The stable was dark.'' Her protest sounded ridiculous even to her own ears.

''There was enough moonlight for me to get a hell of an eyeful of you, sweet thing, even if I didn't have the finesse to undress you all the way before I—''

''Trace, I'm not going to stand here and—''

''You wouldn't even look at me, remember?'' His voice was husky, merciless. ''But you sure as hell had your hands all over me.''

''Stop it!'' Annie snapped, her voice cracking beneath the strain of hearing Trace reduce that night into such sordid terms. A night that had been pure magic for Annie, now transformed into one more notch on McKenna's bedpost, one more sexual conquest of the notorious school rebel.

The pain that sliced through her let the next wave of shivers catch her unawares. Before she could brace herself, it racked her with such force her teeth chattered.

Trace swore, and Annie could feel the path his gaze swept down her body. His hazy blue eyes tracked from the clinging wet mop of her hair to where her thin white blouse clung to her skin. She was suddenly, excruciatingly aware that the wetness had made the garment all but transparent. The appliquéd roses on her bra imprinted a perfect pattern against the fine fabric.

Trace's gaze lay heavy on her breasts for long seconds, and Annie was appalled at the sudden realization that her nipples were aching rosettes tightened against the chill. The delicate nubs stirred to an almost painful heat beneath the weight of Trace's stare.

He swallowed as if his throat was suddenly parched, his face twisting in disgust—at her or at himself, she had no idea. "Annie, you little idiot! What did you do? Walk the whole way over here in the rain? You're soaking wet!"

"The rain is the least of my worries at the moment."

"At least let me get you something to dry off with."

"No!" she said vehemently, her gaze flicking, unbidden, to the wisp of white towel slung scandalously low on his lean hips. "I mean, don't feel obligated to give me yours. Your towel, I mean."

"Oh, for God's sake," Trace growled in impatience, his hands going to the knot of terry cloth.

Annie couldn't stop herself from closing her eyes, fully expecting Trace to strip away the length of fabric, and then toss it to her while he stood there, as unabashedly naked as some primal specimen of manhood a thousand years ago.

It seemed Annie hadn't even managed to catch her breath before rough terry cloth, still damp and warm from Trace's skin, was toweling her shoulders, her neck. She made a choked sound of protest, trying to jerk away from Trace's hands, but he only followed her movements, the softness of the towel doing nothing to disguise the inexorable strength of his fingers.

Those fingers rubbed the towel over her shoulders, down her arms. But when he brushed the towel over nipples already agonizingly sensitized, Annie wouldn't have given a damn if they had been standing in the middle of Times Square and Trace McKenna's whole body was lit up with neon. Her eyes popped open as she struggled to find some way to escape him.

She expected to see Trace stripped to his skin. Amazingly enough, in those moments her eyes had been closed, he had not only managed to shed the towel, but had flung the hotel's complimentary robe over his body, knotting the belt rather precariously at his waist. Annie should have been more relieved than she was, but the robe was only marginally better than the towel. It gaped open at his chest, the stark white fabric a startling contrast to the dark tan of his skin. Trace had gone down on one knee. The other tanned leg pierced through the split in the robe, causing the white folds to stream on either side of the powerful sinews of his left thigh, the shadows barely concealing the part of him that made him a man.

Alarm streaked through Annie at the knowledge that the most subtle shift of his muscles could send even that meager bit of cloth sliding away, leaving him bare.

"Trace, don't," she said, considering the merit of climbing over a chair to put some distance between them. "I'm fine. I just want to settle this about April and then go home."

"Fine. Let's settle it. But you're soaked to the skin. I might be bastard enough to want to have a relationship with my daughter, but I'd just as soon not do so at the price of having April's mother die of pneumonia. You could've brought an umbrella or worn a coat."

"I had other things on my mind. I was trying to think of what I could say to you, how to make you understand—"

Annie placed her hands against his chest to shove him away, but the neck of the robe had gaped and her palm collided with the heated plane of Trace's chest.

The texture of his skin seared itself into her palm. If she had just touched a white-hot iron Annie couldn't have been more shaken.

Apparently her touch startled Trace in a way that her words had been unable to. He sprang back. She saw his face turning dull red, his hands tugging at the robe, pulling it tightly closed where it flowed over his hips. But not before Annie glimpsed a tell-tale bulge beneath it.

Her whole body felt afire with disgust at herself for being unnerved by mere sexual attraction when the man was a very real threat to everything Annie had worked so hard for these past nine years. When he could very well hurt April....

"Looks like I'm still all hormones when it comes to you, Brown-Eyes." Trace broke through her thoughts with his acid sneer. "You'd think I would've learned the hard way to stay clear of you. But then, hell, I was always a slow learner."

"You were too smart for your own good," Annie shot back. "But this isn't some game you're playing, Trace. You're forcing your way into an innocent child's life. I don't want April hurt."

Trace jammed his fists into his robe pockets. "I don't want her hurt, either. That's why I'm here, Annie. I'm sure you don't believe that, but it's true."

"You've always had great reasons for everything you've done, haven't you, Trace? You blew off school because you decided that the teachers were all jerks. You threw away your chance to play professional baseball because of your father."

Trace's gaze slashed to hers. "I didn't throw it away because of my father."

There was something hidden in those words, an undercurrent Annie didn't dare explore.

Trace swore, waving one strong hand in dismissal. "What the hell, believe whatever you want. It doesn't matter anymore. The only thing that matters is April." He planted his hands on his hips, and Annie wondered how a man standing in such posh surroundings could look so utterly primitive.

"So, what's it going to be, Annie?" he demanded. "Are you going to let me have her?"

"She's not a stray puppy, to be yanked between two squabbling kids. She's not anyone's property—not mine and certainly not yours."

"Do I get time with my daughter? Or do I have to fight for it? It doesn't matter to me either way. I'm used to fighting for what I want. But I'd better warn you. I've only lost one time."

"We have to do things my way," Annie cautioned.

"Do you mean you're actually considering meeting my demands?" Annie almost thought she heard a tremor in Trace's voice.

"I don't know," she said. "Yes, I guess I am. But there would have to be certain conditions."

"Name them," he demanded tautly.

"First, you have to swear you won't tell April that you are her father."

"So you want me to be a liar, too?"

Liar. It was a hard word. One with the power to make Annie wince. She deflected the brutal honesty of it by saying, "I don't want April to be traumatized."

"Neither do I. I'll agree not to be honest with the kid for the time being. But there will come a time when all bets are off."

She would worry about that later, Annie tried to tell herself. She just had to get through one crisis at a time. She'd manage to keep Trace silent somehow after Colorado. Truthfully, it was her other term that made her the most uneasy.

She sucked in a steadying breath, facing him as if he were her executioner. In some ways he had been. The Annie Brown who had played the piano and dreamed of Juilliard and concert stages had ceased to exist because of him. "The second condition is that I come with you to Colorado."

An unreadable expression darted into Trace's gray-blue eyes. "What the—" He started, then stopped. Whatever emotions had jolted through him were wiped away. They were replaced by a nasty smile.

"You sayin' you want to come play house with me, Brown-Eyes? Let's see, I'll be the daddy and you can be the mommy. Just think of the games we can play in bed once April is asleep."

"I don't want anything to do with you, Trace. But I don't intend to abandon my daughter in the care of a man who is practically a stranger."

"So you're coming to Colorado to—what? Make sure I don't feed the kid ground-up glass instead of sugar on her cereal?"

"That's not fair."

"You've had her for eight years, Annie. I had nothing. I didn't see her first smile, hold her hand when she was trying to walk. Damn it, I deserve a little time alone with her!"

"You can have it. You have my word that I won't interfere with things between you and April, unless—"

"Unless what? I do something you consider dangerous? Despicable? Like not making her wash behind her ears?"

"I can't believe you could really expect me to just hand April over to you without a word. As far as she knows, you're just some creep she beaned with a baseball because he was scaring her mother. She doesn't trust you. She doesn't like you. And even though she'd die before she'd admit it to anyone, she's downright frightened of you."

"Because you—"

"No, Trace," Annie snapped. "She's afraid because of you. You had me pinned against the wall, struggling when she came into the room. It terrified her. She knows that something is wrong. If I pack her bags and stick her in a plane with you, how do you think she'd react?"

"There's nothing you'd like better than to see me fall flat on my face with April. If I screw things up badly enough you'd never have to see me again."

It cost Annie more than Trace could ever know, but she told him the truth. "After you left today, there was nothing I wanted more. I wanted you to fail with April so I could keep her safe, protected from you. But I've had some time to think about it, and if your meeting is a disaster, the one who comes out a loser is April. No matter how I feel about you, she has a right to know her father. To decide for herself if she wants you to be a part of her life."

Trace felt as if she'd blindsided him. He eyed her warily. "I suppose you expect me to say thank you for that."

"No, Trace. I learned a long time ago not to expect anything from you. Make whatever plans are necessary. You can contact me at the shelter." With those words, Annie turned and walked out the door.

Trace watched her, his heart thudding against his ribs in an unsteady rhythm, his skin suddenly sweating as if he'd run thirty miles.

Oh, God. He could hardly believe it was true. He closed his eyes, picturing April's winsome face, down to the bandage on her chin. He imagined what it would be like the first time she slipped her hand into his. The first time she smiled at him—hell, the first time she looked at him without appearing as if she wanted to kick him in the ribs.

However grudgingly, Annie had given him a chance to forge a relationship with April. He'd made a disaster of so much of his life. He'd screwed up in school and on the baseball field. He'd snarled up his relationship with his parents, his sisters. His relationship with Annie.

But this time, Trace would find a way to make things right.

During that brief, precious time in Colorado, Trace would make certain that April had the time of her life— everything she'd ever dreamed of, including a father who loved her.

But what if she doesn't want you any more than your father did? a voice whispered inside Trace. *Any more than Annie wanted you?*

Annie.

Trace's muscles tightened, burned at the memory of how she had felt under his hands—damp and trembling from the rain, her eyes like some woodland creature's, mysterious, luminous in spite of her fury. His fists knotted at the memory of the feel of her wet blouse and the towel sandwiched between his hands and her breasts, the sensual abrasion as he felt her nipples harden beneath his palms.

She still had the power to rock him to the very core of his soul. And she would be there with April, still beautiful, so damn tempting. Still far beyond his reach.

No. He didn't want to reach Annie anymore, Trace thought fiercely. And he wouldn't fail April. He wouldn't let himself.

But as Trace stared out into a night that was haunted with April's blue eyes and tousled pigtails, her adorable scowl, he felt a chill race down his spine.

For the first time since the day Annie Brown had walked out of his life, Trace McKenna was afraid.

Annie sat at her desk and stared down at the red-inked schedule she'd been working on for two days, mapping out arrangements for volunteers and other shelter employees to take up the slack while she was gone. It had been a gargantuan task. She'd recruited the three people necessary to handle the mayhem that was Annie's workday, the schedule exposing with ruthless clarity the fact that she had become a workaholic of the first order.

She had crammed every corner of her life with commitments, running the shelter, mothering April, counseling the girls who came to her with problems ranging from what color nail polish to put on to whether or not they should put their babies up for adoption. She had filed paperwork and checked homework, helped in the snack bar at the softball field and made presentations to companies, fought for scholarships for BabyPlace moms and spent more nights than she could count trying to soothe heartaches too grownup for teenagers to handle.

She loved her work. Adored it. And as for April... that little girl was the most wonderful thing in her life. And yet, staring down at the schedule that closely resembled a NASA flight plan, Annie couldn't help but remember the conversation she'd had with her father with increasing regularity during the three years since they had reconciled.

You'll never find a man if you continue on this way, Annalise, Colonel Brown's warning echoed in her head. *You need someone to take care of you and April. Someone steady, dependable, responsible. But men like that don't come strolling through the door of a shelter for pregnant teenagers!*

Maybe not, Annie thought, her mouth twisting wryly. But a dangerous, compelling, reckless man had ripped through this place like a typhoon two days earlier, leaving disaster in his wake.

She couldn't even imagine what Colonel Brown would say when she told him that Trace McKenna had swept back into her life. No, Annie corrected herself mentally, she could imagine *exactly* what he would say, which was why she'd been completely out of character, procrastinating like crazy about placing a call to Arizona.

A sane person—translated "coward"—would have merely refused to call the Colonel. Annie and her father had gone a month without talking on the phone before. God knew, Annie was having enough trouble balancing her feelings about Trace's return without throwing her father's sheer loathing of the man into the mix. But the Colonel had made one of his rare generous gestures, buying tickets to the White Sox game during his vacation, planning to take April there next week as a surprise—a fact Annie had forgotten in the craziness of Trace's return.

She stared down at the phone a long minute, then forced herself to pick it up and punch in the number. Two buzzes, and it was answered in a voice crisp as a blizzard wind.

"Colonel Brown here."

"Dad? Hi, this is Annie."

"Annalise! This is a surprise. Is April all right? Nothing's wrong?"

It had always astonished Annie how this man who had been so adamant about his daughter having an abortion or giving April up for adoption could have changed so drastically in the five and a half years since Annie had first met J.T. and Allison James.

There had been plenty of rocky times in the beginning, made worse by the fact that Annie's mother had been dying of cancer. But by the time Mary Brown was laid to rest and April was five, Annie and her father had reached a tenuous truce. Now they were bound by their love for the little girl whose appearance had so drastically changed their lives.

Still, Annie couldn't tamp down the knot of unease that lodged heavy in the pit of her belly. A sensation all too familiar from childhood, those moments when she'd known she was about to disappoint or anger her perfectionist father.

"Dad, as a matter of fact, I've run into a little scheduling problem," Annie began. "I know you wanted to surprise April by flying up and taking her to the game. And it was a terrific idea. Really. But something has come up, and—"

"Something has come up?" There was a bite in the colonel's voice that had made chief petty officers hit the deck. "You've known about these tickets for months!"

"I know. If there was any way to avoid this snag, I would. But there isn't."

"Something's come up? A scheduling problem? Snag? What the devil is it, girl? You're talking like you've lost your mind!"

Maybe I did, Annie thought grimly, *somewhere between the time when Trace stormed into my office and when he kissed me.*

"Dad, I'm not sure how to say this, so I'm going to blurt it right out. April can't go to the White Sox game because we're going to Colorado to spend three weeks with..." She drew in a steadying breath.

"With who?"

"Trace McKenna."

The curse was foul and disbelieving. "McKenna? That son of a bitch! Don't tell me you went looking for that—"

"Of course not. He found me. And April. He saw us on a docudrama on cable TV. He figured out the truth, and he came here determined to meet his daughter."

"You aren't going to let him see her, are you? My God, Annalise, he has no right to just charge back into your lives—"

"He has every right under the law. And he has the money and the power to pursue his rights to the bitter end. He made that crystal clear. Either I let him get to know April or he'll go to court to claim her legally."

"I'll kill him with my own hands! After what he did to you—"

"Dad, that's enough. I don't think he wants to hurt April. He's agreed not to tell her the truth for now. He's only asking for three weeks."

"Don't tell me you believe that! If you give him so much as a toehold in April's life you're a fool."

"Dad, I don't have any choice. Of course I'm not thrilled about this. Of course I'm worried about April, what effect it might have on her when...*if,*" she corrected herself stridently, "she discovers the truth about who Trace is. But I've thought about it a lot, and I've decided that she deserves a chance to know her father."

"She can come to me and I can tell her everything there is to know about him! How he got you pregnant and didn't give a damn."

"Dad, you know he—" Annie stopped, too tired to argue anymore. Her father hadn't listened before when she'd tried to tell him how shattered Trace had been at the news she was carrying his child. Colonel Brown wouldn't listen this time either. Annie sighed, "whatever Trace felt before, one thing is certain. He cares about April now. I have to go now, Dad. I'm really sorry about the Sox game. Please try to understand. I have to do this."

Please understand, daddy...I have to do this...keep my baby... Trace's baby.... The words echoed in her mind, whispers from the past.

Colonel Brown hadn't understood then. It was beyond hope that he could understand now, no matter how many strides he'd made these past three years.

"Annalise, listen to me! You can't trust this jerk. He's proven that once, hasn't he?"

"I'll call you when we get back."

"Back? From Colorado?" Colonel Brown's voice blazed.

It was excruciatingly hard to sacrifice the slight shadings of approval she'd managed to gain from him. "I'm not a little girl anymore, Dad. I make my own decisions."

"The last time you made a decision where McKenna was concerned, you ended up pregnant and on the street!"

Annie gritted her teeth and pressed her fingertips to the sudden headache that was beginning to hammer behind her temples. "I'll call you when we get back. And I won't let anything hurt April. You know I won't."

"Annalise? Don't you dare hang up—"

"Goodbye, Dad." Annie could still hear him bellowing into the phone as she gently placed the receiver in its cradle. She'd barely withdrawn her hand when the telephone began to ring again. Her father, no doubt determined to convince her he was right and she was wrong. Some things never changed.

For a heartbeat, Annie considered picking the phone up, letting him bulldoze her into telling Trace to go to hell. God knew, she didn't want to expose April to any trauma—or traumatize herself, for that matter. And just the brief time she'd spent with Trace had made her feel like a twig tossed in gale-force winds, out of control, helpless against powers too strong to resist.

But she kept remembering J.T.'s face, so solemn, his eyes steady and brutally honest. *What are you going to tell April ten years from now when Trace McKenna walks back into her life and she knows that he wanted a relationship with her, but you kept them apart? She might hate you....*

But hadn't Annie already kept April and Trace apart? a voice inside her whispered. Hadn't she concocted elaborate lies, hidden the truth, tried to pretend Trace didn't exist?

To protect April, Annie asserted fiercely. To keep her from feeling abandoned by her father.

Or had she done so in order to protect herself from the rush of emotions Trace had always inspired in her? To numb the hurt, the grief, the pain that was nine years old. And now she still felt raw, torn wide open again, in the brief time since she'd looked into Trace McKenna's eyes.

It was a disturbing thought, one that made Annie squirm inwardly. The ringing of the phone pounded against Annie's raw nerves, and she reached down, switching off the ringer.

If only it was that easy to shut off the sensations that were still catapulting through her, knocking down all the defenses she'd erected around her heart.

Trace paced outside the airplane hangar, oblivious to the beauty of a dozen private planes gleaming in the morning sun, oblivious to everything except the raw sense of anticipation eating inside him, the triumph that was tempered by unease.

Any minute now, his daughter was going to walk through the gates, see him, see the plane. Hell, even if the kid hated him, she'd have to be excited by the prospect of flying, wouldn't she? And Annie—she'd take one look at the aircraft and know that Trace McKenna hadn't been the screwed-up failure everyone had predicted. That he had fought his way to the top in spite of everything. He raked his hands through his hair, angry that her opinion of him still mattered when he'd prided himself on the fact that he didn't give a damn what anyone thought of him, of Fire-Storm, of the size of his bank account.

He had tried to pretend that he wasn't trying to prove anything to anyone—least of all the girl who had betrayed him. And yet, with every risk he took, it was Annie's face he'd see when he closed his eyes at night. Every success against incredible odds made him feel as if he'd somehow gained back a piece of himself that had slipped through his fingers the day Annie had run away from him.

He had taken those pieces and tried to fill the gaping hole she'd left inside him. But it hadn't mattered. They'd just slipped into the darkness and made him feel more empty than ever.

"Everything looks good, boss." The sound of a mechanic's voice made Trace jump, a guilty heat flooding his cheeks, as if somehow the fresh-faced twenty-year-old had been able to see past McKenna's daredevil facade into the weakness that was Annie.

"I tightened up a few bolts," the youth said, wiping grease-stained hands on a rag. "And I replaced the fuel line. It was cracked in a few places."

"Terrific."

"You might want to talk to whoever maintains this bird and tell them to straighten up. You could've had a problem."

Trace frowned, the kid's words reminding him that FireStorm's head mechanic had all but begged Trace to let him give the plane a badly overdue checkup. How long ago had that been? Two months? Three? Maybe he'd give old Ratso a go at it when he got back from Colorado.

He glanced down at the name stenciled on the kid's coveralls. "Thanks for the reminder, Mike, but I'm pretty sure she'll hold together. My head mechanic was putting engines together with hairpins and duct tape while you were still building with Tinkertoys. He's the best there is."

"Maybe," the kid said, unabashed. "But maybe he needs glasses, 'cause this bird was cruising for a crash landing. Maybe not the next time you took it up, or the next. But sometime soon, things were going to get real interesting."

Trace flashed Mike a smile that was more than a little dangerous. "When you're at a thousand feet and the engine cuts out, or you're free-falling into a canyon that's only thirty feet wide—that's the only time you're really alive."

The mechanic shuddered. "No, thanks. Changing the channel to football when my wife is watching a Mel Gibson movie is the closest I want to get to a near-death experience."

"You're married?" Trace couldn't keep the surprise from his voice.

"Yeah. Got a baby, too." Mike dug around in his back pocket and withdrew a billfold. Before Trace could protest, the kid was shoving a picture under his nose. A girl who couldn't be more than eighteen sat a little stiffly in a cheap wicker chair with an infant cuddled in her arms. The baby's pink dress had obviously gone through several owners. The ruffles were limp and the color washed out. But the child's eyes were wide and wondering. Her mother's smile was soft and knowing.

A fist squeezed around Trace's heart. "She's beautiful."

"Yeah. My friends told me I was crazy for getting married so young. You know, chaining myself down and all. But I love Lisa and Megan, and—hell, hanging out with a bunch of guys at bars and chasing women and stuff didn't have much appeal in comparison." As if suddenly aware of how much he'd revealed, the kid grew sheepish. "I suppose a guy like you thinks I'm nuts—I mean, you go tearing all over the world, private planes, gorgeous chicks, all that adventure."

"No," Trace said softly, handing back the picture. "I don't think you're crazy at all." Trace dug into his own pocket and took out two one-hundred-dollar bills. He stuck them in the kid's hand.

Mike's eyes bugged out. Trace sensed how much the kid needed the money, but Mike held his hands up in protest. "Whoa! This is way too much."

"Take your lady out for dinner and buy that baby..." Trace hesitated, at a loss. He shrugged. "Buy her whatever babies like."

Mike grinned. "That's real nice of you, Mr. McKenna. There's this baby swing Lisa's been wanting to get to hang in the tree outside our apartment, but you know how it goes. Money only goes so far." Mike shoved the bills into his wallet, then stuffed the bit of leather back into his pocket. His gaze tracked to the gate and he smiled. "Looks like I better head out. Your company's coming."

Trace wheeled toward the gate and his stomach plunged to his toes. A somewhat battered van with HomePlace lettered across the side was parked outside the fence. A tall, dark-haired man in a bomber jacket was helping Annie roust a pair of disreputable-looking suitcases out of the vehicle, while April hung back a little, her eyes wary, her chin set with McKenna stubbornness. Trace had expected worse in the first moment his gaze again locked with his daughter's. Considering the way Annie left the hotel three days ago, he'd banked on major hostility from both her and the kid. But April regarded him with grudging curiosity, while Annie... Annie had the same uncertain, almost shy aura about her that had hit him like a fist in the gut the first time he saw her.

The leather-jacketed guy didn't make a move toward the plane. He just squinted in Trace's direction and waved a hand in greeting before he climbed back into the van. The engine roared to life, then wheeled away, leaving Annie and April standing on the expanse of concrete. Trace's muscles knotted. It was as if the woman and child were surrounded by an aura of love and unity that no one could breach. Just the two of them. Trace tried not to be bitter about the fact that he was not a part of that precious enchantment.

His palms suddenly sweating, Trace strode toward them, trying to concentrate on April—his child, the only stake he had in this mess. But no matter how hard he fought it, his eyes were dragged back to Annie time and again, watching the way the breeze plastered her dainty white blouse against her breasts and tangled her calf-length rose skirt against her legs.

It was crazy to watch her—some kind of sadomasochistic torture to glimpse the lacy bit of slip peeping from beneath the billowing fabric, while her hair blew in a misty halo around her delicate face, the strands as hazy gold as a summertime dream.

Trace was close enough to see that she was smiling—that brave, fake smile she'd worn the first time Trace had stalked into their study hall. But he'd always been able to see past it, beyond the smile, to what lay in her incredible green eyes. They were wide and wounded, frightened and soft. He wanted to cup her pale cheeks with the palms of his hands, whisper into the silky curls at her temple.

Don't be afraid of me, Annie. Don't be afraid. I won't hurt you....

Trace stiffened, the words echoing those he had said as a pain-fevered seventeen-year-old, shaking with desperate need in the ruins of an abandoned stable. But he had hurt her when he hadn't bothered to protect her from the consequences of their night's passion. And she had hurt him when she had walked away.

"Hello, Trace." Annie's voice. Quiet. Her fingers were white-knuckled on the handle of her suitcase.

"Hello, Annie." Trace turned toward the little girl, hating the squeezing sensation in his chest at the uncertainty in Annie's voice. "Nice day to fly, huh, April?"

"How would I know?" There was still an edge in the kid's voice, but it was a little more blunted. "I've never been in a plane before."

"Is that so?"

"We have to fix the car and stuff, and I need braces even though I think my teeth are fine, so we don't go on vacations far away. Sometimes my mom takes me to the water park, though."

Braces. Trace hazarded a glance at Annie. At least that was some concrete benefit she could get out of this mess— he could pay for braces with his pocket change. And a new car. Hell, he didn't want his kid stranded somewhere in a broken-down car in the middle of Chicago . . . or *Annie,* he was forced to admit.

"My friend Tyler James gets to fly all the time 'cause his grandpa's rich," April piped up. "Tyler's grandpa said he'd give us a car, too, but Mom says we'll make it on our own. Just me and her. We don't need anybody else. You know, like a boyfriend or step-dad or anything."

It was a none-too-subtle laying of boundaries. Trace didn't have time to speak before Annie broke in.

"April, I told you that Mr. McKenna is just an old friend of mine."

"Yeah. I guess." April regarded him a little suspiciously. "Mom showed me the monkey you won her at the carnival. She said you threw baseballs and knocked junk down to win it."

The carnival. Trace felt like April had nailed him with a stun gun. His gaze collided with Annie's; her cheeks were suddenly pink.

He'd forgotten the night Annie had confided that in all her world travels as an army brat she had never been to a carnival. Trace had slammed a book of Shakespeare's tragedies shut and swooped Annie off to sticky cotton candy and dizzying rides with lights that flashed and tinny music that grated on the ears.

When he'd stopped at one of the game booths, he hadn't known why it had seemed so damned important to win her that ugly neon stuffed animal. He'd worked harder at winning it than he had his last ten times on the pitcher's mound. When he'd tucked the monkey in Annie's arms, she'd smiled at him. It had been the first time he'd seen past her shyness and realized how damned beautiful she was. He could remember the sensation of slipping her small hand into his.

He wondered if Annie remembered that night the same way he did. No, she must've remembered it even better, considering the fact that she'd kept Mozart Monkey.

"April was understandably nervous after what happened," Annie attempted to explain. "I wanted to show her . . . tell her . . ."

Suddenly, Trace couldn't think of a damned thing to say.

April's impatient voice yanked him back to the present. "So, are we going to get in the plane or stand here all day?" she demanded. "Bet the pilot's going to be real ticked that we're late."

"I think we're safe on that score. See—" Trace couldn't figure out why his cheeks heated a little "—I fly my own plane."

"You? You mean, you're a pilot?" Annie's choked exclamation might have been comical under other circumstances.

Trace shrugged. "Got too many complaints about the places I like to fly and the stunts I wanted to pull, so, what the hell? Decided it was less trouble to learn to fly myself."

He let his eyelids slip to half-mast, the corner of his mouth tipping up in subtle mockery. "What's the matter, Brown-Eyes? Scared to go up with me?"

"My mom is not scared!" April jumped in.

"Don't be so sure about that," Annie corrected her. "The few times I rode with Trace in a car I spent the trip with my life flashing before my eyes."

"If my life had been as bland as yours was, that would have been enough to scare the bejesus out of me, too. Annie, did you ever do anything risky, just for the hell of it?"

"Once." There was a sting in that single word. Trace winced as it struck its mark.

"Oh, yeah. I almost forgot. You fell from grace big time with me, didn't you, Brown-Eyes?"

"Trace, please," Annie said with a tremor in her voice. Trace's nerves were buzzing with the need to lambast someone, anyone, to get rid of the sizzling waves of tension burning inside him. But Annie's eyes flicked to April. The frown of confusion that puckered the little girl's face made Trace grit his teeth.

Unless he watched his mouth, everything was going to spill out in the ugliest possible way—the whole sordid story of how Trace McKenna knocked up Annie Brown. Even edgy and angry, Trace could easily imagine just how damaging such a revelation would be to April.

Besides, the truth was that Annie had given him a gift— somehow she had eased April's fear of him, softened the child's hostility by sharing a memory that must have been difficult for Annie. He owed her a helluva lot for that.

Trace moved to scoop up the suitcases, but April swept into the breach, a determined look on her face. "I can carry them. My mom and I take care of ourselves, remember?" Again, the drawing of boundaries.

"Terrific," Trace said. "I can see you're a big help. Maybe you'd like to help me fly the plane once we're away from Chicago."

The kid's eyes all but popped out of her head, a visible shiver of anticipation going through her. "You're joking, right, Mr. McKenna?"

"No I'm not. I'll show you what to do, and then you can help."

"Trace—" Annie started to interrupt.

But April burst in, nearly killing herself with the effort to stifle a grin—after all, Trace realized, it would never do to surrender points to the enemy without a fight. "I guess if it'd make you happy I could try it, Mr. McKenna," April told him. "But don't blame me if I crash it into a mountain or something."

Trace grinned. "I won't."

"Trace," Annie interrupted firmly. "There's no way I'm going to let my daughter fly a plane."

"Mom!" April drew the single syllable into two long ones in the age-old sign of childish displeasure, her eyes flashing. "You said I was s'posed to try and get along with him 'cause everybody loses their temper sometimes. Well I'm trying, but you're already arguing again!"

Annie gave Trace a helpless look, but he only met her eyes levelly.

"You said you wouldn't interfere."

"As long as it wasn't dangerous!" Annie sputtered.

"It isn't. I can have the controls back in my hands in a heartbeat. I'll be right there to help her if she needs it."

"Is that supposed to make me feel better?" Annie groaned. "You can't even get a sane pilot to do the things you want, so you get your own pilot's license. And now you want to put an eight-year-old behind the controls— No, wait—" Annie waved her hands in frustration "—we'll probably be a lot safer with April as pilot."

"Probably." Trace grimaced. It would be a helluva lot safer. If April was handling the controls it would give him something to concentrate on besides the soft, baby-powder scent of Annie in the morning, the velvety cream shadows that clung in the hollow of her throat. Far better to crash into a mountain than feel this gut-deep yearning to drag her against him, see if she still felt so small and delicate and if she still fit in his arms so perfectly.

As if she could read his thoughts, Annie's fingers trembled. "All right, then. Have it your way."

Trace knew just how much that assent had cost her.

April gave a whoop, then scooped up the suitcases, hauling them toward the plane.

"Trace?" Annie's voice was a jolt of pure sensation along nerve endings that were already raw. "Are you sure it's safe to let her do this?"

"She'll be fine. I promise." He didn't trust himself to look at Annie. It would be too easy to reach out to her, squeeze her hand. The need was elemental, a physical pain that pulsed mercilessly in places he'd thought deadened to all emotion.

He wanted to look into those incredible forest-hued eyes and tell Annie that he wouldn't let anything bad happen to her or to April ever again.

He wanted to forget that Annie hadn't wanted him, that she had run away.

Instead he whispered, his voice low, ragged, "I know what it cost you, giving me this chance. I promise you won't be sorry."

"You don't owe me anything, Trace. This is all about April, only April."

Trace tried to shake the feeling that Annie was trying to convince herself.

"Yeah. It's about April." Trace murmured as Annie's voice slid beneath his skin causing awakenings. But it wasn't the little girl Trace was speaking of. It was April, that long-ago month in spring when, for a moment, just a moment, Trace had almost dared to believe that Annie Brown's love could save him.

Chapter 4

Annie huddled in the rear seat of the plane, her eyes gritty and half blinded from the sun that had streamed into the window at her side. She had stared through the plate of glass for hours, the glaring light far less painful than watching the first real moments April shared with her father.

But in spite of Annie's efforts, she kept catching glimpses of the two of them together. And those brief images had branded themselves in her mind until every time she closed her eyes, she could see Trace's big hands closing over April's small ones, guiding her, teaching her with that rare, offbeat patience, that heartbreaking sense of humor that had enchanted a shy bookish girl so many years ago.

Time and time again since they had left the Midwest, Annie could hear Trace's murmurs of praise, see his smile flashing with unbridled delight at his daughter. His eyes glittered with pleasure and pride and something so tender and vulnerable that Annie wanted to run from it.

Don't be kind! Oh, God, Trace, please let me keep despising you, judging you. Let me keep this distance between us. It's the only way I can survive!

Annie's chest felt as if it were crushed in iron bands, her throat raw as April banked the aircraft over clouds gleaming like spun sugar, but not sparkling with half the brilliance of the little girl's laughter.

They were so much alike—the rangy, dark-haired man and the child with braids the same mahogany hue—that it seemed impossible they hadn't known each other forever. It seemed impossible that the little girl hadn't blinked up at her father from her cradle.

But April hadn't had a cradle to sleep in as an infant, only an orange crate Annie had lined with a blanket.

And April didn't know Trace McKenna was her father.

If Annie had her way, April wouldn't know for a very long time. Until she could understand grown-up mistakes and lies that were meant to shield instead of slash at the spirit. Until April could understand that Annie had had no choice.

Until April could forgive her.

Annie raised trembling fingers to the knot that seemed lodged in her throat. Every time Trace smiled at April, every time he touched her, murmured to her in that husky voice, Annie could see April opening up to him a little more. And it hurt her more than she could acknowledge even to herself, because it was one more undeniable sign that the life Annie had made for her daughter was going to change whether Annie was ready or not.

Her stomach fluttered as the plane dipped, piercing the clouds, a chorus of hushed whispers and giggles emanating from the front of the plane. And then just that suddenly, the plane was plunging beneath the clouds. Annie shrieked at what seemed to be a solid wall of mountain rising up three hundred yards before her, blotting out the plane's windshield. "April! Trace, my God!"

In the next breath, April tipped the wings at a dizzying angle, the craggy wall of stone vanishing into a sweep of azure blue.

April whooped with delight. "That was great, Mr. McKenna! Just like you said! Bet I scared you worse than that time Tyler and I jumped out at you in the basement, Mom!"

The notion that the mind-numbing, throat-freezing terror had been some kind of prank Trace had cooked up made Annie furious. Her heart was still three miles back where she'd dropped it when she'd been certain that they were all about to be killed.

"Was that your idea of a joke?" Annie demanded in such cold accents, April went still. The little girl looked back uncertainly.

"Chill out, Mom," Trace said. "The Ape and I just wanted to see if you were still alive back there. You've hardly said a word since we left Illinois."

"I wasn't supposed to interfere, remember?" Bitterness, anger and fear cut through the words. Annie hated herself for the swift burning of tears against her eyelids. She would not cry. Damn it, she would not, no matter how badly that little stunt had shaken her.

Trace angled his face toward her, and for a heartbeat she saw a shadow cross those dangerously handsome features. "Annie, I—"

"Mr. McKenna?" April's voice came, a little alarmed. "Mr. McKenna, look! It's not doing what you said it would. This thing. It's blinking real weird."

Trace wheeled back around, his gaze sweeping the instrument panel. Annie's blood ran cold at the expression on his face the instant his eyes fixed on the high-tech instrument April's finger was pointing to.

"No more jokes! I mean it! This is not funny!"

"It sure as hell isn't." Trace growled, slipping his hands in front of April's. "You have to let go now."

"But you said—" April insisted.

"Let go!"

April yanked her hands away as if the metal beneath them had suddenly heated a thousand degrees. Hurt streaked across April's face, and something like fear.

"Trace, what is it?" Annie's voice sounded like a stranger's, even to her own ears.

"The landing gear. It's not responding...."

"Mommy?" April's voice cut Annie like a blade slipped beneath her skin. "Mommy..." The little girl tried desperately to squirm around, her hand reaching back to Annie, straining.

Annie couldn't reach her fingers... oh, God...

Annie started to climb out of her seat toward the child.

"Sit down and belt in. Now." Trace ordered.

Annie started to protest, but one glare from Trace and she hastened to do his bidding.

"I want you both to listen to me," he said firmly. "It's going to be okay. I've done this before."

Brought a plane down without landing gear in the middle of a mountain range? What was it? Annie wondered a little hysterically. Something Trace and his nut-ball friends did for fun after they skydived with parachutes picked up at a rummage sale?

"First I'm going to circle around, slow down as much as possible...." Trace worked with fierce intensity. Annie followed his gaze to one of the gauges. Her stomach plunged. Fuel. The indicator was dropping at an alarming rate.

"Are we running out of gas?"

"No. I'm jettisoning the fuel."

"Why?"

"We're better off without it."

To lessen the risk of fire, Annie knew suddenly, her head filling with hideous newsreel images of passenger jets exploding into flames.

She wanted to retch as the plane began its descent, the cushion of air between its metal belly and the jagged, tearing rocks below growing narrower. Annie's eyes locked on a landing strip that seemed impossibly tiny even for an airplane in perfect working order. It didn't take much imagination to figure out what would happen to an aircraft skidding and careering toward the end of that strip.

Trace grabbed the radio, his voice low, tense. "Mayday. Mayday. Rob, do you read me?"

A static-laden voice sputtered back. "Tra—Lin—Spotted you—in view. Wh—"

"Gonna be coasting in on my belly. Damn landing gear jammed. Get your butt over here. Pronto."

Annie heard garbled words that must be swearing. What was this Rob supposed to do to help? Run out and catch them on a feather pillow?

Trace glanced at the white-faced child beside him. "Don't worry, April. I'm going to set her down real easy. Just like a paper airplane you glide in for a landing on your teacher's desk."

Except paper airplanes weren't firebombs with wings, Annie thought wildly. They weren't metal shells ready to break apart.

Helpless, Annie watched Trace's jaw clench, his long, strong fingers guiding the plane downward, slowing its speed. April had given up trying to speak. She was watching Trace with wide eyes. A child's eyes, edged with fear, yet not truly believing anything bad would happen to her. Her mother would somehow magically save her. Her mother or the man gripping the aircraft's controls.

"Ape, listen to me," Trace's voice came, bracing. "I'm gonna show you how the pros do this. The guy who taught me emergency landings was a pilot in Vietnam, a real war hero. Brought down a loadful of injured men after a bunch of the ba5 guys had shot off his—"

Annie didn't even hear the rest of the story. All she could do was watch the narrow bare strip of land looming before them, a bank of trees waiting at its end.

All she could do was pray.

"Hold on to your butts, people," Trace ordered. "We're about to make contact."

The plane hit. Annie's teeth cracked together with enough force to dislodge every filling she'd ever had. Her elbow slammed hard into a metal brace to her left. Her stomach rebelled at the crazy tilting, the horrible grinding sound of bare metal scraping the surface of the airfield. The wings were waving with the same frantic energy of a bird trapped in a fox's jaws, while the end of the landing strip raced toward them with deadly speed, in spite of Trace's effort to slow the plane down.

Trace was swearing, low, maybe a little desperately, as if the plane were a person he was trying to bully into submission. Annie could see the corded muscles standing out like iron strips against his skin, she could feel the almost savage force of his will as he held on, fighting.

The battle seemed to have lasted forever, but it was over in seconds. The plane skidded, listing to the right, then bumped to a stop.

Annie didn't even have time to mutter a prayer of thanksgiving before Trace was struggling out of his safety harness, battling to turn around in the cockpit. "Annie?"

Trace's face was ice-white, beaded with sweat. "My God, Annie."

Strange, Annie mused through a web of nausea, that he hadn't first called out to April. But then, April was obviously fine—squirming from her own harness like a terrified monkey.

"Mommy? Mommy, don't die!"

Annie struggled to beat back the dizzying waves of darkness that accompanied the pain in her arm. "I'm not...going to die...." Annie choked out, her stomach sloshing around like a barrel hurtling over Niagara Falls, her fingers fumbling with the safety harness. "I'm going to...be...sick—"

Her skin went clammy, cold sweat sopping through her blouse, her fingers unable to obey her mind's commands. She glimpsed Trace forcing the door to the plane open, felt him unsnap her belts, his strong arms dragging her over the seat, out into a blast of fresh air.

Oh, God, please don't let me throw up on him, Annie thought numbly, her legs giving out on her. She struck the landing strip on her knees, retching, Trace's arm looped beneath her ribs to support her. His other hand caught back her tumbled hair.

She should have been furious, humiliated. Instead, she leaned against Trace's hard-muscled strength for a long moment, grateful that they were all still alive.

Trace released her long enough to grab a clean bandanna from his back pocket, then he gently tipped her face up, swabbing away the beads of sweat as if she were no older than April.

Annie might have been able to yell at him if he hadn't looked so damned shaken himself. "You call that...safe?" was all she could manage to squeeze out as April all but bowled her over in a terrified hug.

Trace's smile wavered at one corner as he reached out, tucking a wisp of hair behind Annie's ear. "Safety is highly overrated, Brown-Eyes."

She should have been angry, but she'd heard that legendary Trace McKenna bravado a hundred times before. From the beginning she'd realized it was just a mask to hide his vulnerability. As she looked into Trace's eyes, she was suddenly certain he had been every bit as terrified as she was.

"Mommy, I don't like flying! P-please, can we go home?" April was shaking so hard her teeth were chattering. "I wanna go home!"

It was all Annie could do not to join in her daughter's wailing. She would have given ten years of her life to be a thousand miles away from this airstrip with its wreckage of Trace McKenna's plane, away from Trace's hands and face and rough, whiskey-warm voice that had left her heart devastated to the same magnitude nine years before.

They hadn't even arrived at his blasted retreat, and he'd almost gotten April killed.

"April, accidents happen," Trace said, attempting to soothe the little girl. "We're all right. That's all that matters."

"My mommy's not all right! She throwed up and she never throws up! I thought she'd be dead, just like my daddy."

Trace flinched as if April had driven a knife into his chest. Annie could feel him withdraw, his touch no longer bracing Annie, soothing her, but rather chilling into something detached, impersonal. No, not impersonal. Annie thought she could sense the tiny shiver of something like disgust.

But before anyone could fill the jolting silence with words, a spray of gravel shot up beneath the tires of a Jeep that was roaring toward them on the narrow road. A razor-thin man of about thirty all but vaulted out of the vehicle while it was still moving.

"Is everyone safe? Anyone else in the plane?" the man shouted.

"No. All accounted for," Trace assured him.

But instead of relaxing, the man raked his fingers through hair already standing on end. "McKenna, you crazy bastard! I can't believe you got that bird down in one piece."

"You know me, Rob. I'm a blasted miracle worker."

"What the hell happened? Did you have the thing strung together with baling wire again?"

Trace winced inwardly, remembering the warning the young mechanic had given him. Unfortunately, the fact that Trace's own negligence had endangered Annie and April wasn't as easy to dismiss as the countless other stunts he had pulled over the years.

"Just some kind of malfunction," Trace said gruffly attempting to cover his emotions. "Something jammed. It happens."

"Yeah. But why does it always seem to happen to you?" Rob looked bone-deep worried—like someone who had spent a lot of sleepless nights stewing over a friend who didn't have the common sense God gave an ant. Trace knew he'd given the man more than enough headaches during their friendship.

"Rob, I'd like to introduce you to Annie Brown, and this is April, my... guests."

"Bet you'll never be crazy enough to fly with this nut case again," Rob said. "This guy should come with a warning label from the Surgeon General. Hazardous to your health."

"Yeah, well, no one knows that better than Annie," Trace said.

"Can you get up, miss?" Rob started to extend his hand, but Trace blocked him and scooped Annie up onto her feet himself. She still felt about as stable as a leaf in a windstorm. April was working hard at stifling her tears.

"You sure nothing's broken? Maybe I should call the doc—"

"No, I'm fine," Annie said faintly. "Just...a little shaken."

"Yeah, and the San Andreas Fault is just a tiny imperfection in the earth," Trace muttered. "I'll take care of her, Rob. Take care of the bird for me. I need to get these two in and settled. You did take care of the project I called about, didn't you? I mean, when I called from Chic ago—"

"Yeah. Took my daughter with me to give me a read on what a girl this age would like, and—"

"Okay, okay. Great." Trace cut in. He slipped an arm around Annie and started toward the edge of the landing strip where his own Land Cruiser was waiting.

"Trace, let me know if you need anything," Rob called after them.

"We won't." The only thing Trace needed at the moment was to get Annie and April inside, make sure he hadn't hurt them. God, maybe his father was right—maybe Trace did destroy everything he touched.

No. It had all worked out. He'd brought the plane down safely. Annie and April were unhurt. It was a miracle considering how damned scared he'd been. Scared in a way he hadn't felt in nine years—a deep fear that had sickened him instead of exhilarated him.

Without another word, Trace lowered Annie into the passenger side of the hunter-green vehicle, then loaded

April in the back. He sped down the access road as if he thought the plane disappearing behind them would explode any moment.

"Trace," Annie said, fumbling for her seat belt. "I'd be...real annoyed if we...survived a plane crash only to smack into a tree. The plane would have made much more...interesting news copy."

Trace looked at her long and hard, seeming to drive by instinct alone down the twisted, tree-lined ribbon of road. "You sure you're okay?"

"I whacked my elbow pretty good, but nothing broke—" her words ended in a gasp, punctuated by April's sudden cry.

"Mommy, that cliff is a house!"

Annie gaped at the structure as Trace pulled to a stop. Had it not been for the glare of sunlight on the windows, she could have passed the house without noticing its existence. Planes of stone followed the contours of the abutment, stark, breathtaking, as if the man who built it had wanted to be one with the rugged beauty all around him.

Or, Annie thought with sudden insight, as if he wanted to disappear altogether...cease to exist.

That was absurd. From the first moment she'd met Trace McKenna he had thrived on being center stage. He hadn't minded risking expulsion, or breaking his neck to get attention. Likely the man had merely tossed down an obscene amount of money and directed an architect to build him a house where he could go rock climbing from his front door.

Annie was so lost in her thoughts she didn't even notice that Trace had stopped until he wrenched open her door.

She started to climb out on her own, stunned that she was still pretty wobbly in the knees, but Trace only swore softly, then scooped her up into his strong arms. Annie protested, her cheeks heating as she caught a glimpse of April. But it seemed that the child's fear at their near-death experience had been considerably dulled by her first glimpse of Trace McKenna's "totally awesome" house.

In a second, Trace had Annie at a door adorned with stained glass insets portraying an Indian astride a paint stallion at the edge of this very cliff. The warrior's arms were stretched toward the sun, as if to embrace it.

When Trace shoved the door open with one shoulder, Annie realized that he embraced everything the warrior symbolized.

The interior of the house in the cliff looked as if it had been spun on a Navaho's weaving loom—colors of earth and sky, a hundred different bronzes and golds and turquoises splashed across the huge, sunken great room.

Nubby homespun textures tempted fingers to touch overstuffed couches and chairs. Gnarled wooden tables, scarred by the spurs of cowboys a hundred years ago, were polished to the mellow sheen of old gold. Nothing hung on the walls of the room. But if there had been a veritable museum display of Rembrandts and Monets and van Goghs, Annie doubted any visitor would notice them when confronted with the picture framed by the giant sweep of windows that formed the entire front of the house.

Sky. Mountain. A crashing silver river so far below, it looked like a trickle of water from a child's hand. The wild beauty reached into Annie's chest, squeezed her heart so tight she couldn't breathe.

But hadn't Trace McKenna done that from the first time she'd seen him? And the compelling aura of the boy she had known was a thousand times more potent in this man— this man who was a stranger to her. This man whose name she'd cried when she was terrified and alone in a hospital in

Cincinnati and labor pains were tearing through her like the claws of some raging beast.

"Can I look around, Mr. McKenna?" April piped up, trailing in Annie and Trace's wake.

"This is your home, too," Trace said, then quickly amended, "At least for the next three weeks. Check the place out. See if you can find the bedroom I had set up for you."

The child disappeared down the corridor, and Annie felt more than a little light-headed as Trace carried her to the spacious couch and set her down on it. He looked so worried Annie forced her lips into a quavery smile.

"This has been quite a day, huh, McKenna?"

"Yeah, well." He shrugged. "Let the good times roll."

"The good times, the plane, the Jeep . . ."

"The plane didn't roll. Thank God." The words were low, a little rough.

Annie wanted him to smile. Instead, those incredible eyes of his darkened, fierce, intense.

"You're sure you aren't hurt? I heard a helluva thump back there."

"Might've been the plane hitting the runway."

"I've heard that sound before. This was more like an elbow whacking something metal."

Unbidden, Annie's hand went to her left arm. She swallowed hard as Trace took her wrist in his loose-fingered grasp, unfastening the tiny mother-of-pearl button at her cuff, rolling the fabric back, away from her skin.

It was a simple gesture. It should've been a relatively impersonal one. Why was it that the nerve endings beneath the bruising on Annie's skin were suddenly charged, not with pain, but with a sensation far different? Why was it that she felt as if Trace had stripped away more than her sleeve? Maybe the first layering of the defenses she'd erected around her heart.

No. She couldn't afford to weaken where Trace was concerned. It would be far too easy to be swept up in the wild rushing magic that had consumed Annie before. She was older now, armed with wisdom gained on the mean streets, and with the need to keep her wits about her, to protect her child.

But Trace's callused fingers were probing the slight swelling, moving the joint as if he were a surgeon instead of a professional daredevil.

"It's all right," he affirmed at last, his thumb stroking a slow circle over the bruise. "Annie, I'm sorry I scared you so damned bad."

"I got my revenge once you got me out of the plane. Dramamine might have saved me on the double Ferris wheel, but I guess it doesn't cover motion sickness when the motion in question is an airplane plummeting to the ground."

She saw something flicker in Trace's eyes. The thick, dark fans of his lashes drooped to the ridges of his cheekbones. He hesitated for a long moment. "Why'd you keep it, Brown-Eyes?"

"Keep what?"

"That stupid monkey from the carnival?"

She'd left herself wide open for that one. But then, even if she'd never said a word, the question would have come sometime. Knowing Trace, it was inevitable he'd ask when she was the least prepared.

Annie's cheeks burned. *I kept it because it made that magical night seem real, with the colored lights reflected in your eyes, the lemonade sweet on my tongue, your fingers threading through mine as if we belonged together....*

Annie looked away. "I've always been a pack rat. Someday, when April was older, I wanted to be able to give her something that was linked to her father." The revelation made Annie's cheeks sting, and she would've walked across hot coals to get away from the haunting light in Trace's eyes. "I should go find April," she stammered. "Make sure she's okay."

She got up, her balance shored by her need to flee. It seemed this time he was willing to let her retreat, because he stood, too, and jammed his hands into the pockets of his jeans.

"Bet I know where she is." He started down a wide, cool corridor that branched off in three directions.

Annie glimpsed a kitchen with adobe walls and hickory cabinets, copper pots and dried chili pepper wreaths dangling from iron hooks. The door to the master bedroom stood open, a massive hewn-oak bed in the center of the room, covered with an exquisite handwoven spread.

There was something almost shy about him as he took the fork in the hallway that angled to the right, and Annie could sense the tremor of anticipation that seemed to throb beneath his careless aura.

"Trace, what's this all about?" Annie asked.

His voice was more than a little gruff. "I, uh, wanted to give April a surprise she'd never forget, so I—"

At that moment they rounded the bend. April stood in the center of a room, her face frozen like that of a bad child actor on the stage of a grade-B horror film.

She was silhouetted against a decor that was all pink and lace and ribbons. The curtains had more froth on them than a wedding gown, the bed was painted with ballerina bunnies, a gorgeous canopy stretched above it. Enough fashion dolls to populate Macy's lounged around a pint-size penthouse that would have done Donald Trump proud.

Dress-up clothes were mounded in a life-sized treasure chest, glittering tiaras and feather boas spilling over the rim. Most horrifying of all, a white-painted vanity table stood against the wall, its top littered with a supply of fake jewelry and Bonnie Buttons makeup for pre-Teens.

Annie pressed her hand against her mouth, hard. It would be too cruel to laugh at the dazed expression on her daughter's face, and the equally thunderstruck one on Trace's own.

Annie turned away from them to regain her composure, but her gaze collided with an open closet door, proudly displaying dresses. A dozen dresses and matching shorts sets decked out with sequins and lace were lined up in military precision. Patent leather shoes gleamed next to a peg sporting a matching purse. If the underpants tucked in the drawer had ice-cream cones on them, Trace McKenna was a dead man.

Annie's heart wrenched with sympathy and frustration toward the man who stood behind her. Sympathy because Trace had been so blasted eager to have his little girl love him that he'd gone to all this trouble to please her. Frustration because he hadn't taken the time to find out how to delight April, treating her, instead, like some sort of cookie-cutter child. Annie could almost see the page in some kind of cosmic guide book. Girl, age eight: lace, ruffles and fashion dolls.

This room would have been a dream come true for most little girls. For April it was a nightmare.

Trace had said he wanted to give April a day she'd never forget. He'd succeeded beyond his wildest imagination. The almost-plane-crash couldn't hold a candle to this disaster.

"Mom?" April breathed without turning around. "This time I think *I'm* the one who's gonna throw up."

Chapter 5

Frustration pulsed through Trace's veins. He spewed out a string of oaths, his face burning with embarrassment at his own stupidity. "Son of a bitch! Damn it, I—"

Annie rounded on him. "That's about enough. I understand that you were trying to do something nice for April. It didn't work out the way you planned, but—"

"You think I can't figure that out for myself, Brown-Eyes? I've always been real good at determining exactly when I've screwed up."

"It's not the end of the world, Trace." She sounded like a schoolmarm trying to calm a kid on a rampage. "It's not April's fault that—"

"April's fault?" If Annie had just booted him in the head he couldn't have been more stunned. "Of all the ridiculous—" Trace glanced at the little girl who seemed to have shrunk, somehow, during his bout of anger. She stared at him with round eyes, far more subdued than when they'd been inches away from vaporizing in a ball of flaming fuselage.

Trace started to swear again, then stopped himself. Hell, no wonder the kid looked undone. Any ground Trace had gained with the child on the airplane flight was disappearing fast, and he didn't have the slightest idea how to stop this crash and burn.

He'd wanted the room to be perfect. His first gift to his little girl. He'd wanted to delight her, to dazzle her. To make her love him the way his parents never had. The way Annie never had.

Instead, he'd disappointed her, then scared the daylights out of her.

Trace wanted to go to April, comfort her. Instead, he jammed his fists into his pockets, hating the vulnerability the child spawned in him—a rawness he hadn't felt since the night he'd spilled all his emotions into Annie Brown's hands.

"Trace," Annie bit out, low, "you could've talked to me about April before you—you plunged into this."

"Right." A muscle in his jaw worked and he fought for balance. "After all, you've known her since she was a baby, haven't you? While I—" He ground his teeth, stopping the bitter words. He didn't want to make things worse for the poor kid.

"Take another room for now, April," Trace said after a moment. "I'll get rid of this garbage."

"I-It's okay," April stammered. "I mean, I..." Her gaze flitted desperately around the room, lighting on a stuffed bear almost buried in puffy white kitties. "The bear'll be real cool, once I get that pink ballet costume off her."

"It's okay, Ape." Trace forced stiff lips into a crooked smile. "I know this isn't exactly your style. I wouldn't want both you and your mom throwing up the first day you got here."

"Trace," Annie began, and he could see the irritation, the frustration and the grudging sympathy in her face. It was the sympathy that made him see red. He didn't need anyone to feel sorry for him. Especially Annie.

He waved her to silence with one hand. "I'm gonna go see if I can salvage your luggage from the plane. You two just—hell, I don't know. Do whatever you want."

He started out of the house, heard the bedroom door shut, then Annie's light, anger-quickened steps behind him.

"Blast it, Trace, you just wait a minute. You made a mistake. It's not the end of the world."

"That's true enough." He wheeled on her, fighting to keep his anger bottled up inside him. "I can have that stuff swept out and a whole new batch brought in before tomorrow night."

Something in what he said made ebony sparks quicken in Annie's eyes. "It's so easy for you, isn't it, Trace? Just flinging out money for airplanes and canopy beds and God knows what else! April doesn't need *things*."

Trace reacted like a wolf with a knife in its paw. "Could'a fooled me. Somehow, I don't imagine the Christmas tree in that shelter you live in loaded down with toys. April said your car's about ready for the junk heap, and you don't have a clue how you're going to afford braces."

Annie went ashen and Trace knew he'd hit her right when she was weakest. "April had no right to tell you that."

"She wasn't telling me anything I hadn't figured out for myself the first time I walked in your door. That shelter isn't exactly the Ritz, you know? In fact, I bet you get some pretty ugly characters zinging in and out. Not exactly the kind of surroundings that would get the PTA stamp of approval, if you know what I mean."

"April has always had everything she's needed!"

"Yeah, yeah, yeah. I can tell her childhood has been Disneyland. But that's all gonna change now that I'm in her life."

"What is that supposed to mean?"

"You're the genius. You figure it out. Now, if you'll excuse me, I've got something to take care of."

"Don't you mean you're running away from this mess, the way you always have when things didn't work out exactly the way you wanted?"

Nothing she could've said would have triggered Trace's fury more completely. His face contorted into a snarl. "As I remember, *you* were the one who ran. That is, after you let me believe that you'd gotten rid of my baby."

She flinched. Sadistic jerk that he was, he was glad.

"Why'd you do that, Annie?" he demanded with velvet menace. "Why'd you have your daddy tell me that you'd destroyed our child? Thrown my baby away?"

Those incredible green eyes grew rounder, what little color remained in her cheeks washing away. "I never told my father that I was going to have an abortion," Annie faltered. "They wanted me to. My parents, and yours, too. But I couldn't . . . My God, Trace, I had no idea—"

No one that pale and shaken could be telling a lie. Trace felt like the biggest bastard on the planet. And the biggest fool for displaying such a raw place in his soul. He fought back the only way he knew how—hard and fast and nasty.

"What the hell did it matter what anyone told me?" Trace scoffed. "You sure as hell didn't want anything to do with me. You made that crystal clear the last time I saw you. I'm sure you didn't want anyone to suspect that Trace

McKenna had knocked you up. No father at all would be better for your baby than a worthless screw-up like me."

Something flickered in Annie's eyes, as if he'd just ripped his fingernails across some half-healed wound inside her. She glanced over her shoulder at the closed door to April's room, raw terror, pleading in her eyes.

Trace felt sick at the possibility April might have heard. He charged past Annie and flung open the bedroom door. Relief shot through him. April was curled on the window seat, industriously undressing the bear as promised, oblivious to the rancor seething between the adults outside her door.

April looked up at him with wary eyes exactly the shade of Trace's own.

Trace tried to force words past the lump that had suddenly knotted his throat. "I just wanted to tell you that you were right," he said, managing to squeeze the words out. "The dress did look stupid on that bear."

He could feel April's eyes on him as he stalked from the room. He shoved past Annie, then stormed to the Land Cruiser and put it in gear. It wasn't until he had driven deep into the shelter of the trees that he allowed himself to slump against the seat in defeat.

He felt more beat up inside than he had when he'd awakened in the hospital three weeks ago. He felt about as helpless as when the explosion had sent him flying through the air. But far worse, he felt exposed, somehow, defenseless against the reproach in Annie's and April's eyes.

That made him feel unnerved, edgy, as if he had suddenly been slung back into the past, into the body of the seventeen-year-old kid who had known little but disapproval and scorn, felt little but anger that hid away the reality of a yawning emptiness inside him, an unquenchable need to have someone, anyone, reach out to him, believe . . . what? That he could do something right? That he wasn't a walking disaster?

Damn! Trace slammed his fist against the steering wheel. He shouldn't still hurt so much, feel so crazy, as if all his insecurities had suddenly been laid bare. He had buried them deep years ago, when he'd walked away from Arizona, and the memories of Annie that had haunted him there.

He'd wanted to stride back into Annie's life—confident, self-assured. A man who had survived the crucible of his past and emerged a success.

Instead, he felt more like a fumbling kid than ever. The constant screw-up. Worthless.

That single word, flitting through his consciousness, galvanized Trace, filling his mind with the bitterest of memories. Colonel Brown's hands knotted in Trace's shirt as he slammed Trace against the support post of the porch, the military man's eyes simmering with hate, with fury, with barely restrained violence that would have terrified Trace, if Trace had had anything left to lose.

You spineless piece of garbage! You think my daughter would have anything to do with someone like you? You may have gotten her in the back seat of your car, Mr. Doctor's son, but she knows what a worthless mess you are now! She got rid of your baby. Threw it away like so much trash—the same way she's throwing you away. . . .

A furious groan parted Trace's lips as he shoved the memory away. The words that had been just one more echoing of his father's angry denouncements, his teachers' jeering put-downs.

Has anyone ever told you that you're wonderful? Annie's shy question rippled through Trace's memory, the lights of the carnival glowing on her skin, her eyes shimmering with pleasure as he laid the stuffed monkey in her arms.

No, Brown-Eyes, Trace could hear his own voice, the unsteadiness in it that had made his cheeks heat with embarrassment. *No one ever has...*

When he'd stormed away from Arizona, after that scene with Annie's father, he'd been in so much anguish he'd come close to flinging himself in front of one of the cars zooming past him on the freeway. Instead, he'd promised himself that he'd show them all that they were wrong about Trace McKenna. All of them...his father, Colonel Brown...Annie. And he *had* proved himself through his spectacular success.

He'd signed on with FireStorm a week later. Within three years he was their number one man. Nothing, no one, was going to take that triumph away from him now. So he'd messed up with the room for April. Big deal. He could still make it right.

A few phone calls, and presto chango. Trace McKenna snapped his fingers and whatever he wanted was done. His bank account was better at granting his wishes than any genie who'd ever been trapped in a damned bottle.

It could buy him anything. Houses built into cliffs, airplanes, friends. Hell, Trace sneered inwardly, remembering his hasty departure from the hospital and his flash-fast arrival on Annie's doorstep. His money had even gotten him his daughter back, hadn't it? After all, if he'd been some poor bastard roughneck, working on an oil well, he would've had to wait God knew how long until he had the money, the ability to go after April.

Yeah, Trace thought grimly. He was one lucky son of a bitch.

Then why did he feel so damned empty inside?

* * *

Three hours later, Trace parked the Cruiser back under a stand of lodge pole pines outside the cliff house. The rear of the vehicle held the suitcases—somewhat worse for the wear. He'd worked hard to excavate them from the wreckage, actually grateful for the chance to battle against the twisted metal—physical exertion having always been his safety valve when his emotions had been getting the better of him.

But as he stared at the windows of the house, now lit mellow gold against the encroaching twilight, Trace still couldn't rid himself of the bitter taste of failure. The gnawing, familiar sense of defeat that wouldn't let him go. A sensation somehow worse because Annie had witnessed it. And Trace knew that he'd never forget the mixture of pity and disgust that had swirled in her forest-hued eyes.

That was, by far, the most grating thing that had happened in this day filled with disaster. Annie had seen him fail big time. Worse still, he'd gotten so angry he'd thrown aside his defenses and let her see just how deep his scars ran. Then, to top it off, he'd hit her own weak spots with all the finesse of a pit bull, left her hurting.

He'd wanted to pay her back just a little for the pain her desertion had caused him. But somewhere, in his anger and embarrassment, he'd forgotten that Annie had given him a gift beyond price—a chance to get to know April. To be part of her life.

She had trusted him that much, at least. Okay, so he'd pressured her. But she'd still decided to give him a chance. After the way he'd acted in the hallway of the cliff house, Trace wouldn't have blamed her if she'd changed her mind.

Sucking in a deep breath, he grabbed the bags, then made his way to the door, shoving it open with his shoulder. He wasn't sure what he expected—Annie, on the phone making arrangements to take April back to Chicago. April tearful and angry and hating him. Or both of them withdrawn and full of censure over his behavior hours before.

Quietly, Trace eased the suitcases to the floor, listening, looking as he made his way down the corridor. He found them in the antacid-pink bedroom. April sat cross-legged in the middle of that ruffly bed, looking as out of place as a catcher's mitt on a trayful of cream puffs. She was dressed in one of Trace's own T-shirts. The thing was gigantic on the kid, the dive-shop emblem faded. April's dark hair cascaded down her back, while Annie sat behind her, drawing a brush through the glorious mahogany ripples. April's eyes were half closed, and he could see her sigh with pleasure, while Annie . . .

Annie's face was wistful, maybe a little bit sad, as if images of the woman April would one day become were tangled in the brown-and-gold strands. As if Annie knew that each stroke of the brush brought her one more heartbeat closer to having to let go.

But at least Annie had had April for a while. At least she had memories of her toddling steps. It was as if they were surrounded in some mystical circle—mother, child. A bond that had been glorified in paintings since the first artist had attempted to capture the Madonna on canvas. It was a circle Trace knew that he could never breach, never be a part of. No matter how many sets of braces he paid for, or how many rooms he designed for the little girl sitting on the bed.

Maybe he was wrong to risk upsetting that delicate balance between Annie and April, a voice whispered inside him.

The thought burned around the edges of his heart, until he couldn't watch them for another minute. He turned and walked away, alone.

Annie glanced up, catching just a glimpse of Trace's features cast in shadow. She stroked a hand down April's silky hair. "Time for bed, munchkin."

"Yeah. But if I have any nightmares about killer pink bunnies trying to skewer me with carrot swords, I'm comin' in to sleep in your bed," April insisted.

Annie tucked the little girl in, then shut out the lights. She hovered there long minutes, her hand still on the light switch, her teeth catching nervously at her lower lip as she peered down the corridor where Trace had disappeared.

It would probably be best for all concerned if she just found herself a bed and went to sleep, left things alone until morning, when they'd both had time to cool their tempers.

If she'd seen even a hint of anger in Trace McKenna's eyes, she probably would have done just that. But the light had snagged on his mouth for just a moment, revealing something vulnerable, something lonely that had reached into Annie's chest and tugged, hard.

Why'd you have your daddy tell me you threw away my baby?

How many times in the past three hours had Trace's words echoed in Annie's mind, painting horrifyingly vivid pictures of the scene that must have transpired between her father and Trace so long ago. No one knew better than Annie that Colonel Brown could wield verbal weapons with far more skill than he'd ever brought to firing an M16. He'd leveled Annie emotionally more times than she could count. And he'd loved her. In spite of it all, deep down, Annie had known her father loved her.

The rigid, military-disciplined Colonel Brown had hated wild, irrepressible Trace McKenna from the first time he'd laid eyes on him.

She had wanted Trace to believe that everything was over—wanted to erase all sense of responsibility from his mind. The letter she had left for him had been firm, and yet she had tried to ease Trace's guilt as gently as possible, to shield him with ambiguities. She hadn't written that she was getting an abortion, although that was what her parents had wanted her to do. She had left it so that Trace could believe that if he chose to, so that he could forget.

But there would have been no gentleness in her father's words. No understanding for the boy who had seemed so tough, but had been so vulnerable underneath it all.

Annie reeled at the image of her father glorying in hurting Trace, the bastard who had hurt his little girl. She reeled at the knowledge that Trace had spoken to her father at all.

God knew, Colonel Brown had never bothered to tell her. Not even years after April's birth, when Annie and her parents had reconciled.

If Annie had had any idea what her father was going to do, she would have summoned up the courage to stay and face Trace herself. But Trace had always made her so weak, so vulnerable, she'd been terrified that if she saw him one more time, he'd manage to talk her into something she knew they'd both regret for the rest of their lives.

Still, if her father had told Annie Trace had come after her, things might have been different.

How? Annie demanded of herself sharply. She and Trace could've settled down in one of those cozy little cottages in the suburbs with a white picket fence and a golden retriever? Trace could've gotten a job swinging a sledgehammer for minimum wage and worked himself old long before his time, while she watched him grow harder and more bitter, restless and unhappy, until he hated her, resented the baby.

No. If Colonel Brown had posted an ad in the *New York Times* that Trace had come looking for Annie, it wouldn't have changed anything. Trace would still have been hell-bent on his own destruction. Annie still would have had to find a way to struggle through the pain of loving him.

It was an exercise in futility to wonder what might have been, weave fairy-tale endings and happily-ever-afters. And yet, as Annie made her way quietly through Trace McKenna's empty, quiet house, she couldn't help but realize just how deeply her father's lie must have cut Trace. How those harsh words must have wounded his spirit. She had seen the boy's pain in the man's eyes three hours ago when he'd been taut with fury, his I-couldn't-give-a-damn aura stripped away.

Slowly, Annie walked through the dimly lit house, searching for some sign of Trace. She found him outside, beyond a sliding glass door that led out onto an outcropping of rock that formed a patio. Rugged furniture hewn of logs blended beautifully in with the woodlands that cupped the house in its palm, while the sunset bled over the rim of the horizon in trickles of glowing crimson.

Trace stood at the edge of the outcropping, silhouetted against the vivid hues. His long, jeans-clad legs were braced apart, as if he were carrying some grindingly heavy weight on those broad shoulders. His hands were shoved in the back pockets of his jeans. His head was flung back, as if he was staring into the sky, his long, dark hair rippling in the breeze. He was every bit as beautiful a male specimen as the Indian worked in stained glass. And, Annie thought suddenly, he was just as solitary, standing there.

Oddly, Trace McKenna had always seemed alone, even when he was in the middle of a crowd of laughing friends and adoring females. Even as a girl, Annie had understood that feeling. She had known it so often herself. In truth, it was what had first drawn her to the rebellious boy who had changed the course of her life.

Even now, so many years later, it made her incredibly sad to realize that while she was finally safe in a circle of love woven by trusted friends and her beautiful daughter, Trace McKenna was still as solitary as he had been from the first moment she had seen him.

Her fingers trembled a little as she reached for the door's gleaming handle. It slid open with barely a whisper, worlds away from the doors in BabyPlace—creaking hinges caked with decades' worth of paint.

"Trace?" She said his name softly, and he stilled. She could feel the waves of wariness rippling from every muscle in his body.

He cleared his throat. "Your suitcases weren't in too bad shape, all things considered. I left them in the hall."

"Thanks. Was there a lot of damage to the plane?"

One shoulder shrugged. "What the hell. If we can't patch it up, I'll buy myself a new one." He was mocking himself, Annie realized suddenly. Mocking everything that he was. Just as he always had.

"Trace, stop it."

"Stop what?"

"Pretending not to care. I'm sorry. Sorry about the plane. Sorry about the room. I'm just . . . sorry."

She heard his breath hiss between his teeth as if she'd struck him with a whip. He turned and the glowing hues of the sunset touched the planes of his face. Annie had seen just that lost expression on his features before, the night she'd found him in the loft of Halloran's stable.

That alone should've been enough to send her racing in the opposite direction.

But Trace's voice came, soft. "Why should you be sorry, Brown-Eyes? I've been a first-class bastard from the mo-

ment I stormed back into your life. The big man, wanting
to impress April. And you." Annie could imagine what that
rough-edged confession had cost him. "Oh well. Guess
you've figured out one thing, anyway."

"What's that?"

"That you did the right thing when you—" He hesitated, dragging his hand through his hair. "What was it
your dad said? Threw me away?"

Oh, God. The words twisted in Annie's chest like a knife.
She couldn't afford to feel this way. Not toward Trace. He
had stormed into her life and threatened to take her child.
His mere presence in April's life could shatter the founda-
tion of trust Annie had built with her daughter. And yet,
she suddenly felt as if she were the one hurting him.

Annie balled her hands into fists, resisting the tempta-
tion to run her fingers down the hard, beard-stubbled line
of Trace's jaw.

She didn't dare reach out to him. She had tried to comfort him once before, and it had led her deeper and deeper
into something she hadn't understood until it was too late
to turn away.

Still, how could she stand here, leaving those pain-filled
words dangling between them? If she did, wasn't she making what he said true somehow? Confirming her father's
cruel words?

"I didn't throw you away, Trace. I only wanted to let you
get on with your future. We were kids. We made a mistake. You had so many dreams. I didn't want you to pay for
what happened between us for the rest of your life."

"But it was okay for you to pay, huh, Annie? What
about your dreams? You know. The big stage. The concert
grand. You worked so hard. Were so damned good on the
piano. Sometimes, when I'd listen, my chest would get all

tight, like . . . like there was something inside me trying to get free. You gave that all up.''

"Sometimes fate chooses paths for us that are different than the ones we'd have picked for ourselves. In my case, the fates were right. I was meant to be scared and alone when I gave birth to April. I was meant to wander into J. T. James's shelter. Because of that, I've been able to do far more good than I ever would have on any concert stage.''

"You could've given me a chance," Trace growled.

"A chance to what? You didn't love me, Trace."

He waited for a heartbeat. ''What if I did?''

A pained laugh squeezed from Annie's chest. ''I was sixteen, you were seventeen. We were infatuated with each other. But love? The forever kind? No.''

Silence. Long. Pulsing. Annie glanced once at Trace McKenna's storm-cloud eyes, then turned away. "Come on, McKenna. Look at you. Mr. Rich Powerful Adventurer. You don't exactly fit the mold of a guy who's been nursing a broken heart for nine years."

For a moment, Annie was almost afraid of what he'd say. His eyes darkened, the mysteries in the gray-blue depths deepening. Then the corner of his mouth softened into that smile Annie had seen so rarely, even on the boy he had been.

"If I'd known how good you'd look, I might have worked harder at acting miserable. You're even more beautiful than I remember you, Annie.''

Hot blood flooded Annie's cheeks. She prayed the deepening twilight would hide it. "As I remember, you always did lay the flattery on pretty thick, Romeo. Funny, all those times I heard you spouting it to your hundred-and-one girlfriends, you never mentioned anything about my looks at all.''

Was it a trick of the sunset, or did those high masculine cheekbones darken. "Maybe you were so pretty I couldn't think of any way to put it into words."

Annie chuckled. "That's an incredible comeback. No wonder you had so many women hanging around your locker. You really are good, McKenna."

"And you really are pretty."

"Marcie Kane, the girl who was your steady when we first met—now she was beautiful. And that cheerleader you dated for a while—what was her name? Buffy? Muffy?"

"Tiffany Jo."

"That's right. Tiffany. If I remember correctly, she was responsible for feeding the fantasies of the male half of Kennedy High."

"Who was responsible for the female half?"

"I'm not going to touch that with a ten-foot pole."

Trace's grin spread wider, a wicked dimple darting into his left cheek. "I knew I impressed you, but I think you're exaggerating a little."

Annie couldn't help herself. She slugged him on the arm. She'd done that more than once in that incredible, brief period when their relationship had shifted from wary tolerance to uneasy friendship, and then, most precious of all, trust.

She didn't want to smile at him, but he was being so...almost, well, sweet. Reminding her too sharply of the Trace who had made her laugh and haunted her dreams for so many years.

Always before when she'd dealt him one of her playful slugs he had retaliated by dragging her into a bear hug and tickling her. Annie felt a shiver of memory work through her. There hadn't been much touching in Colonel Brown's family—no clambering up on parents' laps or snuggling on the couch before bedtime.

The first time Trace had given Annie a quick hug, she hadn't had a clue how to react. When he'd touched her again and again—brushing back a stray tendril of her hair, holding her hand, looping his arm around her shoulder—he'd released in her a hunger she hadn't even known existed inside her. Like someone who had been starved, she'd sought out his touch, delighted in the tastes of physical affection Trace had offered.

Affection. Friendship. Not the hot kind of passion-laced touches Annie had glimpsed Trace lavishing on his girlfriends behind the meager shield of his open locker door.

She had known all along that her relationship with Trace was different. She had tried to convince herself that she liked it that way. But it had been during one of those first playful wrestling matches that she'd become aware of another hunger inside herself, sparked by the hard, lean planes of Trace's body, so different from her own. The silky texture of his hair, the strength in his hands...

Annie shook herself inwardly, forcing herself back to the present—to rugged cliffs and a man who was almost a stranger. To reality and impossibilities she should have let go of a long time ago.

She looked away, not wanting Trace to see that while he hadn't broken his heart over her, she had come terrifyingly close to breaking her heart over him.

Suddenly, Annie couldn't fight the need to beat a hasty retreat any longer.

"April will be up at the crack of dawn," Annie said in an attempt to excuse herself, wanting nothing more than to escape the strange spell that seemed carried on the Colorado mountain air. "We'd better go to bed."

Bed. The word wobbled in her throat, just enough that Trace couldn't miss it. Terrific, Annie, she thought grimly.

Great way to keep him from knowing what you're remembering.

She forced a laugh. "You can race in and think about Tiffany Jo."

"I think she's wearing staples in her navel and very little else anymore." Trace said, but there was no teasing in his voice.

"Wasn't she voted the student most likely to achieve the title of Miss October?" Annie asked.

She jumped as she felt the warm, callused crook of Trace's finger beneath her chin. Awareness sizzled through her, hot, undeniable. Oh, God, why did he still have the power to make her react that way?

She wanted to pull away from him. Instead, she swallowed hard, unable to squeeze words through a throat that was suddenly dry.

She could smell the wind-scent of Trace, the wild, woodsy tang that didn't come from any cologne bottle. He was so close, the tendrils of his hair were tossed by the wind until they brushed against her left cheek.

"Back in Arizona...you looked like an angel to me." His thumb whispered over the curve of her bottom lip. "You still do."

Annie's knees went weak as water at those words, her heart stinging unbearably. "Trace, don't—"

He laid his fingertips on her lips to silence her, and she felt like she was melting. "Don't worry, Brown-Eyes. It was all a long time ago. I'm gonna keep my distance. We both know it's better that way. I just never told you what I saw when I looked at you way back then. I wanted you to know."

Trace turned and walked into his house, toward the bed where he would sleep alone. Annie sank into one of the rough-hewn chairs, dazed at his words and her reaction to them.

I'm gonna keep my distance... we both know it's better that way....

Was it possible that Trace was feeling the same mind-numbing attraction? That he could sense the danger in it?

No, she was being ridiculous. She'd picked up enough clues about the life Trace McKenna led from news clips to fill in the rest. There were probably still flocks of women trailing after him. The only difference was that instead of inhabiting one Arizona high school, his adoring throng was spread out over four continents.

No matter how hard it was, Annie would have to hold on tighter than ever to her original plan in coming here. She'd have to stay as far away from Trace as possible. He could destroy everything she'd built for herself, for April.

No, this new throbbing sense of urgency wasn't because of April. It wasn't even because of the disdain she had first felt for the man Trace McKenna had become.

She'd have to block Trace out of her thoughts, because he could still make her knees wobble, her head spin, make that legendary Annie-Brown common sense fly out the window like a paper airplane. Their lives were totally different. Absolutely irreconcilable. She'd be a fool to forget that, even for a heartbeat.

She had to stay focused. Get a grip on reality.

Reality.

Reality was Trace walking into the glorious master bedroom she had glimpsed hours earlier. Trace, standing in a hot shower, the water pounding on those beautifully sculpted muscles, the steam rising from his skin.

Reality was that huge bed that she had glimpsed hours before, with its homespun coverlet and ice-white sheets and

Trace sleeping there alone, with just one thin wall separating them.

Annie was mortified to feel her breasts tingle, her lip tremble where Trace had touched it. And she wondered if she could close her eyes at all tonight without picturing him in that bed of his, his bronzed skin silhouetted against stark white sheets, his long-limbed body restless.

It was crazy. Insane. And yet, she knew instinctively that even if she leapt from Trace's rugged cliff, she would still be prey to that fierce attraction they had known before either of them was truly ready. It would tug her back as inexorably as any mythical siren's song.

When Annie had left Chicago, she'd been terrified that Trace might be an emotional danger to April. She'd tried to leash that fear by concentrating on the true caring that had been in Trace's eyes when he'd dealt with their daughter. She'd tried to be brutally honest with herself, acknowledging the fact that it was her own relationship with April that could be on shaky ground when the child learned the truth.

But equally terrifying was another fear that reared up inside Annie.

Trace still had the power to take Annie all apart inside.

If she wasn't careful, Trace McKenna would leave her every bit as broken as she had been the night she hitchhiked away from Arizona so many years before.

Chapter 6

Annie stood in the sunny kitchen, whipping up a batch of French toast, April's favorite breakfast. Not that the child would notice if her mother put gold-plated snails on her plate, Annie thought with a grimace.

For the past three days, the little girl had been delighting in a dizzy whirl of activity that was far more fascinating than any egg-soaked bread could ever be. While Annie...Annie was doing exactly what she had sworn she was going to do.

Stay out of Trace McKenna's way.

It should have been easy enough. There was a batch of mysteries Annie had packed in her suitcase so she could catch up on her reading. There were countless woodland trails leading away from the cliff house, offering postcard-lovely vistas to enjoy. There were letters to write and social work journals to go through. Barring that, she could have just slept away the time, napping on the patio to catch up on the sleep she had lost during the turbulent days after Trace had reentered her life.

Even April had done her part. After a rocky beginning, the little girl had decided that Trace McKenna was a kindred spirit. The pair had tripped off exploring an old mine and gone riding on horses that belonged to the man who had come racing to the airstrip three days ago. Rob Carrolton, caretaker of the cliff house, had loaned April his youngest daughter's motley black pony for as long as she stayed with Trace. Cocoa was probably the ugliest pony Annie had ever seen. And the most lovable. April adored her beyond measure.

Annie should have been delighted to play The Invisible Woman. God knew, she'd wanted things to go smoothly. She had hoped—down beyond the selfish, frightened part of her—that April could build some kind of a relationship with her father. And yet, there was something about watching the two of them trundle merrily off together that left Annie feeling wistful. Lonely.

A couple of times, Trace had invited her to come along on their adventures, but April had always leapt in, dismissing the invitations breezily before Annie could reply. *My mom's scared of horses . . . she hates stomping around the woods and getting eaten up by bugs an' stuff. She's real allergic to poison ivy.*

Translation in April-ese: I want to keep you all to myself.

Annie gave the eggs she was beating an extra energetic whip, then slapped a slice of bread into the bowl. She couldn't help but grimace. True, she had legion shortcomings as an outdoors woman. But she didn't exactly relish the thought of Trace McKenna being made aware of every one.

Unfortunately, the strange sensation in her chest had an even deeper source. For eight years, she had had April all to herself. The two of them against the world. It made Annie hurt inside to see just how easily Trace had managed to enter April's life, gain her trust.

It made Annie ache to realize that this was only the beginning. Someday, this child who had been her whole life would walk away from her altogether—a young woman with her own life to lead. Annie could close her eyes now and imagine April striding away with the same eagerness she had when marching off with Trace, she could picture April smiling and flinging her a careless wave of her hand.

Annie stabbed the bread with a fork and set it to sizzle in the cast-iron skillet. Annie had always wanted April to be strong and independent. She'd cherished the girl's stubborn streak, remembering far too many times the girl, Annie, had been bulldozed by her father, other kids who had believed it their sacred duty to torment the shy army brat who had just invaded their school. Annie had been completely blindsided by the niggling resentment that welled up around the edges of her heart when April displayed that independence by accepting Trace.

The truth was, Annie had expected April to be warily tolerant of him. She'd expected the little girl to demand Annie accompany them, or at least occasionally squeeze in time for a cuddle in one of the big chairs. She had hoped that April could put this whole ordeal into perspective— demonstrate that no matter what treats Trace dangled in front of the child, he couldn't woo her loyalties away from Annie.

But with each day that passed, April was more and more fascinated by the man who had brought her to this totally awesome house. This man who climbed cliffs and brought planes in for crash landings. Who rode horses and wasn't afraid of snakes and bats and poison ivy.

It was ridiculous—getting upset because April was distracted during a vacation. Annie should just let her daughter enjoy herself to the fullest and ignore these pangs of something distressingly like jealousy. She should just stand back and let Trace McKenna play Daddy Wonderful until he got restless and bored and wanted to go hang-gliding off the Grand Canyon or something. For all Trace's righteous indignation, it was inevitable that he'd tire of—what had he called it? Playing house? And then, Annie and April could go back to their well-ordered existence in the cozy apartment above BabyPlace.

Trace might check in on April occasionally—a stray birthday card or present. But he wouldn't be a tangible part of their lives. April would go back to scooping up her baseball mitt and running out to play catch with Tyler and J.T. instead of trailing after Trace like an adoring puppy.

The thought should have brought comfort. Instead, Annie felt a stab of unease. She flipped the French toast, remembering Allison James's gentle voice that night at HomePlace, warning that April craved a father of her own.

Annie had never suspected how much her daughter had longed for that kind of relationship until now. That knowledge shouldn't have had such an impact. It shouldn't have made Annie feel like she had failed April somehow. But it did.

She chewed at her lower lip, wondering how April would react if things happened the way she suspected they would, Trace gradually losing interest in his daughter the way he had his countless girlfriends, playing baseball...everything.

There was the racket of running feet in the hallway and April came bounding through the kitchen door. She'd kept the shirt Annie had taken from Trace's drawer that first night. It reached well beyond her knees, but April adored the reggae-spouting crawfish lounging on its faded cotton front.

Annie wondered if, months from now, April would still be wearing that shirt, waiting for a phone call from Saudi Arabia, a souvenir from the Australian outback. Waiting for Trace to walk through the door.

She tried to drive back the image that squeezed her heart.

"Good morning, munchkin. Hungry?" Annie put on her brightest smile.

"Yeah. I found all this cool wilderness food when Trace let me rummage through his backpack. He said I could have freeze-dried oatmeal for breakfast this morning."

Annie's smile turned brittle. "I thought you hated oatmeal."

"I do. 'Cept Trace said it's real good for you, and besides, this isn't some wimpy oatmeal your mom makes you eat. It's the stuff astronauts take on space launches, and— Oh." April's gaze collided with the food her mother was just sliding onto a blue stoneware plate. "French toast. Bet you made that for me, huh?"

"Bet I did."

"I don't want to hurt your feelings or anything. I can eat it if you want me to."

Annie was fighting to keep from snapping at the little girl when Trace came striding in. His hair was damp from his morning shower, a fresh turquoise-blue shirt printed with geometric Indian designs clung softly to his broad shoulders. Jeans that had once been charcoal-colored sheathed his legs, the seams worn white, the edges frayed. His feet were bare and his first smile of the morning was so latently sexy Annie felt a swift stab of desire sizzle along the already ragged edges of her nerves.

She was jarringly certain that April wouldn't be the only one in danger of waiting for Trace McKenna to breeze into their lives.

Nothing could've made her more unsettled. Trace tipped back his head, sniffing the air. "Somethin' smells great in here."

"French toast," April supplied. "I have to eat it instead of freeze-dried oatmeal, 'cause my mom made it for me 'cause it's my favorite back home."

"You make it sound like a form of torture," Annie let slip.

She saw Trace watching her through eyes that saw far too much, and she wondered if he knew that she was stinging, hurting inside.

"Torture me, Brown-Eyes. Puh-leeze!" Trace sauntered over and took the fork from Annie's hand. He scooped a piece of the fried toast into his fingers. He muttered muffled curses, hastily juggling it from hand to hand, blowing on it until it was cool enough to take a bite of. When he did, Annie noted a peculiar expression on his face—like a kid about to take bitter medicine.

Annie suddenly remembered arriving at the McKenna household one morning to go over some English notes with Trace. He'd gone into a dramatic death scene, pretending he was poisoned when his sister, Patricia, had tried to pawn off some French toast on him.

He'd had Annie laughing so hard she was crying by the time he was done expounding on how much he loathed the stuff. Annie's mouth firmed as he braced himself to take another bite.

He made a sound of consummate satisfaction deep in his throat. "This is the best French toast I've ever tasted. Terrific. You don't know what you're missing, Ape."

Damn him to blazes, why did he have to be nice now? Annie took a warped satisfaction in piling up the whole panful on his plate. "You can have it all," she said sweetly. "I know exactly how much you like it."

"Great!" April said, with a skip of delight. "I'm gonna go outside and eat my breakfast with Cocoa."

"Want some marshmallows?" Trace asked.

April groaned and raced outside.

Annie's fingers clenched on the fork. Two weeks ago, April's inner radar would have been locked on the fact that her mother was upset. The child would've been standing on her head, indulging in all sorts of antics in an effort to make Annie laugh. It seemed at the moment, her daughter couldn't see past the end of her nose—that was, unless she was looking at that blasted borrowed pony.

Trace cleared his throat, the sound jarring Annie from her thoughts.

"Well, just me and you and all this delicious toast, huh, Brown-Eyes?" he enthused, taking a seat at the table. She could tell how much effort it took to muster all that enthusiasm. He scooped up a fork and started in manfully.

Terrific, Annie thought. She had a daughter who loved French toast but was eating freeze-dried oatmeal with a borrowed pony. She had a man who was looking green around the gills as he shoveled down mouthfuls of food that he hated because of some warped sense of chivalry. And she was feeling like the only kid in the class not invited to a birthday party.

"Oh, for God's sake!" Annie snapped, yanking the plate from under Trace's nose with a force that bumped the hand holding his fork into his upper lip.

"Yeow!" Trace yelped, rubbing his mouth. "What'd you do that for?"

"I don't need charity."

"Charity?"

"Yes. Trace McKenna saying this is the best French Toast he's ever eaten is a little like Socrates saying he's real thirsty for a hemlock cocktail."

Trace's cheeks reddened. Busted, Annie thought wryly.

He fiddled with the tines of his fork. "I just...well, you worked so hard cooking and all, that I...hell, when April wouldn't eat it—"

"April has been turning up her nose at the four food groups for eight years. I'm used to rejection when it comes to peas, carrots and broccoli. French toast is a new angle, but I'll get over it."

Trace watched her intently for a long moment. "You sure about that?" There was an undercurrent to his voice, something that made Annie stiffen. She had a feeling that he was able to see the sudden crushing sense of hurt and loneliness, a million conflicting emotions that had stormed into her life along with this tall, compelling, relentlessly sexy man she was trying her best to ignore.

"Annie, I know you aren't used to sharing April," he said in an infuriatingly reasonable tone. "This must be a real change for you. I wouldn't mind if you came with us sometimes."

"The agreement was that you wanted time alone with her."

"I wanted a chance to bond with the kid. I figured with you around, April wouldn't have any room for me." Trace's voice softened. "But she does have room for me, Annie."

Annie felt those words pour like acid into an open wound. "Great," she said between clenched teeth. "We'll just set you up in a tent out in back of the shelter, stick the pony in the tree house and import a bunch of poison ivy, and you and April can go on having a whale of a time. That is, if you can squeeze a few hours in between Trinidad and Tibet."

"I'm going to be part of her life, Annie." His eyes met hers levelly.

"I've agreed to letting you spend time with April. You can drop by and see her whenever you happen to be flying past Chicago on your way to Outer Mongolia. April loves palling around with you."

"She doesn't need a pal, Annie. She needs a father."

The words twisted in Annie's chest. "I'd think that after the time you've spent with her, you'd have stopped being selfish, Trace. Think of how badly it would upset her to find out—"

"That she has a father who loves her? Funny, I don't think that would bother her at all." The words packed a dizzying punch, despite the fact that he said them quietly, gently.

"I won't have her confused. Blast it, Trace, I'm trying to accommodate you here. To...I don't know, give you a chance to— But I don't..."

"You don't want things to change. I know. But it's too late, Annie. Everything has already changed and there's no way to turn back now. For you. For me. For April. I've been thinking about this a lot the past three days. To begin with, I want to take care of her financially."

"April and I do just fine—"

"Take that blasted stiff-necked Brown pride and stuff it, Annie. I can make things easier for both of you. Why shouldn't I do what I can for you when it's so damned easy for me? Why shouldn't you take what I'm offering? Security? Freeing yourself from worrying about braces and car repairs and how you're going to afford to send April to college someday."

"Ask April. She's got it all figured out. She's going to Arizona State on a baseball scholarship. She's convinced by the time she's old enough the gender barrier will be broken in the major leagues and she can be the first woman pitcher for the White Sox. Unlike you, she'd work herself to death for the chance."

Trace dragged his fingers through the damp strands of his hair, his mouth tightening. "This isn't about me, Annie. Not about any of the million and one mistakes I've made. It's not even about you. It's about April. About raising the quality of her life."

There had been too many Christmases that Annie had stood like a child herself, her nose pressed against the store window as she stared longingly at the gifts she wanted to buy her daughter. The expensive aluminum bat April had been drooling over for months. The White Sox team jacket in black satin.

There had been too many times Annie had resolutely chosen a less expensive toy or jacket or piece of sporting equipment. April had never complained. But Annie had chafed inside every time, wishing that things could be different. The thought of this man breezing into April's life, carelessly slinging out largesse made Annie's stomach churn.

"In case you haven't noticed, April is a healthy, happy, well-adjusted eight-year-old. There's nothing wrong with her life. At least there wasn't until you came charging into it a week ago."

"It's wrong for me to care about her? You think that's going to hurt her somehow? Dammit, I—"

"Guys! Hey, guys!" April's voice carried along the hallway, the screen door banging as she came charging back into the house. The two adults froze, and Annie sensed that

Trace was battling as hard as she was to keep the raw emotions from showing.

"There's someone coming!" April cried as she burst into the room, her cheeks flushed, her pigtails flying. "It's this humongous truck with this great big trailer."

"A semi in the middle of a mountain hideaway?" Annie asked, confused. She looked at Trace and unease curled in her middle. He didn't look astonished in the least. He looked more like April did when she was at the stubborn-bordering-on-belligerent stage.

"Wonder what a semi would be doing up here, Ape," Trace said, his eyes a little sulky as they met Annie's. "Maybe we should go find out."

Before she could say another word, he crossed to loop an arm around April's shoulders and started for the door. Annie gritted her teeth, determined not to follow. But at that instant, April actually turned to glance back.

"C'mon, Mom! You love surprises!"

Considering that Annie's last "surprise" had been finding Trace standing in her office, her opinion of surprises had dropped considerably. Not to mention the fact that she could use some serious cooling-off time.

"You go ahead. I'm going to clean up in here," Annie began.

"Please! Mommy, don't stay mad at me!"

So April had noticed. It made Annie feel a little bit better. She managed a weak smile. "It's okay, sweetie. You go ahead and—"

April stretched out one grubby hand. The gesture was too precious to ignore, especially in the wake of Annie's own shaken confidence.

She went to April, took the little girl's hand in her own. Trace kept his arm looped firmly around the child. Annie grimaced, remembering the bible-school story of King

Solomon and the two mothers who had been tugging each arm of a baby. Trace had about eight inches and sixty pounds on her, easy, but what Annie lacked in size she made up for in determination.

The one piece of satisfaction she could draw from the whole scenario was that Trace looked more edgy than when he'd crash-landed the plane. His eyes were restless, the lids narrowed, his long muscles radiating unease.

They walked outside, then followed the path to the rear of the cliff house where the big rig had pulled to a stop. One of the men inside it was already unlatching the door. The guy shot April a grin.

"I don't know who you are, girlie, but any kid in Colorado would go on a diet of straight spinach for a month to be in your shoes."

April's brows drew together. "Me? How come?"

The man threw open the massive double doors. The interior was dim for a heartbeat before lights in the trailer's ceiling flickered on.

Annie's knees almost buckled. A little fortress was lashed to a set of bunk beds with electric-blue nylon rope. A life-sized stuffed gorilla sat in round-bellied splendor, its fuzzy arms clutching a bundle of street-hockey sticks, roller blades on its feet.

A mountain bike so elaborate Annie couldn't begin to guess the cost was parked beside a basketball hoop already mounted on a pole, the nylon rope weaving around everything like the ribbons on a Christmas present.

Boxes with clothing-store labels were piled in a miniature mountain in a red plastic bin beside some ungodly-looking contraption that looked like a cross between a four-wheeled bike and a turtle.

Annie heard April's ecstatic shrieks through a haze of disbelief. Heard Trace's sheepish claim, "I wanted to make it up to you about the room. You know, all that lace and pink stuff. I thought these might be more your style."

April didn't even bother answering. She was clambering across the fortress bed, toward the back of the truck.

Trace turned to the driver. "I thought there was supposed to be something else?"

"He should be here any second." The driver stopped, cocking his head to one side at the sound of another vehicle jouncing over the road.

When it broke from the shelter of trees arching over the lane, Annie felt as if someone had rammed his fist into her stomach.

It was a pickup hauling a small trailer.

No, Annie thought in sick denial as the vehicle came to a stop. Trace couldn't possibly have done such an idiotic, irresponsible thing as...

At that moment the sound of a whinny split the air.

Two men were already letting a ramp down, another was backing out of the trailer leading the most gorgeous paint pony Annie had ever seen. Its ice-white tail touched the ground, its mane was caught up in an electric-blue ribbon. There was a saddle on its back—gorgeously tooled leather, with enough silver trimming to fill every cavity in Denver.

At that instant, April glanced up from where she was perched on the bicycle. She let out a sound somewhere between a squeak and a gasp, staggering out of the trailer with the dazed expression of Chicken Little the day the sky fell on his head.

"It's for you, Ape," Trace told her.

"To keep forever and ever?" April breathed.

"Forever."

Never in her life had Annie Brown felt a more potent fury rocket through her veins. She was sick with it. Her whole body quaked, her eyes searing with tears of pure rage. She wanted to pound her fists against Trace McKenna's chest, she wanted to rant and rave.

Instead, she stood as if carved in stone, watching her daughter race toward the beautiful animal. Dreams-come-true sparkled in April's eyes, her face as filled with ecstacy as any fairy-tale princess.

Annie looked at her daughter who was crooning to the pony, then turned to glare into Trace McKenna's face, hating him. Truly hating him for the first time.

"How dare you?" Annie squeezed the words through a throat raw with anguish.

"Let me explain."

"Absolutely. I'll let you explain," Annie choked out under her breath. "You can explain to April why it's impossible to keep a pony in the middle of the city. Why there is no way on God's earth she can keep it."

"There has to be somewhere to board it near Chicago. A stable, a riding school. I don't care what it costs."

"Of course you don't care what it costs," Annie spat. "But believe it or not, there are other things besides money involved here. I work ten, twelve hours a day. What time I'm not at the shelter, I'm running to April's games, helping with homework, driving her to her lessons. Besides, the shape my car is in, even if I wanted to zing her out to the country to ride three times a week, I couldn't do it."

"I'll get you a new one."

"Try it and I swear I'll drive it straight into Lake Michigan."

Trace's brows crashed together in a harsh line. "I'll keep the pony. April can see it when she comes to visit me."

"You're going to keep the pony so that April can ride it two weeks a year? It would hardly be fair—"

"I plan on seeing April a lot more often than that, Annie."

A hot ball of fury, of helplessness, rose in her throat. "Damn you, Trace! I don't care if you're the richest man on earth! You can't buy my daughter!"

"I don't have to buy her. She's mine, too—"

"Trace! Trace!" April's voice penetrated through Annie's furious words. The little girl raced toward them, flinging her arms around Trace McKenna in an ecstatic hug. She clambered up into his arms, the way she had climbed up into Annie's so many times before. Annie's heart shattered as April buried her face against the dark hair that clung to Trace's neck.

"This is the best present I ever had in my whole life! You're the nicest, most radical, coolest man in the whole world! And I was a real brat at first." April drew back, staring into those eyes that were so like her own. Her brow furrowed adorably. "How come you're being so nice to me?"

Trace cradled the little girl in his arms, one large hand stroking her hair. His gaze met Annie's, dark, defiant. For a second she feared he'd tell April the truth.

The words he said struck Annie almost as brutally.

"It's because I love you, April," Trace said, kissing his daughter's tumbled curls.

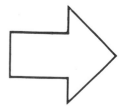

NO COST! NO OBLIGATION TO BUY!
NO PURCHASE NECESSARY!

PLAY "LUCKY 7"
AND GET FIVE FREE GIFTS!

HOW TO PLAY:

1. With a coin, carefully scratch off the silver box at the right. Then check the claim chart to see what we have for you—FREE BOOKS and a gift—ALL YOURS! ALL FREE!

2. Send back this card and you'll receive brand-new Silhouette Intimate Moments® novels. These books have a cover price of $3.99 each, but they are yours to keep absolutely free.

3. There's no catch. You're under no obligation to buy anything. We charge nothing—ZERO—for your first shipment. And you don't have to make any minimum number of purchases—not even one!

4. The fact is thousands of readers enjoy receiving books by mail from the Silhouette Reader Service™ months before they're available in stores. They like the convenience of home delivery and they love our discount prices!

5. We hope that after receiving your free books you'll want to remain a subscriber. But the choice is yours—to continue or cancel, anytime at all! So why not take us up on our invitation, with no risk of any kind. You'll be glad you did!

This lovely heart-shaped box is richly detailed with cut-glass decorations, perfect for holding a precious memento or keepsake—and it's yours absolutely free when you accept our no-risk offer.

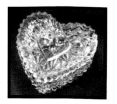

**Just scratch off the silver box with a coin.
Then check below to see the gifts you get.**

YES! I have scratched off the silver box. Please send me all the gifts for which I qualify. I understand I am under no obligation to purchase any books, as explained on the back and on the opposite page.

345 CIS AQML
(C-SIL-IM-07/94)

NAME

ADDRESS   APT.

CITY   PROVINCE   POSTAL CODE

7	7	7	**WORTH FOUR FREE BOOKS PLUS A FREE HEART-SHAPED CURIO BOX**
🍒	🍒	🍒	**WORTH THREE FREE BOOKS**
●	●	●	**WORTH TWO FREE BOOKS**
🔔	🔔	🍒	**WORTH ONE FREE BOOK**

THE SILHOUETTE READER SERVICE™: HERE'S HOW IT WORKS

Accepting free books places you under no obligation to buy anything. You may keep the books and gift and return the shipping statement marked "cancel". If you do not cancel, about a month later we'll send you 6 additional novels, and bill you just $3.21 each plus 25¢ delivery and GST*. That's the complete price, and — compared to cover prices of $3.99 each — quite a bargain! You may cancel at any time, but if you choose to continue, every month we'll send you 6 more books, which you may either purchase at the discount price...or return at our expense and cancel your subscription.

*Terms and prices subject to change without notice.
Canadian residents will be charged applicable provincial taxes and GST.

0195619199-L2A5X3-BR01

SILHOUETTE READER SERVICE
PO BOX 609
FORT ERIE ONT
L2A 9Z9

Canada Post Corporation / Société canadienne des postes

Postage paid   Port payé
if mailed in Canada   si posté au Canada

Business   Réponse
Reply   d'affaires

0195619199   01

MAIL ▶ POSTE

Chapter 7

Annie sat on a giant boulder and stared into the vast expanse of wilderness that rippled out beyond Trace McKenna's cliff.

How was she going to survive this? Another week and a half of watching her daughter fall under the spell of expensive gifts and delightful adventures provided by a man who didn't seem to understand the meaning of the word no? Someone who set no limits—and who had never figured out that living with no limits was every bit as dangerous as being chained down by a raftful of unreasonable rules.

There was no way Annie could make an eight-year-old understand that danger. And unless she got a handle on her emotions, there would be no way to protect April from what was fast developing into an intolerable situation.

Nothing good could come of the increasing animosity Annie felt toward Trace. Or the stubborn, ruthless determination Trace was using to blast into every corner of their lives. With every hour that had passed since the disastrous arrival of Trace's absurdly extravagant gifts, Annie had grown more certain that she and Trace were merrily flinging burning matches into a gasoline can, waiting for the explosion. It would happen. Annie had had enough experiences wading through disasters to understand the possible ramifications of this one.

She also was undeniably aware that the person in the middle of this firing range was an eight-year-old little girl who didn't have a clue what was going on.

How many times at the shelter had Annie attempted to calm down pregnant teens, their often devastated parents, their sometimes angry boyfriends? How many times had she encouraged the warring parties to sit down and rationally, reasonably, come to some sort of compromise? After all, no matter what decision was made—adoption, abortion or keeping the baby to raise—these people would always have a common bond now, a link that no decision could ever completely sever.

What Annie had never faced was that the same rule applied in her own life, with her own daughter and the turbulent past Annie had sectioned off so neatly inside herself. She'd charged off, sixteen and scared, but had emerged completely independent, strong and tough and sure of herself in a way she had never experienced before. She had taken care of April, built a life for herself, and she had given Trace McKenna what she'd been so certain he needed. Freedom. It had never even occurred to her that he might want his daughter, instead.

Even when she'd been confronted by a very real, very angry, very stubborn Trace, insisting that he wanted a relationship with April, she had pretended that she could make him go away. That he would somehow magically disappear again. But he wouldn't disappear. The truth was, he'd never really been gone. He'd been in April's eyes, every time Annie had looked at her, he'd been tangled in the strands of silky hair Annie had brushed so lovingly for eight years. He'd been in April's fastball and her stubbornness and tucked in the box at the back of Annie's closet along with that ridiculous stuffed monkey.

And whether Annie wanted to or not, she was going to have to find a way to deal with him. It was time April was in bed. Once she'd gotten through the precious nighttime ritual she always treasured with her daughter, Annie and Trace McKenna were going to find some way to work this out.

She stood up and stretched, her muscles stiff from sitting so long. A half hour with April—brushing her hair, talking about the secrets of the universe—always put things in perspective for Annie, put her back in touch with what was really important. Then, Annie would be ready to handle Trace.

She entered the sliding glass door and peered into the sunken great room, but the television was off, only a half-eaten bowl of popcorn giving any hint that Trace and April had been there earlier. Annie frowned and headed for the kitchen. It was dark, deserted. Then she caught a glimpse of a light burning at the far end of the hall. April's room.

Annie's muscles knotted. She didn't have a clue what it would look like now. She'd tried not to watch while the truckers hauled the old stuff out and moved the new things in, but she'd been aware of it despite the distance she'd put between her and the house.

Now Annie approached the bedroom warily, padding quietly down the hall. She heard a murmur of voices, saw the corner of the fortress bed. As she moved nearer she saw April perched on the brilliant blue coverlet, legs crossed the way they had been the hundreds of nights Annie had brushed the day's snarls out of her hair.

But tonight, there was already someone else smoothing bristles through the dark locks. The big hands that guided an airplane with such skill looked decidedly awkward clutching the handle of a hairbrush. Annie felt a jab of jealousy pierce through her, her resolve of moments before faltering.

The fact that Trace had taken over even this piece of her relationship with April was more wrenching than Annie could ever have guessed it would be.

"Trace?" April's voice drifted softly into the hallway, and Annie could see the child staring meditatively into the shiny button eyes of the stuffed gorilla.

"What is it, Ape?"

"This has been the best day in my whole life."

"I'm glad." He didn't sound glad, Annie thought suddenly. He sounded the way she felt. Exhausted. Battle-weary.

"Know what?" April continued.

"What?"

"I don't think this was the best day in my mom's life, though."

God. Annie felt April's deduction whack into her solar plexus like a sledgehammer. Trace was silent. Dead silent. Was he searching for something to say? Or was there any point in even attempting to reply to April's observation.

"Trace, why doesn't my mom like you anymore?"

Trace paled under his tan, his eyelids drifting to half-mast. "What?"

"You're always staring at each other like you're real mad, even if you don't say anything. And you don't talk at all unless it's about me. My mom told me an' told me how nice you were to her in high school and stuff. She told me you were friends. That was why you were bringing us on vacation and being so great to us and everything. I didn't believe her, though. I figured you thought my mom was cute and wanted to, you know, date her or something. I figured I'd get real bored because you'd want to talk about old-time stuff, but you barely talk at all."

"Maybe we just don't have anything to say."

"You got a lot to say to me."

"I just want to get to know you."

"Why?"

"Because I think you're really special, April. Because—" Trace swore softly, then fell silent.

"Trace, my mom didn't like all the presents in the truck, and when she saw my pony, she almost started crying and stuff."

"Sometimes people do that when they're surprised."

April frowned and scratched at the freckles the sun had brought out on her snub nose. "Maybe. Sometimes moms are real hard to understand. They cry in those mushy TV commercials and get all weird about kids getting tall and stuff, but they never tell you how they're feeling when they're sad. They make you figure it out for yourself."

Annie raised a trembling hand to her lips.

"Trace, do you...do you think my mom is sad because...well, because you an' me have been...well, 'cause I haven't been paying much attention to her? I get mad sometimes when she's real busy at the shelter."

"Your mom isn't mad at you. Or sad because of you. Your mom is mad because of me."

"How come?"

Annie had been on the receiving end of April's interrogations too often to think the child was going to let up. Annie wanted to rush in, to scoop the little girl into her arms, but tears were threatening. The wrenching, heart-cracking kind that would only upset April further.

Annie saw Trace suck in a shuddery breath. "It's hard to explain what's going on with your mom and me, sweetheart. We just don't agree on some things, and then we get stubborn. I guess we don't listen to each other very well."

April angled her head around until she was peering up into Trace's eyes.

"Know what?" she said with a catch in her voice. "I don't like it when my mom's sad."

Annie's eyes burned. Through a haze of tears, she saw Trace's hand still, the brush poised above the mahogany fall of April's hair.

"I don't like it when she's sad, either," Trace admitted. The brush suddenly slipped from his grip, then tumbled to the floor. Trace turned to scoop it up from where it had fallen, his eyes suddenly sweeping the doorway where Annie stood, half hidden in shadows.

Trace's gaze locked with hers a long minute. But Annie couldn't bear for him to see her so vulnerable, so full of hurt. She turned and walked away. She'd gone into the kitchen and sagged down into a chair when Trace found her.

She'd seen him angry, she'd seen him tense, she'd seen him delighting April. But she hadn't seen this solemn, earnest expression that shadowed his handsome features, this hesitancy that whispered in his eyes, clung around his lips.

"Annie," he said softly. "We have to talk."

"Do we?"

"Yeah. But not with April around. I don't want to risk her hearing anything she shouldn't."

"We can hardly leave her alone on the mountain."

"I'll call Rob. I'm sure he and his wife can keep an eye on her for a little while tomorrow night. I promised April we could go trail riding in the afternoon, take the pony back up the mountain. But once evening hits, you and I could steal away. There's a place we could go."

"Trace, I don't know—"

"Please. We can't go on like this. It's hurting April. It's hurting you. Damn it, I want to get things right this time, Annie. I've already got enough on my conscience."

Strange, she'd seen fury and betrayal, sensed stubbornness and resolve in Trace since he'd charged back into her life. But she hadn't sensed the guilt weighing down Trace's conscience. Was it possible that he was still battling old demons just as she was? Was it possible that those demons were reaching out to hurt, not only Trace and Annie. Could they be hurting April, as well?

There was nothing she wanted less than to be alone somewhere with Trace. But she had to shield her daughter.

"You're right," Annie said after a moment. "We can't go on this way."

"I'll try to set it up with Rob for six o'clock tomorrow night. And I'll clear it with April."

"Fine." Annie climbed out of the chair, wanting to go to her room, try to store up the emotional reserves to make it through tonight. But before she could pass Trace, his hand reached out to stop her, his long fingers reached up to brush a tendril of hair back from her face. The tiny lines at the corners of his eyes deepened with concern.

"You should spend tomorrow in bed, Brown-Eyes. Rest. You look tired as hell."

She was tired. Tired of fighting against Trace, tired of being alone. But she could handle this. She'd get through tonight somehow. She was tougher than she once was. She'd learned the hard way not to lean on anyone else. To do what needed to be done, no matter how difficult it was.

Still, Annie couldn't help but wonder what it would be like to lean on someone else for just a little while. She wondered what it would be like to lean forward, press her cheek against the hard wall of Trace's chest. Feel the warmth, the strength, seep into her spirit.

Instead, she turned and walked away.

Just as he had so many years before, Trace was opening up empty places inside her, showing her a void that left her aching.

The ache wouldn't let her sleep when she lay down on her bed. The loneliness clung to the shadows that moved across her bedroom floor, whispered in the soft night breezes that riffled the curtains framing the open windows.

She staggered out of bed for a few minutes at eight, only to find Trace and April packing saddlebags with breakfast and lunch to take on their ride. Trace shot her a glance and assured Annie that everything was set for six o'clock. April, however, looked less than pleased.

"I don't see why I can't come, too," she grumbled, slapping another glob of peanut butter onto the peanut-butter-and-banana sandwich she was constructing.

Trace tugged at April's neatly combed but lopsided braids. Annie tried to quell a stab of jealousy at the knowledge that he must have painstakingly worked the plaits in the child's hair earlier. "You got a pony, kiddo. The least your mom deserves is a night out."

April peered up at him through eyes suddenly sulky. "Why can't she have a night out with me around?"

"Because then you'd be getting a pony *and* a night out and you'd be two presents ahead of her. Then I don't know how I'd even things up. She might get real jealous and have a temper fit and—whoa, let me tell you, I'm not about to risk that." Trace's eyes tracked to Annie's and clung there for long minutes, a worried crease forming between his brows.

Annie looked hastily away, but what she saw disturbed her even more—April with a strange, wary expression on her face. The little girl snatched up the saddlebags. "Well, are we going or not?" she demanded and stalked out the door. Trace peered after the child, perplexed. "We'll be back around three," he said. "See ya, Brown-Eyes."

Annie stood at the window and watched them saddle up, then ride out—the man, strikingly handsome astride a gorgeous Appaloosa, the little girl, ecstatic on the lovely little paint who had been christened Bo, after April's favorite White Sox player.

Watching the two of them disappear sucked away the last of Annie's energy. She made her way to her bedroom and curled up on a recliner by the window. But as she picked up the mystery on the small table beside her, trying to start the book for the fiftieth time since arriving at Trace's hideaway, all she could see was April's face as she'd stalked from the house. All she could do was wonder what the child's expression had meant, even more disturbing, what would happen when the two grown-ups who loved April confronted each other tonight.

The words on the page circled dizzily before her eyes until she let her lashes drift down to rest on her cheekbones.

She considered dragging herself to her disheveled bed, but her legs were so heavy. She sat in the chair, sunshine streaming over her, until at last she fell into a fitful sleep.

Annie awoke with the suddenness of someone who has just been doused with ice water—that bolt-upright kind of wakefulness born of a certainty that she was late.

The room was pitch black, the shades drawn tight. And she wasn't in the chair, she was curled up in her bed, the coverlets tucked beneath her chin.

When had she gotten up and moved? she wondered vaguely, struggling to catch a glimpse of the clock at her bedside. The red digits proclaimed the hour. Seven o'clock. There could be no doubt it was 7:00 p.m.

Oh, God! She and Trace were supposed to have left an hour ago. Was it possible he was waiting for her? Had he forgotten?

She leapt from the bed and dragged a brush through her hair, ignoring the tube of lipstick on the dresser. She flattened her hands against the soft rose-colored sweater she'd dragged on that morning, making a cursory attempt to smooth the wrinkles from it.

Annie glanced in the mirror and quelled a stab of dissatisfaction with her disheveled appearance. How she looked was not important. After all, it wasn't as if this was a date or anything.

"Trace?" she called as she hurried down the corridor. "Trace, where are—you." The last word escaped from her mouth in a choked gasp as she slammed to a halt in the doorway of the great room. Her gaze locked on the figure silhouetted against the huge stone fireplace.

Annie's mouth went dry, her hands trembled as Trace turned toward her.

She'd expected him to be rumpled from the trail ride—or at most dressed in a casual shirt and faded jeans. But as Trace stood before her the sheer male beauty of him squeezed the breath from her lungs.

Dark blue jeans rose above black cowboy boots decorated with chains of silver conchos. A blue western shirt was buttoned up to his throat, where a hammered-silver bolo gleamed in delicious contrast to the sun-bronzed cords of his neck. The silver on the tie matched the thin silver band encircling the black Stetson he held in one hand, his long fingers curling the hat brim with ill-concealed nervousness.

He looked every bit the cowboy returning to his lady after months on the range—tough, independent, sexy as all get out. His hair fell in rich waves, the sage-brush scent of his cologne teasing Annie's nostrils.

He had obviously taken great care with his appearance. The knowledge made Annie brush her fingers uneasily over her limp sweater.

"I thought we were just going out to—to talk, so...maybe I should slip into something else."

"You look fine." Trace glanced down at his hat brim. His voice grew husky. "More than fine."

Annie felt her cheeks heat.

"I've already dropped April off."

"You should have woken me."

Those gray-blue eyes flickered up for a heartbeat, snagging hers. "I meant to, but you were sleeping so peacefully, I just got you into bed and let you go on sleeping."

Got you into bed. Annie squirmed inwardly. That was what had happened. Trace had found her sleeping, had taken care of her.

The image of those strong arms carrying her to the bed made Annie acutely uncomfortable. The consideration he'd shown in letting her sleep disarmed her. The way he looked made her understand why some women would drive five hundred miles to see a rodeo.

Suddenly, Annie was jittery about going anywhere with him. She gestured to the quiet room. "With April gone, we could talk here."

Trace's mouth crooked in a half smile as he settled the Stetson on his head. "The best treaties are always struck on neutral ground. Besides, The Golden Nugget has the best steak in Colorado.''

To make a treaty, you had to keep your wits about you, Annie thought, not spend the whole time distracted by the way the light played in the rich waves of your enemy's hair. And if she stared at him across the table for any length of time, she had a feeling she'd be hungry for something a lot more dangerous than steak.

But she could hardly tell Trace her real objection to the trip had to do with being in such close proximity to those long legs of his, or that meltingly sexy smile. Or, most dangerous of all, the tentative warmth in eyes so blue they broke her heart.

Annie sucked in a steadying breath. Better to go, get this over with as soon as possible, Annie reasoned. After all, she was a rational, reasonable, intelligent adult who had learned her lesson well. Not once since her long-ago affair with Trace had she even been tempted to put herself at risk. There had been no one else—emotionally or physically— since that passion-filled night in the stable.

The thought should have been comforting. It should have steadied her, shored up her confidence.

Instead, it stirred fears Annie had kept at bay so long, and opened up possibilities more terrifying than anything she'd ever known.

Trace walked to the door, flattening one large hand against the wood to open it for her. Annie wondered if walking through it would be the biggest mistake she'd ever make—except for the one she'd made so many years ago when she had fallen hopelessly in love with a sulky high school rebel named Trace McKenna.

Chapter 8

The Colorado night stretched out like an Indian blanket, woven in rich stripes of dusky purple and raven's-wing black, beaded in designs that might have been stars.

Trace said little the whole way down the mountain, concentrating almost fiercely on the curvy road. Annie didn't even bother to try to fill the silence.

But by the time he wheeled the vehicle into the parking lot of the combination restaurant-Western bar, Annie would've killed to be able to think of a little small talk.

She started to reach for the handle to her door, but Trace leaned over and grabbed her hand, squeezing it gently. He got out of the vehicle and strode around it, then opened her door.

Annie wondered where the boy she'd known had learned to be such a gentleman. Probably from one of the glamorous women who swarmed around rich, powerful, heart-stoppingly gorgeous men as inevitably as mosquitos at a twilight picnic.

The thought sobered her. She managed to avoid the hand he extended to her and climbed out herself.

Trace said nothing.

Despite the Friday-night crowd, the perky red-headed hostess had them seated at a table in record time, her full, crimson-painted lips curved in a seductive smile as Trace slid into his chair. Annie bristled instinctively, and hated the sensation.

"Cheatin' on me already, sugar?" the woman demanded, giving a playful tug on his bolo, then turned to Annie. "Promised to take me into Denver next time he was at the Cliff. Big night on the town, you know. Bought a dress to paint the town red in, and he never even called."

Trace shot her a distracted smile. "I may be crazy, Vera, but I'm not *that* crazy. Farley'd skin me alive and hang me out for the buzzards if I got within fifty miles of you."

"Never figured you for a coward, McKenna. 'Course, I suppose I can see why you'd pick a classy lady like this over a country girl with five kids tied to her apron strings." The waitress winked an eye that was weighted down with a year's worth of mascara. "This guy's not exactly the domestic type, if you know what I mean."

"People change." There was a roughness in Trace's voice that made Vera stare at him in astonishment.

Those thickly painted lips curled like a cat's. "Well, maybe I'll have Farley announce a day of mourning for all the women in the joint. If Trace McKenna's got himself hogtied over you, lady, you'd better watch your back. The women hereabouts take their dancin' partners real serious, and nobody dances as down and dirty as this cowboy. There's about a dozen girls who'll want to scratch your eyes out."

"They can have him. I—we're not seeing each other that way."

The woman let out a throaty chuckle. "If you're ready to cut this cowboy loose, you must not be seeing at all, honey."

"Vera, cut it out. You don't understand," Trace protested.

"The way you were lookin' at her when she walked in, I think I understand just fine," Vera said. With that, she smoothed her red dress over ample hips and sashayed away.

Annie looked across the blue-checked tablecloth to see Trace's face washed in dull red. He cleared his throat. "Maybe this place wasn't such a great idea."

Annie thought about Vera's teasing and focused on the warnings that had been buried in her words. It was vital Annie remember that Trace was no more domesticated than the stallions that used to charge down the canyons. He was dangerous and wild, a man who might have fathered her daughter, but who would never be content living the tame kind of existence most people craved.

Annie had been smart enough to figure that out when she'd been sixteen. Nine years later, she'd be a fool to forget it. If ever there was an environment that would keep that foremost in her mind, the Golden Nugget was it. "This place is perfect," she said.

They sat in silence, perusing the menus, but once the order had been taken by a gum-cracking waitress who ogled Trace like the latest centerfold of *Hunk-o-Rama* magazine, Trace braced his elbows on the table, leaned his jaw on his fists and cleared his throat.

Annie glanced up at those rugged features once, then cast her gaze back to the tablecloth, unable to quell the sudden flip-flopping sensation in her chest.

"I don't know how to start this, Brown-Eyes, so I'm just gonna plunge right in. There's so much I want to know—

about April. About you. There's so damned much to sort out."

"All right. Start at the beginning."

"The beginning." Trace echoed. "Christ, I wish it was that easy. I wish..." He hesitated. "I know you weren't thrilled with the presents I gave April today."

"No, I wasn't."

"Maybe I went a little overboard. But you have to understand, you've had this wonderful kid for eight years, Annie. This incredible, amazing little person. While I've already missed out on so damned much."

"Trace—"

"I'm not trying to make you feel guilty about that, Annie. I'm just trying to tell you how it is with me. Every minute I spend with her, I just get hungrier to know everything about her. What her favorite color is, why she always bites the point off of the bottom of a cone first and sucks the ice cream through it. I want to know when she lost her first tooth, and what she looked like when she was a baby."

"She looked so much like you that it hurt," Annie said softly. "Lots of dark hair, and those eyes... She had your temper, too. Truth is, I think the nurses must've been secretly relieved when they discovered I'd run away from the hospital."

"Do you have a picture of her? I know it sounds crazy, but I feel like if I could just see who she was when she was small, if I could commit it to memory, I could imagine I was there for her."

Pain gripped Annie's chest. She looked up into Trace's eyes, eyes that were intense, almost pleading. "Trace, there are no pictures of April when she was a baby. I was bouncing from odd job to odd job. I barely had money for food." It was one of the lasting scars from the time Annie had spent as a street kid—the fact that she could never look at an image of April's first muzzy smile, those unfocused blue eyes that had enchanted Annie the first moment the doctor had laid April in her arms.

"It wasn't so bad really," she amended, wanting to spare Trace the brunt of the guilt she saw in his face. "April and I got along. Summer and fall, I hired on at farms, picking apples, working at produce stands. April and I could usually stay in a back room. Winters were harder, but there were enough good people, kind people sprinkled among the cold ones to keep me from giving up hope. You must know what I mean. It couldn't have been easy for you either."

Trace's laugh was bitter. "Oh, I'm a survivor Annie. Always was. I landed on my feet a month after I left Arizona. I was pulling down a decent salary at FireStorm, living with a couple of other guys in an apartment."

"I'm glad, Trace."

"You shouldn't be. I spent the whole time being bitter as hell. Trace McKenna, the betrayed. The whole time I was feeling sorry for myself you and my baby were barely getting by."

"You had no way of knowing that."

"Annie, anything could have happened to you. What if you'd gotten hurt or the baby had gotten sick?"

"She did get sick when she was about two and a half. Scared me so badly. That's how I ended up at J. T. James's shelter. They took us in, helped me build a life for April, and for myself."

"I'm glad they were there for you. But that doesn't change the fact that you were alone for so long." Trace gave a snort of disgust. "Here I am, asking you for a picture—as if you had a hundred-page-baby book tucked in your back pocket."

Savage regret contorted Trace's face, born of painful understanding.

There was such desolation in those storm-cloud eyes that she wanted to soothe him, comfort him. Wanted to give him some tangible piece of those lost years, to show him that she and April had been okay. Annie groped for her purse, digging out a picture from the back of her wallet.

"I have a snapshot J.T. took of April on her third birthday. It's the earliest picture I have." She dug in her billfold, then extracted the photograph. Trace reached for it, eagerly. Annie almost couldn't release it to his hand.

Somehow, it had always seemed like the girl holding April was a stranger—a wide eyed child with a baby in her arms. The picture had been taken before Annie had fought her way free of the pain of leaving Trace behind. Sorrow still radiated from Annie's eyes, a fragility wreathing her face in that picture. The lost expression made her cringe even now.

She prayed Trace would only have eyes for his daughter. She saw Trace's gaze move hungrily over the image of April in a candy-apple-red dress Allison James had provided for the occasion. One of April's little fists was digging into the chocolate cake, a birthday hat perched on her dusky curls.

"Did she eat the cake, or did she just demolish it?" Trace asked in an unsteady voice.

"Actually, she threw it at J.T."

"Already working on her fastball." Trace's laugh was harsh, roughened by an undercurrent of loss. Annie knew the moment his gaze skated from April's image to hers. Trace's smile went soft with regret.

"God, Brown-Eyes, look at you. You were a baby yourself."

"I survived."

"You did a helluva lot more than survive, lady. You raised one terrific kid. But what you must've sacrificed—" His voice trailed off. "I didn't want to hurt you."

"Once you gave me your baby, Trace, there was no way to keep either one of us from getting hurt somehow. The key is to keep that hurt from coloring the rest of your life."

"You did that, didn't you, Annie Brown? I mean, look at you, Brown-Eyes. All grown up. You're a helluva lot tougher than I remember you. But you're also... I don't know. There's something deep inside those eyes of yours. Something even more beautiful than I remember. You used to look afraid all the time, except when you were at the piano. Now—you aren't afraid anymore."

I'm afraid of you, a voice inside Annie whispered. *Afraid of what I feel whenever I look at you. Afraid I won't be strong enough to save myself this time.*

"Annie?" Trace reached across the table and covered her hand with his larger one. Annie watched her fingers get swallowed up by his, felt the callused warmth engulf her. "Remember when you told me how it was when you were a little girl? How you never let anyone past your defenses because you always knew that your father would be dragging you off somewhere new?"

Annie's cheeks heated at the memory of that confession—made to Trace on a hot spring night with the scent of rain hanging in the air. He had turned up at the steps of the library by accident just as she was leaving. She wouldn't dare have believed he'd hung around on purpose waiting to walk her home.

"There was no point in getting attached to anyone. The minute I left a school, everyone forgot I even existed."

Trace's thumb skimmed over her knuckles with a tenderness that melted into Annie, hurting her. "Annie, I never forgot you."

The words sizzled past those defenses Annie had clung to for survival. They rippled into places that were still raw. "You felt responsible for me. Guilty."

"God knows that's true enough. The night I found out you were pregnant was pure hell. I didn't have a clue, for God's sake. Just walked into our kitchen and saw your parents, stalking around, raging at mine. You were just sitting at the table, so damned quiet, your eyes all swollen from crying. I couldn't believe what I'd done to you. I was so damned scared and confused."

"The way my father was raging, you should've been terrified."

"I didn't give a damn about your father, Annie, or mine. It was you who terrified me. Sitting there, so damn fragile. You hadn't talked to me since the night in the hayloft. You wouldn't even look at me during school. For a month and a half you'd acted like I didn't even exist anymore. I can understand why. I mean, I'd taken advantage of your friendship. I hadn't thought about consequences. I know that when you came to find me at the stable, you came as a friend."

I came as a girl who loved you... loved you so much, I would have walked through fire to take away your pain. But Annie couldn't tell him that now, no more than she'd been able to that horrendous night in the McKenna family's kitchen. It was all a long time ago. The girl who had loved Trace McKenna to the bottom of her soul was a stranger to Annie now—a wistful wraith who now existed only in the picture of April's birthday party.

"Trace, it was all a long time ago."

"I took from you, Annie. I was hurting so damn bad. Half drunk. When I saw you, standing in the doorway, the moonlight shining in your hair... when you came to me, touched me..." Trace's fingers tightened on hers, and

Annie could almost feel the pulse of his adolescent pain. "I knew you didn't love me, Brown-Eyes. But I needed you so bad, needed you to wash away all the ugliness."

Annie struggled against the old pain Trace's words were reawakening, pain she'd managed to lock away years ago. She didn't want to feel it again. Didn't want to remember. "Trace, there's no point in dragging this all out. I believe everything happens for a reason. I was meant to come to Halloran's stable and make love to a boy I was infatuated with. That way, I would understand the girls who came to the shelter. And I was meant to have April. She is the most wonderful thing in my life. If you're still feeling guilty, think about that. You gave me a gift, Trace. The most beautiful gift imaginable."

Trace's brows furrowed, his eyes darkened. "So beautiful that you ran away from me? Did you ever mean to tell me?"

"What? Contact you at FireStorm and say, By the way, you have a daughter. Now that you're rich and famous, hand over a child support check?"

"I mean when you were sixteen. Can you even imagine what it was like for me to walk into the kitchen, have your father blast me with the news that you were carrying my child?"

Annie swallowed hard, remembering Trace's face—pale as death, his eyes black with shock. The hand that had been clutching his baseball mitt had started shaking and he'd stared at her, as if begging her to tell him it was all a bad dream.

"It was my choice to make love to you, Trace, whatever you might believe. I cared about you. You were hurting. I made the decision—"

"Oh, and I had nothing to do with it?" Bitter self-disgust tainted his voice. "My hands were all over you. And I was good, wasn't I? Mr. High School Stud."

"You were half out of your mind with pain. You didn't know what you were doing." Annie's voice dropped low. "I did."

"Oh, I knew what I was doing, all right. I was taking. Taking just the way I always took what I wanted and didn't give a damn. I wanted to be different when I was with you. Dudley Do-Right. A hero. But when you found out you were pregnant, I guess you figured you were better off on your own, that I'd just make a disastrous situation worse. Hell—" Trace rammed his fingers back through his dark hair "—you were probably right. What could I have given you, but more heartache? But damn it, Annie, you didn't even give me a chance."

She'd thought a thousand times what Trace would have sacrificed if she had stayed behind in Arizona and married him the way he'd kept insisting she do. It had never occurred to her that Trace might misconstrue the motive behind her leaving. That he would believe she didn't think he was good enough, strong enough, to take care of her. Never had she considered the damage her actions must have done to his pride. And his heart? The whisper rose sudden, bittersweet inside Annie. No. Even now, Trace spoke of guilt and regret and pain. Not love. Never in their time together had Trace spoken of love.

"I'm sorry I hurt you," Annie said, reaching across the table, touching his cheek. "And I know you didn't mean to hurt me. But the Annie Brown who came to that abandoned stable is gone, Trace. So is the boy who raged over the end of the dream he'd never dared to have. What happened between us changed everything. But it's over now, Trace. It's time to let it go."

"Is it?"

Annie shivered at the whiskey-rough demand.

"We share April, of course," Annie stammered. "And—"

Trace sighed, his jaw knotting for a moment. "Annie, I—"

"Two steaks, one on the hoof, the other charred beyond recognition." The waitress's saucy voice made Annie jump. Trace looked ready to kill the woman, but he gritted his teeth as the waitress slid the plates onto the table before them.

Annie stared at the prime cut of beef and knew there was no way she could squeeze so much as a bite down her throat.

Trace stabbed halfheartedly at his food. The sudden silence that fell over the table was crushingly uncomfortable. The only sound was the records the disk jockey was sending out over the speakers—country songs that broke your heart. Lost loves and forgotten dreams set to music that sank deep into your bones and stayed there.

Annie endured the mixture of music and Trace's moody silence for as long as she could, then set down her fork. He looked so distant, so strange. Unreadable.

"Trace, what are you thinking about?" she asked at last.

"You'd laugh if I told you."

"No I wouldn't. I promise."

Trace looked at her from beneath thick lashes, his eyelids at half-mast, his mouth curved with something almost like shyness. "I'm thinkin' I don't feel so different from the kid in the stable right now. I'd like to dance with you, but I figure you'll tell me no. Rejection can be hell on the male ego."

Annie fidgeted with her steak knife. "I don't think that would be such a good idea. Dancing, I mean."

"I'm not asking you to marry me, Brown-Eyes. It's just a dance."

"Easy for you to say." Annie didn't want to smile at him. He left her no other choice. "According to Vera, you're the Cowboy King of the Golden Nugget. I'm a city girl who spent every dance she attended holding up one of the walls and watching everyone else. In fact, I seem to remember you being one of the 'everyone elses' I watched. You and Robin and Paula and Linda and Sue and Maureen and—"

"I seem to remember you dancing with the drama club president—Mr. Bow-Tie Teacher's Pet."

Annie was struck by the acid tone Trace used, as if that dance had somehow rankled.

"What'd you ever see in that jerk?"

"I didn't exactly have partners lined up waiting for a turn. You, for example, never got within a mile of me at a dance."

"Not true. I stuck that rose behind your ear at the Sadie Hawkins."

Annie gave a soft laugh. "I remember. You dismembered the boutonniere your main-squeeze gave you. She was thrilled beyond words."

Trace's eyes were soft blue with the memory. "Well, I might not have had the brains to ask you before, Annie, but I'm asking you now. Will you dance with me?"

"We're supposed to be making a treaty here—"

"Absolutely. After we dance, we'll smoke the peace pipe." He pushed back his chair and stood. He towered over her, tall and lean and compelling. Annie knew she should tell him to sit down and finish his steak. They had to settle all this and pick up April. They had to stay focused on the issue at hand.

Instead, she slipped her fingers into his and stood. She could feel her cheeks grow warm, her lips parting. "You're going to regret this, Baryshnikov."

"Yeah, well, I'll add it to my list of regrets where you're concerned." Annie could sense something in his voice. Something that made her heart stumble as he led her onto the floor where three other couples had already begun two-stepping to some upbeat music.

Annie didn't have a clue what she was supposed to do. "This was a very bad idea," she said, hazarding a glance up at Trace.

"Just melt into my hands, sugar. Trust me. Let me take you—" He might have been seducing her toward a far different goal than navigating the dance floor of a Western club. His voice was low, a little rough, a lot alluring.

Annie tried to match his expert movements, but in this, as in so much else where Trace was concerned, she was hopelessly overmatched.

When the song ended, she started to pull away, retreat to the table, but the first strains of a love song drifted out across the smoky room.

This time, Trace didn't ask. He stared down at her with eyes suddenly as fathomless as the heavens themselves. His strong arms tugged her close, one curving in an unyielding band at the small of her back, his other hand coming up to catch her fingers as he pulled her body close to the hard masculine plane of his own.

Fire-hot, rock-hard, Annie felt Trace's body graze hers as they moved—the tips of her nipples brushed his chest, excruciatingly pleasurable sensations awakening in her tender flesh. His denim-covered thighs whispered against hers, hinting at that far-more-primitive dance they had shared once before.

When they'd started dancing, he had told her to melt into his hands. But she'd never suspected how merely moving to music in a man's arms could make you melt into his very soul. She heard Trace groan deep in his chest, then his arms tightened, closing what little space had been between them. The sculpted muscles of his chest imprinted against the soft swells of her breasts, the heavy silver buckle of his belt nudged against her stomach, while beneath that, she could feel a firm swelling of a totally different kind. The most feminine part of her responded so fiercely Annie couldn't draw away.

Trace pillowed his cheek against her hair, his warm breath brushing her ear, his lips like warm, moist silk where they touched that sensitive skin. "Is it really over between us, Brown-Eyes?"

The question reverberated through every desire-tingling nerve in Annie's body, peeling away a thousand lies she'd told herself in an effort to explain her reaction to Trace during the past week. She swallowed hard, tried to think of something rational, reasonable, to say, some way to put distance between them.

"Annie, I tried to forget you in a hundred different places. I raced all over the world, trying to keep my adrenaline running so high I wouldn't notice the emptiness anymore. There were other women. No responsibilities, no ties. Hell, I was the same old Trace McKenna, just taking. But after you, I made damned sure the women were taking from me, too. That it was understood no gut-level emotions were expected, no commitments."

Annie trembled. "I don't need to hear this."

"I need to tell you. What I felt. Where I've been these past nine years, so you'll understand why everything changed the minute I saw you again, touched you. Kissed you."

"You kissed me out of anger," Annie insisted.

He stopped in a pool of shadows, pulled away from her. His hands bracketed her face, forcing her to confront the full impact of that dizzying, passion-hazed gaze. "You want to know the truth? I kissed you because I'm still starving for the taste of you after all these years. Because every time I close my eyes, I can still see the way you looked in the hayloft, moonlight on your skin. I can still hear your gasps, your sighs. That tiny sound you made when I drove myself inside you."

Annie's whole body felt afire, the memories so vivid, Trace's eyes so intense. Heat radiated from every muscle in his body, sparking a wild desire that made her heart pound.

"You want to know what I'm thinkin' now, Brown-Eyes?"

"Wh-what?"

"I'm thinkin' I want to kiss you. I'm still scared you'll say no, but I want it so bad, I'm willing to risk it."

Buried deep in Annie's consciousness was the will for survival, the instinct she'd been ruled by for so long. It told her to pull away from Trace McKenna, get furious or just plain run. Fight or flight—she'd read about it in countless psychology texts. But this time another instinct rolled over her, softening her lips, parting them, pressing her breasts tighter against the front of Trace's shirt.

His mouth took hers with so much tenderness tears stung Annie's eyes, those lips that could be so hard and unyielding, so deliciously wicked, enchanted her, bewitched her.

Trace McKenna had been devastating as a seventeen-year-old. It hardly seemed possible he could be more so now, but he was. The tip of his tongue skated along the crease of her lips, probing gently, offering, not taking, until Annie's knees were shaking, her hand trembling where it curled into the silky lengths of his hair.

It had been so long, Annie thought muzzily, so very long since she'd allowed herself to sink into sweet sensation, taste such soul-shattering pleasure, feel such relentless need.

Need for Trace. Always Trace. Only Trace.

"Hey, McKenna," someone called out. "Get a room!"

Reality crashed in on Annie, sending heat spilling into her cheeks as the other patrons applauded.

She expected to hear one of the famous Trace McKenna comebacks. Some joke that would have everybody roaring with laughter. But Trace's jaw only knotted.

He grabbed her hand and dragged her from the dance floor, pausing only long enough to toss a wad of bills onto the table where the half-eaten remains of their dinner still waited.

Without a word, Trace guided her past the staring patrons and Vera's makeup-laden eyes. The mountain air struck Annie's cheeks as she tried to keep up with Trace. But he didn't head for the Land Cruiser. He tugged her into the shadows where the logs forming the walls intersected.

The gentleness was gone from his face as he whipped her around, pressing her back against the rough bark. Annie stared into those searing blue eyes, seduced by the fierce need that roughened Trace's voice.

"I want you, Annie. I want you so bad I wake up at night, drenched with sweat. I can taste your name on my tongue, know that I've been calling it over and over."

The image made Annie's head swim, her throat dry. "Th-that's crazy."

"I was always crazy when it came to you." He swore. "Nine years, damn it. Nine years I've been starving for a taste of you. I've been trying to forget you because you hurt me so damn bad."

Those eyes that had haunted Annie's dreams blazed with torment. A torment she'd never have believed possible until this moment.

"Trace, it was just a—a reaction to the guilt you were feeling over what happened in the stable—"

"You wanna know the truth, Annie? By the time you climbed up into that hayloft I'd been wanting you for weeks. It was making me crazy how bad I wanted you. Every time you walked into a room or passed me in the hall, I got hard as steel wanting you. It was scaring the hell out of me."

Annie's mouth went dry. "Then why—why were you so—"

"Such a card-carrying jerk? I'll tell you why. The way I was feeling, I knew we'd end up in the back seat of my car. I didn't want that for you, Brown-Eyes. You deserved better. I swear to God, I didn't want to hurt you." His voice broke, a strangled sound rising in his chest. "But I destroyed your life, didn't I, Annie?"

"No, Trace." Annie reached up, stroking his cheek, his jaw, feeling the old pain tearing him apart inside. She'd never suspected she'd left him like this—tormented, shattered.

"I wanted so bad to do right by you. You believed in me—you were the only one who ever did. I thought you could see past the image I worked so hard at. But you didn't really believe in me any more than anyone else. When things got down and dirty, you walked away. You walked away and you took my baby with you. Why'd you do that, Annie?"

"You were raging at your father, at my father—saying you were going to marry me and they could go to hell. I thought that you were just trying to get back at them, at everyone. That you were willing to throw your whole life away to spite them.''

''What life was I supposed to be throwing away? I was a screw-up jerk with nothing. I saw it every time I looked into my father's eyes, or the teachers' or the coach's. But when I looked into your eyes, I saw something different, Annie. Something terrifying. Wonderful. You didn't let me hide behind my attitude, you wouldn't let me lie back and throw everything away. I hated you for showing me everything I could be, but had been too damn stubborn to achieve. And I loved you—''

Annie's breath caught on a gasp of denial.

''Yes, goddamn it. I loved you, but I couldn't say the words because I was scared as hell that you'd give me that sweet, solemn look of yours, that you'd be so damn gentle while you told me that you had your life all planned out. You were going to Juilliard and then to Carnegie Hall. That you were gonna be somebody someday, and I'd just hold you back.''

Annie's throat ached, burned. ''Wh-why didn't you tell me? Oh, Trace.''

''Don't you see? My greatest fear was that I'd take the single good thing in my life and destroy it. And I did. I never was able to trust the fact that you believed in me. I kept waiting for your faith in me to crumble. And it did. I thought you wouldn't want me—that I'd hold you back. And when I gave you my baby, you showed me that everything I'd been so damned scared of was true.''

It would have been far wiser to tell Trace that it had all happened a long time ago. That it was in the past. The pain they'd both suffered had fashioned them into the people they were today—all but strangers to each other, following different life paths. It would have been wiser, and far less painful, to put necessary distance between them. Put things into perspective.

Annie tunneled her fingers beneath Trace's hair, curving her palm gently around the cords of his neck. After all that had happened between them, he deserved the truth.

"It tore my heart out to leave you," she said softly. "I made love with you because I loved you. And I walked away because you'd been trapped all your life, by your own self-doubt and your father's disapproval. I couldn't bear the thought of being one more link in the chains that held you down."

"The baby—"

"I won't lie, Trace. When I first found out I was pregnant, I was terrified. You know what my father was like. And then, there was you. You wouldn't even talk to me after we made love. The only time you said a word to me was to say you were sorry about what had happened."

"I'd hurt you. I hated myself for that. What the hell could I say?" Trace's mouth twisted in bitterness. "But I would've stood by you no matter what you decided to do. Even though I loved you, wanted you and the baby, I'd have supported any decision you made. If you'd wanted to—to end the pregnancy, if you'd wanted to give the baby up for adoption. Whatever. I just wanted to be there to help you get through it. I wanted to be strong for you, Annie. Take care of you."

"I wanted to free you from the responsibility. I wanted to give you room to fly. But never once did I think of giving up your baby, Trace. I had a piece of you to love forever." She could see devastation in his eyes, all the wounds laid open to the night.

"Annie." He whispered her name against her lips. "How the hell did things get so screwed up between us?"

"We were kids. Scared kids. And we created a situation neither of us was ready to handle. We made mistakes. Both of us."

"Is this just one more mistake, Annie?" Trace asked softly. "Me, coming back into your life? Or is this a second chance for us?"

"I don't know." Panic bubbled in Annie's breast, mixed with a wild kind of hope. The kind of blind hope that sent people making leaps of faith.

But leaping into the unknown was Trace's forte. Annie had always been cautious, careful, exploring every possible consequence before she acted. Except for the night she had gone to find Trace....

The thought sobered her as nothing else could have. "Trace, no matter what we felt for each other nine years ago—we're different people now. With different lives."

"Then you're saying we should just forget the whole thing? The hell with us?"

"No. I'm saying that the last time we had feelings for each other, we raced in without thinking about the consequences. Look at the pain it caused—you, me and even April. We can't afford to make the same mistake again."

"You're not sixteen anymore. You're a woman. I'm a man."

"That's why we have to sort this all out. To think it through."

"You got everything set up in little compartments, Annie?" Trace demanded, suddenly edgy. "You think you can take what happened between us when I kissed you and stick a label on it? What the blazes is there to think about? Whether or not it was too hot to be real? Was there some other man who made you feel anything hotter?"

For a heartbeat, Annie couldn't meet his eyes. Then she stared straight into that storm-cloud blue. "There hasn't been anyone since you."

"You mean you've never been in love with any of the men you've—"

"I mean that there haven't been any men at all."

Trace stared at her, stunned. "I don't believe it. You're beautiful. So damn smart. There must've been men who—"

"It was my choice, Trace."

He took a step back, one of the lights from the parking lot shining on cheeks suddenly pale, a face incredibly still. "I busted you up pretty bad inside, didn't I, Brown-Eyes?"

Tears formed in the corners of Annie's eyes. Trace cupped one hand on her cheek, feeling the wetness as they spilled free.

"Give me a chance. I'm not asking you to love me. Not right now. I'm not even saying I love you. All I know is that my whole life I've needed something to give me direction. Something to give meaning to all the craziness. All the pain. Maybe, if you'll give me a chance to make things up to you, I can find that something."

"Trace, I don't know—"

"Just think about it, Annie. We have a child together. And God knows, every time I touch you, I need you so bad I can barely breathe. You have to feel it, too." His voice dropped low, pulsing through her nerve endings like warm brandy. "Tell me you feel it, too."

"I don't want to—can't afford to—" Suddenly, Annie needed to deny it, even to herself. "I've never been a very physical person."

"You made love with a boy who was half crazy with pain. I wasn't as gentle as I wanted to be, Annie. And I was so sure you'd turn away from me that I didn't take the time to pleasure you. Next time I have you beneath me, I'll show you what it's like to be loved by a man. I'll make it so good for you, you'll forget that other time.''

Forget? Forget the simmering, slow burn Trace had started inside her? Forget the soaring sensation of feeling him become a part of her? Forget the groping need, reaching for a burning sphere of light, sensation that had danced just beyond her reach in the moments before Trace had plunged into her one last time, his incoherent cries shattering on a sob.

Did Trace even remember how he'd clung to her, his face buried against her bare breasts, his tears running in hot rivulets down her skin? Could he even guess what she'd felt, holding him? Even then, she'd never cherished any delusions of happily-ever-afters with Trace, she'd known their time together would be as fleeting as it was precious to her. But she'd been glad, so glad that he'd been her first. Something that nothing—not time nor distance nor one of Trace's countless other girls—could take away from her.

She'd held on to that in the years that had come after. She'd thought it was enough. But this dangerously handsome, devastatingly vulnerable man before her was offering something more now. Something she hadn't dared to hope for, dared to dream.

"I don't know, Trace. I can't think straight. I—"

"There's time, Annie. Just promise you won't walk away from me again without telling me why."

Why? If she walked away it would be because she was terrified of the feelings he stirred in her. Because she'd already lost him once, and almost hadn't recovered.

Annie stared into Trace's silver-blue eyes, knowing that she was a coward. That she was running from the real truth. She didn't dare fall in love with Trace McKenna this time.

Because if she let herself love him, really love him, she'd have to admit that she'd been wrong to walk away from that rebellious seventeen-year-old boy so many years ago, depriving him of all the time he could've spent with his daughter. Time Annie could never give back to Trace and April.

If that was true, how could Annie ever forgive herself?

"We need to pick April up," Annie said, grasping on to the most logical excuse to get her away from this night with its stars, the soft music drifting from the Golden Nugget. Away from the solemn light in Trace's eyes.

As if he sensed her need for distance, Trace stepped away from her, jamming his fists into his pockets. "You asked me before what I was thinking, and I told you," Trace said. "Now I'm asking you."

"I'm thinking I was crazy ever to come here, that this whole thing is dangerous. So dangerous. That if I had any sense at all, I'd race back to Chicago on the next plane."

"You promised you wouldn't run," Trace bit out, and she could sense the savage fury, the pain of the boy he had been.

"I didn't promise anything. I can't."

"Try it, and I'll track you down, Annie," Trace growled, his hands catching her arms, a primitive light in his eyes. "I swear I'll come after you."

There was a time such a declaration from Trace would've been the answer to Annie's most secret prayers. Promises of dreams come true and fairy-tale reunions. Now Trace's words only tightened the coil of uncertainty in her chest.

"I'm not going to let you walk out of my life again," Trace said fiercely. "Not you or April. It's too late for that now."

Annie looked deep into those storm-dark eyes. There were a thousand methods of running away, places to go where no one would ever find you, places to hide your heart. In her years at the shelter, Annie had learned every one of them.

The trouble was, Trace was right.

It was too late. She had run from Trace McKenna once before.

This time, there was no place left to hide.

Chapter 9

Trace paced the night-dark confines of his bedroom, low-slung jeans clinging to his freshly showered body, shivers from the icy water he'd used still skating across his bare skin. Two hours had passed since he'd guided the Land Cruiser out of the parking lot of the Golden Nugget on the way to pick up April.

He'd been fighting to regain his emotional balance during the whole ride. But even two hours' distance and a shower frigid enough to turn a polar bear blue couldn't cool the sensations let loose the moment he'd kissed Annie Brown again.

Shattering. Primal. They gripped him again every time he closed his eyes. Raw, blinding need had shot through every fiber of Trace's being, bursting self-control, igniting fires far more dangerous than the raging infernos Trace had plunged into so many times before. Trace knew from harsh experience that the key to survival in a perilous situation was keeping your head. No matter how bad things got, you couldn't give in to the fear. But when Trace had tasted those lips he had dreamed about, agonized over for nine long years, the fear that shot through him was visceral, devastating. Terror that he could lose himself again in Annie's arms. Terror that he wouldn't be strong enough to hold her, resourceful enough to keep her.

Terror that she would turn and walk away.

"God!" It was half curse, half plea, as Trace stalked to the open window. What was he doing, putting himself on the line again like this?

He'd wanted to work things out with Annie. Wanted to find some way for them to share April. He'd even toyed with the idea of sex with her—toyed with it? Hell, he'd been consumed with the idea from the moment he walked into the shelter office. But he'd thought he could keep his head through it all, that he could maintain enough distance to keep him from being shattered the way he had been so many years before.

But the truth was, there had never been any distance between Annie and him. No safety nets. No anchor ropes. When it came to Annie Brown, he'd been free-falling from the first moment he'd met her. It had been glorious. Incredible. But then he'd hit the ground. In a hundred bone-crushing accidents, Trace had never felt any impact so crippling.

He must be crazy even to consider throwing himself back to the most glorious, most agonizing, time in his life. He must be insane to even consider . . . what?

Loving Annie?

A giant fist squeezed his ribs. He stalked to the open window in an effort to catch his breath. The breeze stirred the damp webbing of hair that spanned his chest—a chest aching for the imprints of Annie's fingers, the heated press of her palms.

Stars spilled across the heavens like rhinestones snapped from a child's play necklace. Moonshine fashioned silvery sliding boards for dreams to skim down on.

Night and dreams of Annie.

Would they ever be separate in his mind? Would he ever be able to look out and see darkness instead of black velvet curtains that had sheltered them from the harsh realities of the world for just a little while? Would he ever forget that stunning moment of joy, so blindingly brilliant, when he'd put his hands on Annie's body and known she wanted him, too?

For years it had infuriated him to feel the tightening in his sex whenever he thought of that moment. He'd tried to drown the sensation in gallons of whiskey, beautiful women, a thousand wild rushes of adrenaline as he pushed himself to impossible limits.

But now he felt that same crushing desire with a kind of wild hopelessness, a dizzying plunge that made him wonder if he'd be the one who turned coward this time.

Trace McKenna, daredevil *extraordinaire,* adrenaline junkie who never felt alive unless he was blazing at Mach 10 on the ragged edge, might finally have rammed into a risk he wasn't brave enough to take.

But there would be plenty of time to gather his courage where Annie was concerned. The woman had made it clear she was going to be damned careful when it came to starting anything physical between them. Hell, she hadn't let any man touch her, taste her, since the night he'd taken her virginity with all the finesse of a rutting stag. He'd known he hadn't been any fantasy lover that night. But it must've been pure misery to have scared her off men altogether.

Hell. He'd thought he'd been acquainted with hell's most searing flames when he'd lost Annie so long ago. But that couldn't compare to the agony of watching her now, not being able to crush her in his arms, kiss her, make love to her.

She still broke his heart. The woman who sat, even now, on the side of April's bed, stroking back her daughter's hair, singing snippets of lullabies the child was no longer aware of. Lullabies that Trace sensed were to comfort Annie, soothe Annie, not the little girl slumbering, oblivious to the emotional turmoil all around her.

Annie was still quivering inside. Even through the walls that separated them, the years that made them strangers, Trace could feel her whole being resonating with reawaked pain and a thousand unanswered questions, terrifying possibilities that could open the door to something both of them wanted desperately, but feared soul-deep.

Trace wondered what it would be like to feel free to go to her, kiss the tender dip of her temple. To tell her everything was going to be all right. And to believe it, down deep where his nerves were raw.

She'd come to Halloran's stable so many years ago to offer him comfort. God knew, he wanted to do the same for her. And yet—wasn't Annie right to counsel caution? They were both so tense, so uncertain. And then there was April. Their actions in the next few months would alter the course of her life forever. Any change that profound was a precarious one, filled with danger.

Damn. Trace swore and stalked over to his bed. He sat down on the edge and lowered his face into his splayed hands. It had all seemed so simple when he'd stormed out of the hospital three weeks ago. April was his daughter. Annie had betrayed him. Betrayed him even more vilely than he'd believed all these years by stealing his child from him. He had intended to bulldoze his way into April's life, give her everything his vast wealth could buy, and all the love Trace had never known as a child himself. Love he'd only entrusted to one person for such a brief, precious time.

Yes, the whole mess was disturbing. Unsettling. That first week he'd been mad as hell, and hadn't been too particular about getting back at Annie Brown for all those sleepless nights that had left him weak and wanting.

But the ache that had started down deep in his chest tonight was far more lethal than what he had known before. He'd been a boy when Annie had walked out of his life last time. A kid who had believed he could obliterate the emptiness she'd left inside him by living life on the edge. A kid who had been so damned determined to show the world that he didn't need anyone. Trace McKenna, Mr. Live for the Moment.

He'd had nine years to learn that it didn't take any guts to fling your life away when there wasn't anyone waiting for you, wanting you, loving you.

But Annie had loved him once. Nine years ago when he'd been too much of a coward to tell her how he felt, too much of a tough son of a bitch to admit to the tender, soft places she'd touched inside him. Telling her how he felt would have been the greatest risk Trace had ever taken. In the end, it would have been the only risk that really would have mattered.

The knowledge burned, relentless inside him, churning up self-doubts, self-loathing, a primal kind of helplessness and a sense of futility that left him more torn up than he'd ever been before.

He'd told Annie it was too late for them to run. But wasn't it even more likely that it was too late to pick up the pieces of the dreams they had abandoned? There hadn't seemed to be any common ground between them years ago. There was even less now. April. Only April. Unless they could build something stronger, something new....

"Damn it, Annie, why'd you run away from me?" Trace groaned into his hands. "Why didn't you tell me you loved me? Why couldn't I tell you I loved you? Oh, God, things could've been so different."

"Trace?"

The tentative sound of his name on her lips made Trace jump to his feet, his cheeks burning with the fear she might have heard his anguished words, the rest of his body heating with another kind of fire as his gaze skimmed down Annie's body.

She stood, framed in the doorway. When she'd left April's room, he couldn't guess. But the rose sweater and cream-colored slacks had been stripped away. Her hair was long and loose and honey-gold, flowing over a simple white-cotton nightgown with a touch of old-fashioned lace edging the high neckline. The hem of the gown skimmed her thighs, her legs stretching long and golden-tan to small bare feet. Her eyes shone huge and soft. Wary in the moonshine.

Trace fought against the pulsing need that started in the core of him. His voice sounded like that of a stranger. "I thought you were still in with April. Is there—was there something you needed?"

She caught that full, dusky-rose bottom lip of hers with her teeth, and Trace felt the pulsing inside him turn to thunder. "I guess what I need . . . needed to say is . . . thank you."

"Thank you?"

"For giving April this time. For trying so hard to make her dreams come true. I'm still uncomfortable with a lot of this. The pony, all the money you spent on toys. Everything. I've prided myself on taking care of her. Giving her love. I've told myself that material things didn't matter."

"Take it from someone who's got everything money can buy. You're right. This stuff doesn't matter a damn when you've got no one to love." The words slipped out before Trace could stop them, leaving him raw, exposed, vulnerable. Damn, hadn't he ripped himself open enough for one blasted night?

"I know you're right. If a person had to choose between love and material things, there would be no contest. But if you can give April things I can't...if she can have both...who am I to say no, just out of some stupid, stubborn pride."

"You have a lot to be proud of, Annie. She's incredible. I can't tell you how much I respect you for the way you've raised her. I'm the one who should thank you for all you've done for my daughter."

Tears were forming in Annie's eyes. Trace could see them, glinting, sapphire-blue in those sad green eyes. "Funny, the things you never think about until it's too late," Annie whispered.

"Tell me about it." Trace crossed to where she stood, so alone. Alone the way she had been when she bore his child. Alone and scared and trying so hard to be brave.

"Late at night I—I always sit at the edge of April's bed for a little while. Watch her sleep. She's so busy during the day. She hardly ever sits still."

"I don't know where she gets all that energy. It's like she can't wait to explore everything. Conquer the world."

"She reminds me so much of you, Trace."

Her words touched him, deep. "She's more together than I'll ever be, Brown-Eyes. Because of you."

That should've comforted her. Eased the tension in her delicate frame. Instead, Annie's hands curled into fists against him, a shuddery sound coming from her throat. "Don't say that, Trace. Don't..."

"Tell you the way I feel?"

"Don't feel that way. Don't you see? I was sitting by April's bed, and kept thinking about the moment you asked me for a picture of April when she was a baby. It always made me sad. I wanted to be able to take out a photo album like other mothers do, look into those big, wondering eyes of hers, see that crooked little smile, that one that was like yours just before you did something to make people laugh. But even though it hurts me not to be able to hold the picture in my hand, it doesn't really matter. I have her image in my heart."

"I'm glad, Brown-Eyes."

"But don't you see? You don't. You'll never be able to see how beautiful she was. I took that away from you."

Trace felt his own chest go rigid at her pain. "Annie, you did what you thought you had to do. You can't look back. Neither of us can. We can't change what happened."

He cupped her face in his hands, felt her tears burn his palms. "Don't cry, Brown-Eyes. I can't stand it when you cry."

"I'm so scared, Trace. I had everything all figured out. My whole life. April's life. Annie Brown, who had triumphed over her painful past, turned her mistakes into something worthwhile. I believed that I had done the right thing by leaving Arizona all those years ago. Even just a few weeks ago, I convinced myself I wanted to keep you away from April because you would traumatize her somehow, or disrupt her life by bouncing in and out of it whenever it was convenient for you."

"I don't blame you for having reservations about me. You just wanted to protect April."

"No. I wanted to protect myself. The hardest thing I've ever had to admit is the fact that I'm not scared you'll hurt April. I'm afraid April will hate me for lying to her. And

I'm such a coward that I can't risk losing her love. Even if it means I'm cheating you out of the joy of telling her she's your child."

"Oh, God," Trace dragged her against him. "Annie, I don't want to take her away from you."

He felt her slender body shaking where it pressed against his. She buried her face against him, her hair feathering in silken waves against his skin. Her breasts were soft, fluid, pillowed against him.

And he knew the same immeasurable need he'd known so long ago—the need to take care of his sweet, sweet Annie. To protect her from anything that could hurt her—most of all to protect her from himself.

"I won't let anything hurt you, Brown-Eyes. I promise." It was the same vow he'd made as a boy so long ago. Would he fail her now, just as he'd failed her then?

He sought out her chin, cupped it in his hand. He forced her to lift her face toward him. "If it ever came to a choice between the two of us being in April's life, I'd turn and walk away. And I'd never look back."

"I just want to fix things...find a way to make them right. But I can't think of any way to—"

"Maybe I can." The idea appeared out of the mists of Trace's mind, the most secret, hidden places. It was so fragile, so daring, he could barely put it into words. "Marry me, Brown-Eyes."

She pulled back, incredulous. Trace winced inwardly as a ragged laugh tore from her throat. "Trace, you can't be serious."

He braced himself, stunned by how damn serious he suddenly was. "Is it really such a crazy idea? If we got married, I could be a part of April's life. I could adopt her, Annie. Be her father—emotionally and legally. The only father she's ever known. I'd be satisfied with that tie. Hell,

I'd be grateful for it. If I had it, there would be no reason to demand more."

"More?" Green eyes went misty, uncertain.

"You'd never have to tell her that I'm the brainless kid who got you pregnant."

Stillness. It engulfed the room. Pulsed in it. Trace was stunned to see Annie's eyes brim with tears. He'd always figured he was no matrimonial prize, but it hurt him somehow, seeing that rejection in her face.

Then she spoke, barely above a whisper. "You would make that sacrifice for April?"

"I'm not doing it for April. I'm doing it for you."

"Why?"

"Because I loved you once. Because I think there's a chance I could love you again." This time he laughed, a low, ragged sound. "Maybe I never stopped."

Wisps of her hair clung to her tear-streaked cheeks. Trace brushed the strands away with the tips of his fingers. Then slowly he lowered his lips to the salty-wet streaks, tasting Annie's sadness, pressing kisses against the pulse of her deepest fears, his fiercest regrets.

Trace felt something unfold inside him as he tracked his lips down to the corner of her mouth. He felt the bitterness, the anger, he'd kept closed in a rock-hard ball in his vitals soften, open and flow into Annie's own most private anguish. A mating, not of bodies, but of yesterday's wounds, tomorrow's promise, today's stark uncertainty.

Nine years ago, when he was emotionally battered, Annie had come to him and embraced his agony, taken it into herself. He'd given her his baby that night. Blinded by his own desperation and need, he'd filled her with his child.

Was it possible that tonight they could be conceiving something almost as precious? Something fragile and new and miraculous after so many barren years?

Trace would have joyfully sacrificed ten years of his life just to be able to settle his mouth over Annie's trembling lips, kiss her long and deep and slow and hot. But he didn't want to risk pushing her, trampling on this new trust that had sprung up between them, this honesty that was as frightening as it was filled with hope.

He wanted to give Annie a chance to sort through what he'd said, to decide . . . he wanted to give her the rest of his life. His whole future. A future that had been barren, empty, until he'd looked up from his hospital bed and seen Annie Brown on a television screen.

He was reaching down inside himself, seeking the strength to pull away, when Annie made a soft, wounded sound in her throat, and sought out his lips with her own.

It was the first time Trace could remember Annie seeking out his kiss. The gift would have been too precious to sacrifice even for a man with three times the noble impulses Trace had.

He threaded his hands through her hair and let her explore his mouth with her own, let her seek out comfort, surcease, the way he had when he had first kissed her so many years ago.

"Th-this is crazy," Annie breathed against his mouth.

"I know."

Her tongue stole out, pressed against the corner of his mouth. Jagged desire ripped through every fiber of Trace's body.

"We don't even know each other."

"Maybe we know enough."

"Trace, I—"

"Think about it, Annie. All these years, I couldn't forget you. Did you forget me?"

"How could I, with April staring back at me with your eyes, flashing me your smile—"

"Is that the only reason you thought about me? The only way you remembered me? As April's father?"

He felt her shudder, as if the admission was tearing something inside her. "No. I thought about that night at the fair. The way you held my hand. The way you grabbed my ribs in the spook house and made me scream. And then, when you realized you'd really frightened me, how you dragged me back against you and made sure nothing else could make me afraid."

"If you were my wife, Annie, I could keep all the ghosts away. From you and from April."

"I'm not a scared girl anymore."

"Well I'm scared. Damn scared. Scared that tomorrow I'll wake up and you'll be gone again. Scared that April will just be a dream. That I'll still be left with an empty place in my heart, the memory of a baby that never got a chance to laugh and smile and love still eating inside me. You think it's easy to admit that, Brown-Eyes? Mr. Living on the Edge scared out of his mind?"

"We both have our own lives—"

"I don't know about yours, but my life sucked."

Annie laughed aloud, a thousand voices of reason clamoring inside her. A thousand wild dreams beating butterflies wings against her sanity. "You're insane," she breathed, battling against the smile Trace McKenna had always won from her so effortlessly. Her mouth wobbled into a grin.

"Yeah, Brown-Eyes. That's me. Certifiable. The question is, are you crazy enough to marry me?"

"I live in Chicago. You flit all over the world."

"That's the beauty in being the boss, sweetheart. I can move FireStorm's base headquarters to the goddamn moon if I want to. I want to marry you, Brown-Eyes. The same way I do everything else in my life—fast. Real fast."

"You can't just—just rush into something like this."

"Got no other choice." Dangerous, seductive lights played in the storm-cloud depths of Trace's eyes.

"Why not?"

"'Cause I don't want to make another mistake with you. I don't want to push you. Risk hurting you again. But every time I touch you I get so damn hot, what little willpower I have melts. If we don't settle this—and soon—I'm gonna lose my grip, Annie. Do what comes naturally."

The gruff tones of his voice shivered down Annie's spine. "What's that?"

"I'm gonna scoop you up in my arms and carry you to my bed. I'm gonna strip away that nightgown and kiss every inch of you—pleasure places I never even knew existed ninc ycars ago."

Annie bit her lip, hard. But her mouth still tingled from Trace's kiss. She couldn't drag air into her lungs. Shadowy images from the hayloft slipped across her mind like black satin. Trace had been pure trouble back then. The years had hardened him, toughened him. But they hadn't tamed him.

There had been only one brief snippet of time Trace McKenna had let another spirit touch his, Annie realized suddenly.

Once she had had the courage to walk away from him out of love. This time, did she have the courage to walk into his arms buoyed by something as ephemeral as hope?

It was terrifying. Mesmerizing. The thought of having Trace McKenna as her lover. Of stripping away all the layers of her life—social worker, friend, mother, daughter— leaving only the secret part of her, the woman part, the lover part, bare to Trace's hands. Hands so strong, so callused, so potently male, they awakened something primitive in the darkest recesses of her soul.

Annie couldn't reach the words that were locked so deep inside her. She did the only thing she could to show Trace what she was feeling, trusted him with emotions she didn't fully understand.

Her hands were unsteady, her cheeks fire-hot as she grasped the short hem of her nightgown. Trace's gasp of surprise broke on a groan of raw need as she slowly drew the garment over her head and let it slip from her fingers to pool on the floor.

Chapter 10

Trace's body went rigid as a bronze statue, the only flicker of life the desire raging like a brushfire in his eyes. Annie stood there, frozen, fragile in this new daring, feeling as if she might shatter under the intensity of Trace's gaze.

"Annie, are you sure?" he rasped.

"Don't make me say it, Trace."

He wheeled away from her, and for a heartbeat Annie thought he intended to walk away. Be the cautious one, this single time. But Trace's long-legged stride only ate up the distance between where he'd stood and the door to the bedroom. His hand was unsteady as he grabbed the knob and jammed the door shut.

He stood, silhouetted against the panel, his body as hard and tough as the oak the door was hewn from. Rugged beauty. Primitive strength. A dream ages old.

"I'm almost afraid to touch you," Trace whispered. "After what happened last time—"

Annie's cheeks burned. "You mean you don't keep...uh, protection handy?"

His mouth ticked up in a ghost of his old wicked smile. "You probably won't believe this, but I don't. Not here, anyway. Not...until I knew I was bringin' you here."

"You must've been pretty sure of yourself."

"No. But when I touched you in that office of yours, it was like the time we were in the stable, only ten times stronger. Spontaneous combustion, Brown-Eyes. Over the edge. I tried to convince myself that it was anger, that I wanted revenge, pure and simple. Kissing the hell out of you was a way to shut you up and drive that damned look off your face. The one that said you were totally in control when I was falling apart. But I guess my gut didn't believe all those excuses. So I..."

"Made certain you could take care of me?"

"Yeah, well, I don't buy that line anymore—you know, the one that says if you only do it once a girl can't get pregnant." Bitterness edged his voice, along with ruthless self-blame.

Annie shivered as the breeze from the open window flowed over her skin. Her cheeks stung, and she was suddenly excruciatingly aware she was standing there, naked, while Trace McKenna stared at the door.

Reflexively, she grabbed up her nightgown, pressing it against her bare breasts just as Trace turned. Those beautiful eyes probed past embarrassment, into her most closely guarded insecurities.

"Ah, no, sugar," Trace breathed. "Don't hide from me. I've been waitin' so long to see you. Dreamin' of lookin' at you all over."

Just the sound of those husky-warm tones made Annie's breasts tingle, her nipples pearl. She fixed her gaze on the thick carpet, uncertain, unsure. She hadn't been a beauty when she and Trace had been together last time. But now a faint webbing of stretch marks from her pregnancy feathered across the gentle swell of her stomach, her breasts had changed from nursing a baby.

It suddenly seemed so unfair that Trace was even more compelling, more arresting, in his raw masculine beauty than he had been so long ago. That he would know all the secrets to this game of lovemaking, while she had only hazy memories of awkward gropings, half-formed caresses, needs she hadn't fully understood.

She turned away from him, suddenly afraid. "It's not fair," she whispered. "I don't—don't know what to do. And look at you—you look even better than you did in high school, while I—"

A raw jolt of sensation speared to Annie's center as Trace's callused hand cupped her naked shoulder, smoothed down the vulnerable curve of her arm. "You're the most beautiful thing I've ever seen, Annie Brown. Except for that little girl in the other room."

Annie's heart soared at the fierce honesty in his voice.

"You know why April's even more beautiful to me?" He asked, turning Annie to face him. She drowned in gray-blue eyes. "'Cause April is a part of you and a part of me, together forever. In a way that nothing—not my stubbornness or your pride or your daddy's hate—can ever break apart."

"Oh, Trace." Annie quavered.

"You wanna know something really crazy?" He nibbled kisses along her cheek.

"What?"

His fingers tangled in the nightgown she was still clutching. He tugged it away from her and dropped it onto the floor. "I wanna make a dozen babies with you. I want the whole damned world to know I can't keep my hands off you."

Hands... his hands were all over her, sculpting the contours of her breasts, her belly, her waist, as if he were blind and was learning her by heart.

"I never got to see you carrying April. Never got to put my face against your stomach when it was swelling with my baby. Never got to whisper to her..."

Trace's fingertip wisped over one of the faint white marks on Annie's abdomen. His lashes dipped low, dark shadows of regret on high cheekbones.

Annie reached out to cup his cheek in one hand, threading her fingers into the silky strands at his temple. "What would you have said to her?"

"That I was her daddy. That I'd take care of her. And that—that her mommy was the most beautiful thing that ever came into my life...." The words ground to a halt. Annie couldn't bear the raw emotion in Trace's face, couldn't bear the answering anguish in her own heart as she pictured the precious image he'd woven.

His words had only torn open the wound, laid it bare to the sun. Annie reached out to heal it the only way she knew how. She cupped Trace's face in her hands, and pressed her trembling lips against the pain-hardened curve of his mouth.

He groaned, a shudder working through the hard planes of his body. Annie felt his lips open against hers. He scooped her into his arms, the sensation of her skin against Trace's naked chest making Annie feel as if she were melting. Melting into the wild, carnal magic carved into every sinew of Trace's body. He carried her to his bed as if she weighed no more than a wildflower, his mouth seducing her with long, slow, hot kisses as he rasped earthy words of praise, silken promises.

The coverlet was downy soft against her bare back as Trace followed her down onto the mattress. He eased one jeans-clad leg over her naked thighs, drawing her hard and tight into the unyielding contours of his body, letting her know with vivid clarity just how hungry he was to bury himself inside her.

"Feel me, Annie." He pressed himself against her. "Feel what you do to me. How much I want you."

Annie felt his arousal pulse against her in a primitive rhythm that made her feel achingly empty, as if she'd perish if Trace didn't fill her. Even the slow dragging of his tongue down the slope of her breast, the seeking, melting kisses that circled her nipple, couldn't stop the need she suddenly had to strip away the single layer of denim that kept her from being skin to skin with this bone-meltingly sexy man.

"T-Trace, you're not—not playing fair," she managed in throaty accusation.

He opened his mouth over the rosy point of her nipple, sucked it deep into the heat of his mouth. Annie almost came off the bed at the sensual jolt it sent rocketing through her. "You know me, Brown-Eyes. Never play by the... rules. But if you've got any objections, I'm listenin'."

"You have too many clothes on." Annie reached for the frayed waistband of the denims.

She could feel his smile spread against her passion-heated skin; his lips were damp and firm and warm, his jaw lightly stubbled. Wicked. Devilish. He rolled onto his back, his fingers going to the fastenings of his jeans. She watched as he worked a metal button through its frayed hole, then another.

Annie's mouth went dry as the fabric spread, tugged apart by his impressive arousal, revealing a wedge of dark hair. In Halloran's stable she had been timid, tentative, pliant, following Trace's lead, but afraid to give in to her own impulses. Annie had had nine years to imagine what she might have done, could have tried, if she had just had the courage to risk.

She caught her lower lip in her teeth, her hand curving over Trace's where his fingers were poised at the next metal fastening. Trace shot her a piercing glance, searching her face for some sign. Annie suddenly knew he was certain she'd changed her mind. That she was going to start stammering out excuses, reasons why they should pull back from what they'd begun here.

His whole body was rigid. A bead of sweat trickled from his temple down the lean line of his clenched jaw. He didn't say a word, and Annie knew he wouldn't. If she chose to break off their lovemaking, Trace McKenna wouldn't breathe a word to convince her, no matter how savage his need was pulsing through him, no matter how much he ached for release.

The knowledge ran soothing fingers through her tangled emotions, making her suddenly bolder than Annie Brown had ever been in her life.

And she realized she wasn't trying to recapture the magic night she had found Trace in the stable. She wasn't trying to find the innocence and wonder of the wide-eyed girl she had been. She wasn't trying to right past wrongs with the boy she had loved, then lost.

She wanted to make love as a woman with this man—the man who had stormed into her life to claim his daughter, the man who had showered his little girl with every gift imaginable, but hadn't realized that the most beautiful thing he could give April was the glow of complete acceptance, fierce, unconditional love. Trace's awe when he looked at April had made Annie look past worries about homework assignments and braces and a hundred other mundane concerns, so that she could marvel again at the child who was the legacy of one enchanted April.

With slow deliberation, she peeled Trace's fingers back from the straining fly of his jeans and laid that beautifully shaped hand on his thigh. Her eyes snagged his for a second, then she reached for the next metal button.

She'd expected the tingle of embarrassment that stung her cheeks, the bounce her pulses took to a higher notch. She hadn't had any clue how hot Trace would be as her knuckles grazed the steely evidence of his maleness. She hadn't suspected how the sound of his hoarse groan of pleasure would empower her, embolden her.

The button slipped from its hole, the vee of denim spreading wider. Annie saw Trace's hands knot in the sheets as she ran the tip of one finger ever so delicately down the length of him, then stripped his jeans away. He looked so tough, so pain-ravaged, so beautifully vulnerable, she succumbed to unfathomable impulse and pressed a soft kiss against that fire-hot flesh.

Her honey-gold hair swept in a silken veil across the rigid muscles of his stomach, brushed against the hair-stippled skin of his inner thigh. A ragged, animal sound rose in the back of his throat. "Annie...oh, Annie...you're making me crazy."

"You're already crazy," she breathed, smiling into his eyes. "Maybe it's contagious."

"Like hell!"

"You're dangerous, Trace McKenna," Annie taunted, feathering her splayed fingers up the ridges of his belly into the dusting of hair that spanned his broad chest. His nipples were pebble-hard, tickling her palms as she rubbed her hands in slow circles. "You've told me that time and again.

Bad to the bone. But if that's true, why do you feel so good?''

"I'm not good, Annie. You know that better than anyone. I'm a taker who—''

"You're not taking from me now, Trace. Look at you. You're giving me the chance to touch you, to explore…when I know you're ready—more than ready to…''

"I don't want to take you the way I did before. I want to go slow, savor every kiss, every touch, draw it out until it seems like it'll go on forever,'' Trace growled. "But damn it, Annie, you make me feel like I'm gonna explode.''

"That's what you're best at, isn't it?'' She pressed her lips against his heartbeat, skimmed her mouth to his nipple. "I want you to. Explode, Trace. Set me on fire the way you did in the hayloft. But take me all the way, this time, to the place where you were burning.''

She touched his nipple with her tongue. The wet, delicate contact shattered something in Trace. Annie could feel it snap, feel the raw desire arc through him with awesome power.

Then he was dragging her up and into his kiss, rolling her beneath him, every work-toughened sinew of his body branding itself into the softer contours of Annie's own. He swallowed her up, fire-hot, straining against her as if by will alone he could fuse them together for all time.

His mouth was all over her, hot, wet on her throat, his hands hungry as they caught the aching swells of her breasts. He reached the straining points with his mouth and sucked greedily, as if he'd been starving for the taste of her, dreaming of the texture of her against his tongue.

"I've thought about this so damned many times, Annie, dreamed of it,'' he groaned against the hollow between her breasts as he trekked his way up the trembling slope to her other nipple. "Damn it, I want it to be right this time.''

She was arching her hips against him, tangling her fingers in his hair. The feel of his mouth flexing beneath her hand, against her breast, was the most shatteringly erotic sensation she'd ever experienced. Until Trace thrust his arousal against her thigh, showing her the depth of his need.

She slid her thighs apart, meaning to cradle him, wanting to draw him inside her. But Trace only frustrated her by shifting to the side, the cool air filtering over skin hot from his passion, damp with his sweat.

Annie started to protest, but it ended on a strangled gasp as those long, beautiful fingers slid from her belly into the dark gold down at the apex of her thighs. She stiffened, wanting, needing, that insistent caress, but feeling awkward, vulnerable. Then Trace touched her. One finger, gentle, tender, seeking, found the most delicate part of her, opening her as if he were folding back the petals of a rose.

Annie felt a trembling in the core of her, a heady anticipation that made her breath catch, freeze in her lungs. Ever so slowly, Trace stroked upward, catching the nub of her desire with the tip of one callused finger. Nothing that had happened in the abandoned stable had prepared her for the burning intensity of that caress.

"T-Trace..." She breathed his name, pleading for something she didn't fully understand, knowing in that instant that there were a hundred dimensions of her own sexuality Trace McKenna could unlock for her.

His finger dipped into the moist heat of her, swept up again to circle, seduce, his mouth murmuring words of praise against her hip. "You feel so good, Annie...so damn good. Don't be afraid, angel, I'll take care of you."

Kisses linked his sweet, sweet promises, like a golden thread slipped through the heart of a handful of pearls. Annie felt herself sliding into Trace's caresses, into the seduction of his voice, the need she could feel in him. His mouth dragged long, lingering kisses down her hip, to the lily-pale skin of her inner thigh, his fingertips teasing her most tender flesh, making it throb and burn, pulse with an almost frenetic need.

Trace's long, dark hair brushed the curls that shielded Annie's feminine secrets, his mouth tracking along the line that drew downward, an arrow pointing to where she wanted Trace to touch her...claim her.

He curved one hand beneath her thigh, opening her more completely to his passion-heavy gaze. Then ever so slowly, he kissed her. Slow and wet, tender and yet full of earthy hunger.

Annie came undone.

She writhed against the coverlet, tiny, desperate sounds rising in her throat as Trace McKenna brought every fiber of her being into sizzling, bone-melting, soul-stealing awareness. The control she'd fought for, hidden behind for so long, tore away from her on a gasp as Trace's inferno consumed that hidden, closed, fiercely leashed part of her. She was teetering on the brink of something magic, something beautiful. She wanted Trace with her. Annie tangled her fingers in the silky waves of his hair, broken pleas forming on her lips. "T-Trace—now, please, oh, sweet heaven, I need—"

Trace rose up, loomed above her, starkly beautiful in his masculinity, awesome in the potent power of his need. His eyes were black with desire, his face glistening with sweat. But the strongly sculpted planes of his face were still scarred with regret, with self-blame, with so much pain Annie wanted to erase.

She saw him grope with something in the drawer of his nightstand, his hands fumbling, awkward as if it were the first time he'd ever performed the ritual of protecting himself and his lover.

Annie knew with bittersweet certainty he'd done so more times than she would ever want to know. But the trembling in his hands, the low curse in his throat, made her smile, then gently finish for him.

She wanted his eyes to be sizzling bright with passion, fierce hunger. She didn't want to see the self-blame darting through the blue-gray depths.

"Trace, what's wrong?"

His mouth twisted. "If I'd just had the brains to do this last time—"

"I wouldn't change anything about that time. Or—or this one," Annie whispered. "Except... I want you to show me... take me over the edge with you, Trace McKenna. Show me how to fly."

"Ah, Annie...." His voice broke as he positioned himself between the restless columns of her thighs. He braced himself with one hand on either side of her, holding his weight off her as his arousal nudged the damp satin he'd readied with his kiss. He eased himself into her center.

She felt him straining to bring her all the tenderness he'd been too tortured, too anguished, too inexperienced, to give her that first time. Knew that he was completely unaware of what that single night of lovemaking had meant to her. There was something so endearing about this life-scarred man, treating her as if this was her first time. But it wasn't. She wanted more from him than gentleness. More than caresses filled with regret, desires leashed by a misguided sense of blame.

He was shaking, pushing farther in, withdrawing, pressing deeper, letting her become accustomed to the thick, heavy length of him stretching her. She wanted more.

"All of you, Trace," she breathed against his chest. "I want all of you."

"I don't want to—to hurt you again—ah, Annie!"

She arched her hips up against him, just as he made another gentle stroke, her movement driving him deeper, her fingers against his bare buttocks urging him down into the wet heat of her.

A cry tore from low in his throat, his control snapping. He drove deep, full, hard, the length of him touching the mouth of her womb, the potent strength of him making Annie's head swim, everything that was feminine inside her rising up like Eve the temptress to embrace him, to revel in him, to mate with him.

Crazy Trace McKenna—she'd heard him called that a hundred times. She hadn't known Trace could produce insanity, with the fervent, worship-filled sips he took of her neck, her cheeks, her throat. She reeled at the sheer power of him thrusting deep, urging her higher, forcing her to let go of any inhibitions she might have clung to.

Pressure built until Annie was biting her lip not to cry out, drinking in Trace's fierce passion like some life-giving potion, feeling it carry her along like a raging river. White waters of response sprung up wild in her center, making her sob with yearning. At that moment, Trace's hand slipped between their bodies, found the glowing hot ember of her need. He pressed it, seduced it, toyed with it, his voice husky, intoxicating, as whiskey as he breathed, "Over the edge, Brown-Eyes. You feel so damn good. So...God, I can't hold...on much longer. Fly with me. Just let it all go."

She felt the tremors erupt in him with a savagery that stunned her. He thrust deep, a groan of regret in his throat that told her just how much he'd wanted to take her with him. Just how hard he'd fought to hold himself back.

But at that instant, Annie shattered on a cry of mindless pleasure. It caught her in its fist, crushed the air from her lungs, the pain from her heart, the last drop of control from her head. She writhed against Trace, clutched at him, tears slipping down her cheeks, sobs balling up under her ribs, bursting there, too painful to keep inside.

The sob shook its way into Trace's body. She felt it lodge in his heart.

He rolled to one side, pulling her with him until she lay atop his lean frame. Her feminine sheath still clung to him, cradled him, as if on some deep, psychic plane. She was afraid that the instant they were parted, he'd slip away from her again, be far beyond her reach.

She buried her face in the hot lee of Trace's shoulder, wishing she could bury a thousand vulnerabilities there, a thousand regrets. And fear. Fear of opening something to Trace McKenna far more dangerous than merely her body.

"Screwed up again, didn't I, Brown-Eyes?" Trace's gruff tones reverberated through her. "Christ, I didn't want to hurt you again, make you cry. After all I took the last time we were together—"

"You didn't take anything, Trace," she choked out, clinging to his trembling shoulders. "Do you know why I came to you that night? Why I made love with you?"

"Because you were an angel who trusted me, wanted to comfort me."

"I didn't do it for you, Trace. I did it for me." Annie raised her face from the damp satin of Trace's skin and stared deep into his eyes. "I knew I could never keep you, never hold you. I always knew that you'd fly away from Arizona and never look back. It was what you needed to do. The only way you could save yourself from all the ugly labels they'd put on you. You said you used me. Took from me. But I took that night from you. I wanted it more than

I'd ever wanted anything. I wanted you to be my first, Trace McKenna. You could've had any of the girls, prettier girls, more—''

"There was no one prettier than you in my eyes."

"I thought that the only way you'd want me was when you weren't . . . when you were—''

"Drunk enough to be reckless? Drunk enough to leave you unprotected? God, Annie!"

"Don't you see? That's what I mean when I say it was my choice. That's why I couldn't let you pay for what happened. Yes, I wanted to comfort you after what you'd been through. Yes, you wanted to . . ." She hesitated, swallowed hard.

"Brown-Eyes, you don't have to rake this all open."

"Yes I do. You wanted me to understand why you came to find me, Trace. I want you to understand why I ran away. There was a part of me that always knew that when I opened myself to making love with you, it was for selfish reasons. Because I thought it was my only chance to be with you. Before you came into me . . . I even thought about the fact that we needed some kind of birth control, but I was certain if I left you to get it, by the time I came back, you would've realized it was just plain Annie who was there with you. Shy, awkward Brown-Eyes."

Trace cupped her cheek in his palm. "There was nothin' plain about you—moonlight in your hair, your face, like an angel, your eyes so soft. I couldn't believe you were really mine, even for that tiny space in time. That was what hurt so much, letting you go. Don't make me let you go tonight, Brown-Eyes."

It seemed impossible, it seemed incredible, to feel the tension build again between them. Need—different flavors, different colors, different fantasies—took root inside

Annie and fed on the simmering heat that rose again in Trace's eyes.

"Wh-what about April? When she wakes up in the morning—"

"We'll be up and dressed by then. I want to go into town before we tell her we're going to be a family. We are going to be a family, aren't we, Annie?"

"I—I want to. I just…there are so many things to work out first."

"You think too damn much. Everything'll be all right, Annie. Nothing can come between us now. As long as you believe in me."

Nothing can come between us… believe in me…. The words were a fierce vow, a plea. Annie knew just how much they had cost him. She curled close to Trace's chest, her thigh over his hips, and tried to revel in the hardening evidence that he'd not yet gotten his fill of her. She should have felt secure, filled with hope and wonder and a sense of rebirth.

But Trace was right. She did think far too much. She thought of the little girl sleeping in the other room, oblivious to the fact that her whole world was about to shift off its axis. Everything was going to change. For the better, Annie promised herself. For the better.

April would have a father….

A father.

Annie winced at the image of another place, another man, spine straight as the barrel of a rifle. Colonel Brown. War hero. With a code of honor as immovable as the Rocky Mountains and a fierce protectiveness of his only granddaughter. And his daughter, Annie thought with a sudden pang. The only time Annie had seen a crack in her father's rigid facade had been the day he walked into her room and discovered the home pregnancy test she'd used. His face had held the expression of a man whose heart had just been ripped from his chest.

Pregnant? Who did this to you, Annalise? That low-life scum, McKenna? I'll kill him! I swear to God—

It wasn't Trace's fault, Daddy, Annie's pleading voice echoed in her head.

He forced you! He had to force you! I'll have him arrested for rape.

It wasn't rape, Daddy. I knew what I was doing.

Damn it, girl, do you have any idea what you've done? No college is going to give a scholarship to a pregnant girl! We'll take you to a clinic, get rid of this—this problem. And as for Trace McKenna— He'll pay for what he did to you!

The scene that followed had been a nightmare that had haunted Annie for nine years. And even though Annie had managed to reconcile with her parents for April's sake when her daughter was five, Colonel Brown's hatred for the boy who had "ruined" his daughter burned with the same intensity as his hatred of those who had protested against Vietnam years ago. For nine years Colonel Brown had nurtured his hate for Trace McKenna, hardened it over time.

Annie had found it daunting enough to tell her father that Trace wanted to be a part of April's life. The mere idea of telling him about the impending wedding made Annie's stomach twist itself into knots.

Annie's own years as a parent had taught her about the dreams that came from staring into your child's eyes—seeing a little being so full of promise, a thousand possibilities. She had grown to understand that her father had had to blame someone for Annie's fall from grace, or he would have to blame himself.

At first, Annie had made great effort to change Colonel Brown's attitude toward Trace. Then she'd surrendered, met by his indomitable will. She'd comforted herself with the knowledge that Trace didn't need her father's approval. That they were so far separated, it didn't matter anymore. She'd even comforted herself with the certainty that Trace might feel a wicked amusement at her father's ire. The same amusement he'd felt at the principal's loathing, the disgust he felt toward any authority figure.

Nothing can come between us now, Trace had told her.

He was right. She was an adult. She'd made more than a few choices her father hadn't approved of—starting with bringing April into the world. And now, her father positively adored his granddaughter.

Her father would be angry. Hurt. No doubt his first instinct would be to mount a campaign to rival the Tet Offensive in an effort to stop this wedding. But in the end he'd have to see that this was best for April, wouldn't he?

And best for you? a voice inside Annie queried.

"What's the matter, Brown-Eyes?" Trace murmured against her temple. "You seem like you're a thousand miles away."

Not a thousand miles, Annie thought. Just nine years away—a dozen mistakes away—facing a hatred that had grown only more virulent with time.

She pressed closer to the hard strength of Trace's body, unable to keep the tiniest quaver from her voice.

"Trace, make love to me again."

I need to feel you inside me, a part of me. I need to know that you're really here and I'm not going to wake up from another dream about you. I need to keep my doubts at bay.

She swallowed hard, stammered, "I mean if you can...if you want to...."

She watched a smile spread over his face, his eyelids slipping to half-mast. "Oh, I want to, lady. I'll never get enough of you. Never."

His mouth closed over hers, driving back the shadows, spinning her into a world of dreams-come-true and happy endings.

Annie wanted to stay there forever, away from the harsh reality she'd been forced to face inside the walls of BabyPlace shelter, while she stood among the fragments of her own most cherished fantasies.

Dreams faded with morning light.

They rarely lasted forever.

Chapter 11

Annie stood at the kitchen window, a cup of coffee growing cold in her hand, one of Trace's T-shirts hanging down to the middle of her thighs. He'd awakened her just as sunrise was staining the rim of the cliff magenta, and Annie had had the odd suspicion that he hadn't slept at all, merely held her in the darkness, alone with his thoughts. He had reached for one of his soft cotton T-shirts, smoothing his hands over her breasts, her waist, as he draped the faded fabric over her.

"My nightgown—" Annie had protested weakly. "It's around here somewhere."

"I want you to wear this until I get back from town," Trace had murmured against her ear, sending a shower of sparks to places that still thrummed from his touch. "I want you to feel it against your skin...feel as if I was still touching you all over."

The husky words had dripped over Annie with blatant sensuality, making her nipples ache against the soft fabric.

Trace had drawn her against him, felt the response of those rosy crests nudging against his chest. "God, how am I ever going to wait until tonight?" he had groaned, then with a kiss, started out the door. "Annie, not a word to the Ape about our plans. You promise?"

"As long as you promise there'll be no more ponies, McKenna. Not even a hamster. Nothing that requires housing, feeding or changing bedding."

"What about diapers? The way we were carryin' on last night, it won't be long before..." He'd stopped, looked at her with an endearing uncertainty. "It's not a requirement to marrying me, you know, Brown-Eyes," he said suddenly.

"What?"

"Having my baby...again. But, God, how I'd love to see you carrying my child. Holding it to nurse at your breast. You'd be so damned pretty. Beautiful." The wistfulness that tinged his voice whispered things he had left unsaid. Told her Trace had pictured that time and again, unable to quit picking at the image like an old wound. It unnerved Annie, made her ache for him, made her think of possibilities that hadn't occurred to her since the day she'd left Arizona behind.

For eight years, Annie had had all she could do to provide for April. She'd worried over necessities like school clothes and braces. Prayed for a scholarship that could clear April's way into college. When she discovered that the salary the Jameses wanted to pay her was three times that of any other social worker she'd refused their generosity, determined to make her own way, indisputably earn every penny she and April lived on.

She'd adored the babies at the shelter, cuddled them and cooed to them more than she'd cared to admit. She'd looked at the stair-step James children with an empty ache inside her. But she'd accepted that April would be her only child a long time ago. The images Trace's words had painted were both beautiful and terrifying.

"Trace, this is moving so fast already, that I—"

"Shh." Annie savored the memory of how Trace had laid his fingertips on her lips. "Guess I'll have to slow down," he'd admitted. "It won't be easy. But then, with us, nothing's ever been easy, has it?"

The corners of her mouth had wobbled into a smile. He'd kissed the tip of her nose with exquisite tenderness. "I'll be back as soon as I can. Start figuring out where you want the wedding, who you want to be there. That's one place you're just gonna have to keep pace with me, sugar. I intend to have you in my bed every night. April's one smart kid. It won't take her long to figure out what's goin' on. By the time she does, I'd just as soon have my ring on your finger."

Trace's wedding ring. That whiskey-warm voice repeating vows that would make her his wife. The mere thought still made Annie shiver with a mixture of delicious anticipation and a very real suspicion that she had finally gone over the edge.

"Last night I was thinking about where we could hold the wedding," Trace had said. "The cliff is beautiful at sunset, like everything good and right is pouring over it, setting the mountain aglow. Will you marry me on the mountain, Annie Brown?"

"Yes. I'll marry you on the mountain," she'd promised. *I'll do anything you ask,* a voice inside her whispered. *Anything except the only thing that matters...telling April the truth.*

She brushed aside the thought that pricked at her, clinging instead to memories of the morning, hazy-bright, so beautiful they already seemed unreal. But Trace's shirt still caressed her, clung to her, holding the scent of pine woods and recklessness, sagebrush and leather, showing her in a way nothing else could have that the night before had not been a dream.

"Mom?"

April's voice made Annie start. Disoriented, she spun around, cold coffee splashing her fingers. Her other hand swept up to brush her disheveled bangs out of her eyes.

"Make any French toast this morning?" the child asked in a voice so bright Annie needed sunglasses to field it. "Love that French toast you make, Mom."

Edgy as Annie was, she couldn't help laughing at the reminder of the morning two days ago when Trace's truckload of presents had arrived. It was obvious April was trying her best to make amends.

I don't like it when my mom's sad... the hushed admission April had confided to Trace stung Annie's heart. She crossed to her daughter, caught her in a hug.

"Actually, I figured the two of us could go out and eat oats with the pony. Day before yesterday you ate astronaut food. I figure horse food is next."

The wary light in April's eyes vanished and she made a spectacular face. "Horse food probably tastes better." She glanced around the room surreptitiously, her gaze flicking to the window. Her brow puckered. "Have you, uh, seen Trace this morning?"

"He went into town for something."

"Oh. Did you guys work stuff out about the pony or are you still fighting?"

Fighting? Annie felt her cheeks heat. They'd been locked together all night, but the only thing they'd fought for was to deepen the pleasure, draw out the exquisite sensations.

"No. We're not fighting. We..." Annie stumbled to a halt. It was as if April's words had reawakened the tingling trails of every path Trace had blazed upon her skin with his hands, with his mouth.

She turned away swiftly, as if her eyes might reflect every touch and kiss that had transpired in Trace's bedroom.

"Mom, why don't you like Trace?" April asked suddenly.

"I do like him. I—"

"You like J.T. and you never yell at him or stare at him with that look like Wile E. Coyote gets right before the Road Runner drops an anvil on his head. No matter what, you're always arguing with him, and when I get close you stop."

"Grown-ups don't have to agree on everything to be... friends. Just like you and Tyler don't agree on everything."

"Yeah, well, when I get mad at Tyler I get him in the Iron Jaws of Death hold an' he tries to tie my braids in knots and then we end up laughing so hard we forget the reason why we were fightin' in the first place. Maybe you should try tying Trace's hair in knots. It's about long enough if you work real hard."

Annie laughed.

"Mom, I like Trace," April admitted as if it were some deep, dark secret. "I like him a lot. He's my second favorite man person in the whole world. J.T.'s still my first, but I've known him lots longer. And Trace doesn't get all sour-looking like Grandpa does sometimes. Is it okay for me to like Trace better than Grandpa?"

"Yes, baby. It's okay."

April's eyes got a gleam that was pure devilment. "I wonder if Grandpa will like it that Trace got me a pony. I can't *wait* to tell 'im. Hey!" she burst out with a grin. "Trace said I could do anything I wanted here. Do you think he'd care if I called Grandpa an'—"

"No!" Annie said a little too emphatically. At April's look of surprise, Annie forced her voice to gentle. "I mean it doesn't matter whether or not Trace would mind. I mind." Annie's stomach plummeted. Colonel Brown's phone number was one of the first April had memorized.

Annie saw her sudden shift in mood impact April's expression. The child's face suddenly stilled, those eyes, so like Trace's, seeming to peel away pretense to see the unease that lay beneath Annie's now-brittle smile, that stubborn McKenna chin jutting out at an ominous angle.

"If Trace doesn't mind, how come I can't—"

"Because I'm your mother, young lady." God, Annie hated it when she used the term "young lady," but a hundred warning rattles were going off in her head. April wasn't above cooking up mischief. She was, after all, Trace McKenna's child. And though she was the most reasonable little being imaginable when it came to logical limitations, April had never had any patience for what she called "stupid rules."

Annie sucked in a steadying breath, thinking about Trace on his mysterious errand down the mountain, and of the news they would break to April later that day. Telling Colonel Brown about the impending wedding was inevitable, no matter how much Annie would have liked to postpone it. And God knew, it wouldn't get any easier if Annie waited an eternity.

Better to get the initial confrontation over with. Let her father blow up and rant until he got used to the idea. Then when he had calmed down, April could call about her pony and about the man who was going to be her daddy. As long as Annie laid clear ground rules about how her father was to treat Trace, everything would work out in the end, she assured herself. After all, her father loved her, didn't he? He adored April. . . .

Annie turned back to her daughter. "April, speaking of the pony, have you fed it this morning? Maybe you should go check on her. I . . ." Annie groped for an acceptable lie. "I have some papers I need to go through for BabyPlace. Some work I brought along."

"You've just been sitting around ever since we got here," April observed, her brows lowering. "How come it's so important now?"

"April, if you're not going to take responsibility for that pony—"

"All right, all right, I'm going," April said with a formidable scowl. "Geez!" She stomped out of the room. Annie watched her cross to the paddock where the pony stood cropping grass.

Quickly, Annie walked to Trace's master bedroom and shut the door. There was a phone in almost every room of the Cliff House, but being in the room where she and Trace had made love somehow bolstered Annie's courage, steeled her for what she knew would be a daunting ordeal at best.

She took the phone off the cradle and punched her father's number. It buzzed once, then a voice crisp as winter air came through the line.

"Colonel Brown's office." Milla Yates had been her father's secretary for years. There had been a time Annie had almost hoped that the spritely widow would charm the colonel into marrying her, but both Milla and the colonel had kept their relationship strictly professional.

"Hi, Milla. This is Annie."

"Annie! Why, what a surprise!"

"I was wondering if I could speak to the colonel?"

"Of course you could. That is, if the colonel were here."

Annie's brow crinkled in puzzlement. "Did he step out of his office?"

"No. He won't be back on the base for two weeks. This is his vacation time. I was sure you knew—after all, he bought those baseball tickets. He's been so looking forward to spending time with you and April."

Guilt gouged Annie. "There was a mix-up. The plans just didn't work out. I thought he might've stayed on the base."

"Actually, he left a day early. He was in quite a state at the time. He didn't say anything, of course. That's not his way. But when you've worked for a man as long as I've worked for your father, you can tell when they've been cut off at the knees by something."

"Terrific," Annie muttered. "Do you have any idea where I can reach him?"

"No. He might have gone up to that fishing camp he used to frequent with your mother. And then, there's that Crawfish Jubilee he's always loved down in Mississippi." Willa paused. "Are you sure he didn't go to Chicago? He didn't ask me to change any of his flight plans, and if you'll excuse me for saying so, your daddy might be able to command a warship, but he couldn't make a plane reservation if it were the last flight off of an active volcano."

Annie pressed her fingertips to her temple, rubbing the throbbing knot of nerves that was gathering there. Was it possible her father would have flown to Chicago? Why? He knew she and April would be gone.

"Willa, if you hear from him could you have him call me? I'm at Trace McKenna's Colorado cabin—"

"Did you say... McKenna?"

"Yes."

There was a beat of silence, and Annie could feel efficient Willa riffling through index cards in her mind, trying to find the name she'd recognized. Annie could tell the instant the woman found it.

Trace McKenna—failed pitcher, troublemaker, impregnated Annalise Brown in the month of April...

Milla cleared her throat. "I'm sure there are plenty of McKennas scattered all over the country. Bet if I looked in the phone book right now I could see half a dozen."

"Don't bother, Milla. The man I'm staying with is April's father, if that's what you're wondering about."

"That one who...Annie, I'm not one to interfere in other people's lives, but are you sure this is wise? I mean, getting tangled up with that boy again?"

"He's not a boy anymore, Milla." Annie didn't have the energy to pursue the conversation another moment. "I have to go now. If my father checks in with you, please tell him to call." She rattled off the number on the phone, then swiftly set the receiver back in its cradle.

Annie sank down on the edge of the bed, wishing with all her might that she could turn back the clock eight hours. She could still be curled up next to Trace's naked body, her cheek pressed against the steady drumming of his heart. Everything had been so clear last night. Trace's insistence that she marry him had seemed so logical. He'd told her that he had loved her long ago. Had even offered hope that he might fall in love with her again.

Maybe I never stopped...

But what if we're making a terrible mistake? Annie thought, a twist of pain in her heart. What if he can never love me again? What if I can't love him?

So much time had passed. Time filled with pain, loss, a sense of betrayal. Was it possible to heal wounds that cut so deep? Or would they merely fester, hidden away, until they burst free?

Annie paced to the window and flattened the palm of her hand against the glass pane, staring out across the Colorado mountainside. Everything had seemed so simple when she'd been in Trace's arms. She wanted him here now, wanted him to smile at her that devilish, bewitching smile of his, wanted to hear that little catch in his throat, that sound of pleasure as his mouth molded itself to hers.

She wanted him to drive away a thousand doubts and fears that buzzed inside her like irate bees, stinging and making her burn with their poison.

No! Annie brought herself up short. She was being ridiculous. She and Trace had finally worked things out. True, Annie hadn't had a chance to speak with her father yet. Nor did she have the courage to face April with the fact that she'd lied when she'd told her stories about the little girl's father. Trace was undeniably making a sacrifice in allowing his true relationship to April remain a secret.

But he would be the little girl's father in every other way. April would carry Trace's name, be legally his. How much could that single secret matter in the face of the future Trace would share with his daughter? And with Annie? How deeply could those secrets cut when Annie spent every night in Trace's bed, trying to heal the wounds she'd left on his spirit?

The sound of Trace's Land Cruiser rumbling up the road was the most welcome sound Annie had ever heard. She shook off the troubling thoughts and raced out, wanting nothing more than to feel his arms around her, see April's smile when they told her about the wedding.

For once, Annie was going to believe in dreams. In miracles. In second chances that might blossom into love.

What had Trace said?

Nothing could come between them now.

Trace swung the car door open, his breath snatched away by the sheer pleasure of watching Annie hurry from the house and rush down the path toward him, her hair wisping like enchanted skeins of gold over her shoulders. He must have dreamed a scenario like this a hundred times during the weeks after he'd admitted he'd fallen in love with her, obsessed on such visions with the single-mindedness of a seventeen-year-old in the throes of emotions he couldn't control and didn't begin to understand.

But this Annie—a woman whose beauty had been honed by compassion and intelligence, hardship and strength, despair and triumph, was more lovely, more compelling, than any sixteen-year-old innocent could ever be.

Trace dug one hand into the pocket of his jacket, feeling the two velvet boxes he'd tucked there after a marathon session with Denver's finest jeweler. His lips curved into a smile edged with an optimism he hadn't dared to feel before this moment.

She was still dressed in his T-shirt, the worn cotton swallowing up her slender frame, her slim legs encased in a pair of jeans, her shapely feet bare.

For a heartbeat, a knot of raw gratitude, of total awe, welled up in Trace's throat, leveling him with the knowledge that never in his twenty-eight years had he known the sensation of having someone waiting for him this way, anxious for his return home.

But as Annie drew near subtle differences in her appearance trickled unease down his spine.

A worry line was carved between her delicately arched brows. Her mouth was smiling, but there was a brittle quality to it that hadn't been there when he'd kissed her this morning.

Trace tamped down a wave of panic that fluttered unbidden in his chest when he noticed the pale cast to the cheeks he could remember were blooming and rosy—the legacy of a night so shatteringly beautiful, he was still shaken to his very core by the wonder of it.

Was she already having doubts about marrying him? The thought stole into Trace's mind. Damn, he should've scooped her up like one of the old frontiersmen, and dragged her in front of a preacher before she'd caught her breath.

It was ridiculous to be so shaken when she hadn't said a word. It was absurd to start reading into her expression some kind of disaster. But Trace couldn't seem to shake the tension creeping up around his neck and shoulders, tightening like a vise in his belly. As if he were waiting... waiting for what? For Annie to run away?

The thought jolted through Trace with a force that stunned him. He crushed it, ruthlessly, furiously.

No, Annie was coming toward him this time, reaching out....

Trace caught her in his arms and kissed her, deep and hard, as if the mating of their mouths could banish all the secret doubts inside him. But despite Annie's soft whimper of pleasure, she flattened her hands on his chest and pushed against it to put some space between them.

"April," she breathed, gesturing toward the paddock.

Trace delved his fingers back through the hair at Annie's nape, tilting her face up to his. "We'd better get her blessing, and fast," he growled, his eyes shifting to where the little girl stood, brushing her pony's coat. "I've only been gone a few hours and I feel like I'm starving for a taste of you."

Trace wove his fingers with Annie's. Then together they walked to the paddock where April was tending her beloved Bo.

The instant April saw Trace, she flung the currycomb into her tack box and came running. Five steps from Trace's arms, the little girl's gaze locked on Trace's and Annie's joined hands. April slammed to a halt, staring, her forehead puckering in puzzlement. A wary look darted into the little girl's eyes.

"I thought you guys were fighting," she said, a little grudgingly.

"We were, but we're not anymore," Trace cut in, excruciatingly aware that this tough-talking little girl was far more fragile than she seemed. "See, your mom and I...well, we were kind of thinking that...since we both love you so much, and we...care about each other...we might..." God, he was making a mess of this. He swore softly, and dug in his pocket, taking out the rectangular velvet box. "April, this is for you."

The little girl took the box and nibbled on her lower lip. "What is it?"

"Open it and see."

Trace held his breath as the little girl untied the gold cord bow, then lifted the lid of the box. An exquisite gold necklace was inside, the charm suspended from the chain was shaped like the mythical horse Pegasus in flight.

"It's real pretty," April gasped, running her fingertip over one wing.

"It's a locket. See?" Trace took the delicate necklace in his hand, the dainty chain pooling in his callused hand. He flicked a hidden latch, and the locket opened.

Annie gasped. April gave a little cry of surprise. Inside the locket was a picture of Annie, nine years ago, staring out at the world with such shy sincerity, such gentleness. On the other half was a picture of Trace that could've been titled The Quintessential Adolescent Attitude.

"Oh, Trace!" Annie breathed, reaching out to touch his picture. But April was already looking up at the flesh-and-blood Trace, suspicion curling like smoke across her features.

"Where'd you get that picture of my mom?" April demanded.

"Out of one of her old yearbooks."

"How come you put your picture and her picture in the locket?"

"Turn Pegasus over and you'll find the answer."

April took the locket in her hand, turned it over carefully. Trace watched the sunlight sparkle on the engraved lettering the jeweler had done that morning.

Now We Are a Family.

"Can you read it, angel?" Trace asked softly as Annie's hand linked tightly with his. He glanced up at her to see tears trickling down her cheeks.

"'Course I can read it! I just..." April looked up at Annie. "Mom?" Just a single word, uttered in a small voice.

"April, Trace—"

"I asked your mom to marry me," Trace finished for her, hunkering down on one knee so he was eye-level with the little girl. "I haven't had much practice at this dad stuff, but I'd like to try it, if it's okay with you."

Silence, filled with hopes, dreams, fears. Annie could see April thinking hard. "If my mom married you, I guess I could keep the pony, huh?"

Trace chuckled. "You can bank on that."

"Stacey's mom got married again, and the man was all sicky-sweet to Stacey until after the wedding, then he couldn't stand to be in the same room with her for five minutes."

"April, there's nothing I want more than to be..." his voice caught. "Be your father."

"My daddy's dead."

"I know. But maybe I could take care of you for him since we're both down here and...he's off somewhere in heaven. That's what I want to do, April. Take care of you. Take care of your mom."

April fiddled with the gold chain. "I always wanted a daddy like Tyler's dad. He has this totally awesome motorcycle, and Tyler gets to ride around the parking lot in front of him sometimes. J.T. took me once, too. I wished he was my daddy, but he wasn't."

She seemed to be working so hard, trying to puzzle things out. "Trace?" she said, looking up at him with big eyes, a mirror image of his own.

"What, sweetheart?"

"I like horses lots better than motorcycles."

"I like you lots better than horses," Trace replied. The little girl gave him an uncertain smile.

"You take your time and think about this, April. I know this is a big surprise for you. You might have lots of questions you want to ask us. I want you to ask every one."

"If you get married to my mom, do I still have to go to bed at eight o'clock?" April asked soberly. "And do you like brussels sprouts? 'Cause if you do, my mom'll make 'em all the time, and they make me feel like I wanna barf."

Trace laughed, catching the child in his arms. "Brussels sprouts are definitely disgusting. As for bedtime, we'll have to see about that, you little con artist."

"Will you come live with us at BabyPlace?"

"I'm not sure." Trace looked at Annie. "Your mom will still work there, and you can go visit anytime you want. But we might buy a house somewhere nearby. Or build one."

April nibbled at her lip again, her gaze flicking toward the glass-and-stone magnificence of the house at the edge of the precipice. "We don't have many cliffs in Chicago, y'know."

"If your mom and I got married, we could come to the mountains whenever we wanted. We'd just hop in my plane, and—"

April drew back, her eyes wide. "I don't think I like planes much after last time."

Trace laughed and cupped his hand on his daughter's velvet-soft cheek. "What happened with the landing gear was a freak accident, precious. And look, we're all safe."

"Yeah, well, just barely. And you made my mom throw up. I think I'm gonna ride Bo up in the pasture and think about more questions. Can I wear Pegasus while I do? He'll help me think."

With long, gentle fingers, Trace fastened the necklace around the child's throat. April's grubby fingers settled the necklace against the front of her shirt, the locket hanging low enough that she could see it.

"Trace?" she asked softly.

"What darlin'?" Her eyes were so serious, Trace braced himself for some profound question.

"If you were my daddy, would you help me beat Johnny Belmeyer as first string pitcher?"

Trace grinned, the beautiful sound of Annie's laughter tugging at his heart. "Ape, I can show you how to throw a knuckleball that'll singe the number right off Johnny's jersey."

April's grin was a mile wide. She flung her arms around Trace's neck and held on tight. "I'm a little bit scared," she confessed, "but I'm a whole bunch happy."

"Me, too, Ape. Me, too."

"You want to go riding with me?"

"Absolutely. But first your mom and I have some things to talk about. I'll meet you in our favorite pasture, okay?"

"Okay."

Trace stood as April went dashing toward the paddock where Bo was contentedly munching grass. He and Annie watched in silence until the little girl and her pony went trotting off up the trail.

"I've got something in here for you, too, Brown-Eyes," Trace said as April disappeared behind the trees. He turned to face Annie.

The jeweler's box he dug out of his pocket this time was faded, the corner of the velvet box a little worn. A bright gold ribbon around it only accented its age.

Trace unfastened the ribbon and opened the box. A small gold band was nestled against the velvet, a modest diamond solitaire winked brightly beside it.

"I know it's nothing flashy, Brown-Eyes. If you want a hundred carats to wear on your fingers, just say the word. But this…well, this is what I bought before I came to your house the night you ran away."

Annie slipped the diamond ring out, saw it was set in the petals of a golden rose. "Trace, it's beautiful."

"It seemed so right for you way back then. I guess it still does."

"You kept it all these years?"

"Oh, I tried to get rid of the thing a dozen times, but somehow I always ended up tucking it back in my drawer." He shrugged. "Read the inscriptions."

Annie tilted the ring until she could see curling script that had obviously been there a long time. To Brown-Eyes With Love, Trace. Under that script a single word was freshly engraved: Believe.

Annie's eyes filled with tears. They spilled free, trickling down her cheeks. "Oh, Trace."

"Let me put it on you, Annie."

Annie touched the ring with one trembling finger, silence stretching out until Trace's nerves burned. "Annie?" he squeezed her name through stiff lips.

Those green eyes found his, the depths troubled as she slipped the ring back into the velvet box before handing it to him. "I want to let you put it on me, but when you do, I want it to stay there forever."

"Why wouldn't it stay there forever now?"

"I don't know, Trace. It's just that April hasn't had time to really think this through. She'll have to deal with a lot more pressing issues than whether or not I cook brussels sprouts."

"We'll work it out, Annie."

"I know. I..." Annie raked her fingers back through her hair. "I'm being ridiculous. I know." She forced a wobbly smile and held out her hand. "This is absurd. Go ahead, Trace. Put it on."

"You sound like someone telling the firing squad they can fire."

Hurt vibrated through Trace's voice. Annie felt sick because of it.

She caught his face in her hands, looked up at him, begging for understanding. "Trace, you have to be patient with me. This has all happened so fast. I want a future with you. I do. And I want to wear this beautiful ring. Put it on. Please."

Annie wanted to banish the stormy lights from his eyes, the pain. She wanted to sweep up the doubt-filled words she had said, hide them away, so he would still be looking down at her with such indescribable tenderness.

But there was no way to erase what she had said. Silent, Trace closed the velvet box and jammed it into his pocket. His mouth was set in a taut line, his brows were drawn together.

Annie tried to think of something to say, but before she could speak, the sound of another vehicle rumbling up the road intruded.

"Don't tell me you've got another truck coming here?" Annie tried to keep her voice light.

"No."

"Then who..."

At that moment a rental car came into view. Trace swore, and Annie's hands knotted as the driver became visible through the car window.

Colonel Brown was glaring through the windshield, his eyes flashing with the same dangerous light that had illuminated them when he was going into combat.

Chapter 12

Trace stiffened as if he'd taken a punch to the gut. His eyes narrowed as he glared at the rental car and the man climbing out its door.

The last time he had seen Colonel Marcus Brown, the man had had him by the throat, shattering him with lies that had left hideous scars in Trace's soul. But the rage he felt now had little to do with wrongs Marcus Brown had done to Trace himself. The hate that pumped through Trace—hot and thick and dangerous—was because of what Colonel Brown had cost April and Annie.

"How the hell did that old bastard find us?" Trace rumbled. "The blasted CIA?"

Annie looked a little sick, a lot pale. "I had to call him the morning after I came to see you in the hotel. He'd gotten tickets to a Sox game as a surprise for April and had planned to visit us for a few days this week."

"That doesn't explain how he found this place."

"I told him we were going to your place in Colorado. I'm sure he just checked around, found where you had land. Or he might have asked at the shelter. I had to give them some idea where I was going in case of emergency."

"Perfect. Just goddamn perfect," Trace muttered caustically. "I'm sure the Colonel was thrilled to hear I was back in your life."

Annie caught his hand and squeezed it, hard. "Trace, please let the past be over and done with. He's my father. April's grandfather."

"Yeah, and he's a real prince of a guy, your dad. The most tyrannical, arrogant son of a bitch I've ever known." The words were hard, bitter. But Trace took one look at Annie's ashen face and attempted to wrestle the red haze of his fury until it was back under control.

He sucked in a steadying breath and looped an arm possessively around her shoulders, the tension in Annie seeming to sizzle its way into his body to mingle with his own.

"Dad," Annie managed to say as they started toward the rental car. "This is a surprise."

Colonel Brown marched toward them, his face drawn. Dark circles of sleeplessness ringed the older man's eyes, but his gaze still snapped with that fierceness that had aided him in countless battles in 'Nam. Just the sight of the man made Trace's gut clench.

"Colonel Brown. It's been a long time." Trace forced his voice to stay calm, even. He gritted his teeth and extended his hand for the Colonel to shake.

The man linked his hands behind his back, his lip curling as if Trace held a rattlesnake. Trace's fingers curled into a white-knuckled fist and he let his arm fall to his side.

"Where is April?" Marcus Brown demanded. "I've come to take you and April back to Chicago, Annalise."

"She's not going anywhere—" Trace began, but Annie squeezed his arm, a pleading look on her face.

"April's out in the south pasture, riding the pony Trace got her," Annie started to explain.

"Pony?" The colonel sputtered. "You let that child race off alone—"

"She's perfectly safe, Dad," Annie interrupted. "The pony's gentle as a lamb."

"Not really," Trace put in. "April's just a helluva rider."

"Trace, let's just all go inside," Annie suggested, her gaze flicking warily from one man to the other. "I'll fix some tea and we can talk."

Trace wanted to tear into the old man whose lies had cost him eight precious years of April's life. Instead, he looked at Annie, his jaw knotting.

"She's right," he managed to say. "No sense making this any worse than it has to be." Trace turned and strode toward the doorway.

Annie hurried after him, the colonel following as if he were being led in front of a firing squad.

As Annie ushered them back to the kitchen, the room bright and airy, Trace was suddenly glad as hell that the Colonel had chosen to force their meeting here, on Trace's own Turf.

Annie hurried toward the kitchen entrance, with its screen door. "I set some sun tea to brew this morning," she began with a nervous catch in her voice.

Trace caught her by the arm, his voice as gentle as he could make it under the circumstances. "Annie, nobody gives a damn about tea right now."

"I suppose not." She brushed back a strand of honey-gold hair and gave a laugh that was choked up with nervousness. She turned toward her father.

"Well then. I suppose we should just... just get straight to..." She sucked in a deep breath, her fingers tight on the steely muscles of Trace's forearm. "Dad, I have something to tell you. Trace has asked me to marry him."

What little color had been in the Colonel's face drained away, leaving him gray as a corpse. "No."

"It's true, dad."

"You can't—you didn't say yes?"

Hot spots of color appeared on Annie's cheeks. "Not exactly. But I'm going to."

"My God." The colonel squeezed the words out faintly. He sank onto a bench at the harvest table, looking suddenly weary and old.

"I figure this isn't the greatest news to you, Colonel," Trace said tautly, "but this time I can take care of both Annie and April, give them anything they want financially."

"But that's not the greatest gift he's bringing to this marriage," Annie said. "Dad, you should see him with April. He's wonderful with her. He's taught her to ride, let her fly his plane. She adores Trace."

"She's an eight-year-old child," the colonel said. "Of course she'd adore someone who charged into her life, buying her ponies. That's not in question. What's in question is what is going to happen when McKenna runs out of presents to entertain her."

"Dad, April's relationship with Trace isn't about the presents he gives her," Annie said, trying to intervene. "It's about—about taking her hiking in the mountains, about teaching her to read trail sign and playing Monopoly until his eyes fall out. Reading her stories and—"

"I intend to be a father to April in every sense of the word, Colonel Brown," Trace cut in. "This isn't some impulsive decision that will pall when the newness wears off. I want Annie for my wife. April for my daughter.''

''It isn't impulsive?'' the colonel growled, raking his fingers through the short strands of his salt-and-pepper hair. ''You've barely been back in my daughter's life and you're wanting to marry her? What do you know about Annalise, McKenna? Besides the fact that you got her pregnant?''

''I know she's the mother of my daughter. That was something you neglected to tell me in our little interview on your front porch back in Arizona.''

''McKenna, I would've told you she'd been dragged to hell by the devil himself before I'd have told you where Annie was. You weren't man enough to be my daughter's husband when you were seventeen. And you sure as hell aren't man enough now!''

''Dad, stop it!'' Annie burst out. ''Trace, please don't let him ...''

She didn't finish. She didn't have to. *Don't let him push you over the edge,* her eyes pleaded. *Don't let this erupt into a confrontation poisoned with hate that should've been buried long ago.*

Trace knew what Annie wanted of him, needed of him. But fury was setting Trace's lungs afire, zinging into every nerve ending in his body, filling him until he felt like a mine about to explode. One trip, one more misstep by the colonel ...

No, Trace resolved. He wasn't going to give the son of a bitch the satisfaction.

''Whether I'm *man* enough to be Annie's husband is her decision. Not yours.'' His voice vibrated with dangerous overtones.

''I drove you out of my daughter's life because I love her,'' the colonel roared. ''I wanted what was best for her.

Everything she ever dreamed of was shattered because of you."

"I would've worked myself to dust to give her what she needed. What she deserved. You threw her out of your house." Trace could see the colonel flinch, but he didn't relent. "Where the *bloody hell* were you when Annie and my baby were living on the streets?"

Trace heard Annie protest through the fire-bright haze of his fury. The colonel reared back as if Trace had slashed a whip across his face. Annie went to him, stood behind the old man. Trace's mouth filled with bitterness, hate.

"Trace, that's enough. We won't get anywhere like this. My father and I settled our differences a long time ago."

"Well, that's just terrific, but I didn't settle a damn thing with him, Brown-Eyes. Hell, if I'd had any idea where you were when April was tiny, I would've walked my feet bloody to get to you. This son of a bitch knew where you were, and he didn't lift a single judgmental finger to help you."

"Trace, stop!" Annie cried out. "I don't want to—"

"I want to," the colonel said, jamming his hands against the table and rearing up, his face almost purple with rage. "You try, just try to make me feel sorry for you, Mc-Kenna. Make me regret throwing you out of my daughter's life. Look what you did to her! You lured Annalise out with some damn sob story and got her feeling real sorry for you, didn't you? A decent man would've turned her away. A decent man would've protected her. But you—you just took her, didn't you? Seduced her and didn't give a damn if she wound up pregnant with your child."

"I loved Annie," Trace said tightly. "There's nothing you could say to me, no name you could call me, that I didn't call myself after I found out she was carrying my child."

"Yeah, you were a real prize, McKenna. Flunking out of school, throwing away a career in baseball most kids would've sold their soul to the devil for. But that wasn't enough. You had to destroy my daughter."

The words hammered at Trace, knocking down the shaky sense of self-worth he'd managed to build inside himself. The colonel's diatribe echoed every word Trace had said to himself.

"I never meant to hurt her." Trace grappled to keep his voice from betraying how deep the colonel's accusations had pierced him. "I'm trying to make things right for Annie now."

"You and that baby of yours destroyed Annie's life!"

"April is my life," Annie said in fierce accents.

"And I suppose McKenna is, too? If he was so blameless when he got you into bed with him why did you let April believe that her father was dead? All she had to do was watch the nightly news to see McKenna flinging himself into God-knows-what inferno or parading around on the arm of some glitzy woman!"

"I did what I thought was best for April. I'm marrying Trace, for the same reason."

"You truly believe that?" The colonel gave a bitter laugh. "What are you all going to do? Settle down in suburbia in a house with a white picket fence? He hasn't changed a damn bit in the years since he left Arizona. He's still got women in a dozen different countries. He's still trying his best to break his goddamn neck! What do you think is going to happen, Annalise? You think an adrenaline junkie like Trace McKenna is going to change from skydiving to mowing the lawn for entertainment?"

"Don't judge me, Colonel," Trace said. "You don't know a damn thing about me."

"I've known so many men like you in my time with the army, McKenna, that I could write your goddamn life story and not miss a beat. Hungry bastards, every one of them. Just existing until the next rush."

"Maybe your daughter is the only rush I need anymore. Maybe April is better than any adrenaline high."

"Maybe." The colonel's eyes narrowed, keen intelligence sparking through the slits of his eyelids. "Prove it."

Trace heard Annie's protests as if from a distance, but the room seemed to spin away, until it was only Trace and the man who had all but destroyed his life nine years ago.

"I don't have to prove a damned thing to you," Trace bit out.

"I suppose not. But if you really love Annalise and April, you won't object to making certain this is what they want. What you want."

"Annie said she'd marry me. That's all I need."

"Fine. Marry her."

Trace blinked, suddenly feeling like the old man had lured him onto black ice and he was about to fall through. "What the hell's your game, old man?"

"Marry Annalise, play father to April. But don't just plunge into it now. Wait six months, maybe a year, before you take such a drastic step."

"Dad, that's not your decision—"

"You expect me to give you enough time to talk her out of it?" Trace scoffed. "Poison April's mind against me? I don't think so. Annie is going to be my wife the instant our blood tests come through. I'm not going to lose her."

Trace tried not to feel the weight of the jeweler's box in his jacket pocket, tried not to think of the uncertainty, the hesitation that had been on Annie's face when he'd shown her the ring.

Colonel Brown flashed Trace that arrogant scowl that had always made Trace want to rearrange the man's teeth. "What you really mean, McKenna, is that you're not going to give Annalise a chance to change her mind."

"You got that right."

"Why, McKenna? You think she's going to walk away from you again? You think once she has some time to know you—really know you, away from all your rich-boy toys—that Annalise will refuse to be your wife?"

It was as if the colonel had looked into Trace's darkest fears, had dragged them into the light. Trace felt stripped, exposed in a way that made him feel as if he were teetering on the edge of a cliff, waiting for Annie to reach out her hand, pull him back onto firm ground. Or, Trace thought with a stab of unease, push him from the precipice.

Trace's gaze found Annie, and he hoped, prayed, that she would tell her father that there was no reason to wait, to prove anything. She wanted to marry Trace.

But Annie's cheeks were pale, her eyes uncertain. Fingers of dread closed around Trace's throat, squeezing tight.

"Annie," the colonel said, "whatever decision you make now will impact on the rest of April's life. Think, Annalise! What will happen to that little girl if she lets herself love McKenna and then in a year or two—hell, in a month—he gets hungry to take another dive, another fall, fight another fire. What's going to happen to April if McKenna finally succeeds in breaking his fool neck?" The colonel's voice dropped low. "Annalise, what's going to happen to you?"

Trace swore a dark, vile oath, slamming his fist against the table. "Stop trying to scare her away from me! It won't work this time, will it, Annie?" He spun to face her, his hands closing tight on her shoulders. His voice dropped low, aching. "Will it?"

Annie winced—from his grasp or his fierce demand, Trace couldn't be certain. She looked small, broken, fragile in a way Trace had thought she hadn't been since she left Arizona so many years ago. The knowledge that the hate between him and her father had done this to her burned like acid in Trace's gut, mingling with the pain each second of her silence coiled inside him.

Panic pulsed in the hidden core where Trace, the seventeen-year-old, had hidden away all these years, bruised, battered, betrayed. With each heartbeat of silence, Trace fought to drag breath into his lungs, fought to believe... in what? Happy endings? Second chances? That somehow, some way, this time Annie would trust him? Believe in him?

Trace saw tears welling in Annie's eyes, saw her valiant attempt to blink them back.

He shot a glare at the Colonel. "Leave us alone for a little while."

The colonel stood, his eyes already holding the light of impending victory. Trace grasped Annie's arm, drew her toward the window where pine-swept breezes whispered down off the mountain.

He could barely speak through the knot of uneasiness in his chest. "Go on, Brown-Eyes. Whatever you have to say, say it."

"My father had no right to say the things he said to hurt you. But I can't forget the things he said that were... sensible, Trace."

"Well, being a crazed idiot, I have trouble weeding that out from the bullshit," Trace said tightly. "You're the honor student. You tell me."

"Would it be so terrible to have a-an engagement period? Six months, where we could spend time together, think things through."

If she'd plunged a knife into Trace's heart it couldn't have stabbed him more deeply. The fact that Colonel Brown had put the weapon in her hand made the wound all the more bitter. "I've waited nine years. Without you. Without my daughter. Don't you think that's long enough?"

"We lost contact during all that time, Trace. There are still so many things you don't know about me. And that I don't know about you. What if this is just some kind of magic, a few weeks where things are perfect? What will happen when the magic is gone?"

"You think what happened between us last night is just some sort of fluke that's gonna fade away? You think that someday, when I touch you, you aren't going to sigh, Brown- Eyes? You aren't gonna want me?"

Her cheeks were fire-red, her eyes glistening, over-bright. Tears. He was making her cry again. Hell, he wanted to let the sobs come himself. Let them tear free on the jagged edges Annie's betrayal had left on his soul the first time. He couldn't even begin to imagine what destruction she was leaving this time, as she pulled away from him. Away from the promises, the hopes, the magic. Away from the heaven he had found in her arms, the beauty that had pierced to the very core of him when he'd stared into his daughter's eyes.

"Annie?" The word was ragged. He couldn't keep the anguish from biting through it.

"Trace, I—"

The sudden sound of hoofbeats, loud, almost frenzied, shattered the words. Trace wheeled, looking at the screen door that was wide open. He lunged toward it, just in time to see April and her pony vanishing into the woods. He swore, raced outside, calling April's name, but the little girl had vanished.

"My God," Annie breathed. "Tell me she didn't hear—"

Trace caught a glimpse of something lying on the ground, an object that was golden, glinting in the sun. He dipped onto one knee, his fingers scooping up the locket he had given April half an hour before.

The locket had been flung to the ground, the chain snapped by a child's hands.

Broken like the last of Trace's dreams.

He scooped up the locket, crushed it in his hands until the metal wings bit into his skin.

"Oh, my God," Annie choked out, her gaze shifting to the path where her daughter and Bo had disappeared. "She can't have—have heard.... We have to find her, Trace."

"Oh, I'll find her all right. And if anything happens to that girl—" He didn't finish the sentence, just raced over to the paddock where his horses grazed.

He bridled his big gelding, then threw on a saddle.

"I'm going with you," Annie said fiercely.

"Like hell! You're scared of horses. You'll only slow me down."

"That's my daughter out there, McKenna! I don't give a damn if I have to ride a blasted alligator to find her!" Annie's voice broke on a sob. "Please, Trace!"

Trace swore. In moments he'd roped a gentle palomino mare, saddled it in record time. He didn't wait for Annie to mount it, he just grabbed her around the waist and flung her astride the animal.

Heavy footsteps raced toward them, the colonel's features twisted with alarm. "What's wrong? For God's sake—"

"April. She heard it all, goddamn it to hell." Trace's voice tore on rage and grief and helplessness. "She heard every rotten sordid detail of how she was conceived. Happy now, old man?''

The colonel plunged into the paddock, struggling to grab another gelding. Trace's jaw set, hard. The bastard could go to hell, he wasn't waiting another second.

He swung open the paddock gate, let Annie out, then guided his own mount through it. Fastening the gate again, Trace's fingers tightened on the reins. He dug his heels into his gelding's flanks and sent it thundering down the narrow woodland trail.

It should have been easy to track the little girl. It should've been easy for Trace's big gelding to overtake the pony. But April rode in typical McKenna breakneck fashion, and the pony had been bred with the swiftness of its mustang ancestors. Worse still, the twisted mass of trails tangled around the mountain like a Gordian knot.

Trace had ridden half a mile before he drew rein at a fork in the trail. Annie cantered up, holding on to the horse for dear life, looking pale and breathless, but more determined than he'd ever seen her.

"Trace, what is it?" She asked as he dismounted, examining a hoofprint in the muck. "Where is she?"

He swung back onto his horse, his face grim. "She's going down Warrior Path."

"Wh-what's that?"

"It's the place I go when I'm looking for my hit of adrenaline, dangerous for experienced riders. For a little girl—'' He didn't finish his sentence. He didn't have to. He leaned low over the neck of his gelding, urging it into a run.

Annie's head swam with images of April thrown, hurt, crying. Lying at the bottom of a cliff somewhere, alone, her whole world shattered by the three people who loved her most, who should have banded together to protect her, not poison her with hate and blame that was nine years old.

She urged her horse to follow Trace's gelding, terror pulsing through every fiber of her body. No, she brought herself up shortly. Trace would find her. Trace would make sure she was safe.

"Please God, let her be all right," Annie whispered like a mantra. "Let everything be all right."

But as she stared at Trace's quickly disappearing back, Annie had a sickening feeling that nothing would ever be right again.

Chapter 13

Branches whipped at Annie's face, the rough bark of tree trunks scraping at her jeans-clad legs as she tore down the narrow path after Trace. Dust kicked up by his big gelding's hooves filled Annie's nose and mouth, filtering a fine layer of silt over her sweaty skin.

It was all she could do to cling to the palomino's back, one hand on the reins, the other clutching the saddlehorn as if it were the only thing keeping her from tumbling into a bottomless pit. A pit of despair, of self-blame. A pit of guilt and pure terror.

April knew the truth.

The words pounded in an agonizing litany in Annie's head.

Her brave, tough, trusting little girl had learned Trace McKenna was her father in the most brutal way possible, listening while three adults who loved her, who should've done everything in their power to shield her, raged at one another, tearing at old wounds, gouging out new ones, fresh ones, to mingle with the pain of nine years before.

Trace whisked the gelding around a ninety-degree turn in the trail, the edge nothing but sheer cliff face, dropping onto a deposit of jagged stones below. Annie clung tight to the mare and forced herself to look over the ledge, praying she wouldn't see a tiny figure in Trace's dive-shop shirt with uneven braids lying down below.

Annie sucked in a shuddery breath of gratitude, so distracted by her relief that for a moment it seemed she'd go toppling over the ledge. She barely managed to keep herself astride the mare as it struggled to keep up with Trace's gelding.

"April!" Trace's voice echoed back from the mountain, seeming to reverberate through the trees. "April, where are you?"

Desperation, grim determination, every line of Trace's body was taut, alert. Those blue-gray eyes scanned the woods, checked the trail for sign, as he guided his gelding by instinct alone.

"This is my fault," Annie told herself again and again. "If April's hurt, it's because of my cowardice... my cowardice in not telling her the truth about Trace. But please, God, don't take my little girl away to punish me...."

Trace stopped at another fork in the trail. One fork was blocked by a fallen sapling.

He climbed out of the saddle, searching for traces of Bo's tiny hoofprints. What he saw made his face go pale. He swore, swinging back up into the saddle. Annie had never been so scared in her life.

"Trace, what is it?"

Trace jabbed his finger at a weathered sign that he'd had Rob nail to the sapling to warn away any riders or hikers who strayed onto McKenna land.

Danger. Trail Washed Out.

Annie pictured the path they'd been riding on, racing like the wind. There were a dozen places where a washout could've caused a deadly accident. If Trace had closed this part of the trail—if he considered it too dangerous to risk riding on, Annie couldn't even begin to imagine how perilous it must be.

"Stay here!" Trace barked the command, then urged his gelding to sail over the blockade.

Annie didn't waste time in arguing. She shut her eyes and kicked her own mount hard. The horse cleared the sapling in startled alarm, the jarring landing nearly rattling the teeth out of Annie's mouth.

They had ridden barely fifty yards when April's pony came bolting toward them, saddle empty, eyes wild. A knot of dread shut off most of Annie's breath. Trace's jaw tightened until it was white. He said nothing. He didn't have to.

Bo's appearance could mean anything—April, thrown and a little shaken, making her way toward them on foot, or... scenarios too horrible to think about.

"April!" The desperate edge in Trace's voice fuelled Annie's own fear.

The fifteen minutes they retraced Bo's path seemed like an eternity—Trace's voice echoing through the trees, silence the only reply they heard. Then, suddenly, the faintest of cries came in answer.

"Help me! Help!"

April's voice—ragged with terror.

Annie's heart plunged to her toes. "Trace! Oh, God, do you hear her?"

"April?" Trace bellowed. "Ape, keep talking, sweetheart. Tell us where you're at!"

"Over here! T-Trace, I'm scared!" The cry broke on a wrenching sob.

"It's okay, April! We're coming!" Trace let the horse pick its way through the undergrowth, cursing the slow pace, knowing that if he and the gelding fell, they'd do April no damn bit of good. The trail made a sharp left turn. Then, suddenly, the gelding reared, whinnied in fright, scrambling back from the edge of a trail that had disappeared into nothing but a ragged mud slide that had catapulted down the sheer mountainside.

It was a miracle he stayed on his horse. As Annie caught up, she saw April thirty yards below the drop-off. The child was huddled on a narrow ledge that seemed so fragile it was only a matter of time before it crumbled away beneath her.

Most terrifying of all, the cliff was so sheer it looked as if there were no footholds, impossible to climb.

"Oh, God," Annie choked out. "We have to call someone—a rescue team—"

"April doesn't have that kind of time," Trace growled, swinging down from his horse. As if the cliff itself had heard his words, a clump of rocks and soil broke off the bottom of the ledge, cascading down a fifty-yard drop.

"Then what—"

"I'm going to go down and get her."

Annie's hands were shaking, her heart beating its way out of her chest. "But if you put any weight on that ledge you'll both go down." Both. Gone in a heartbeat. Terror was a living thing in Annie's breast.

Trace worked to unfasten the worn coil of rope that he'd tied to his saddle the day April had demanded lessons on lariat-throwing.

"It's going to be all right, Brown-Eyes," Trace said. "Trust me."

Trust...something she hadn't dared to extend to him an hour before. Something that might have made all the difference. Trace's gaze held hers a long moment, then he knotted the rope firmly to the gelding's saddlehorn. "Annie, you have to help me. Hold Cochise by his reins. Don't let him know that you're afraid of him. I'm gonna lower myself down to April."

"But what if I can't control the horse? What if you fall? The ledge won't hold with both you and April."

"I'm not gonna fall." Trace was checking the rope. His face was grim—so grim Annie could tell he was worried out of his mind. She sensed he was picturing the same horrible scenarios she was. He was feeling the sensation of the cliff giving way, him falling, April falling....

"April, honey?" Trace called out, the sound of the childish sobs stilling for a moment. "I'm coming down to get you."

"Wh-what d'you care if I fall? You hate me! I wrecked up my m-mommy's life—"

"That's not true!" Annie cried, anguish at the child's guilt-filled words leaving her heart in shreds. "Don't you believe that for a second, angel. I love you so much."

"I'm s-scared...my arm...it's got a funny bump on it. It's all turned the wrong way."

"We'll take care of that, sweetheart," Trace soothed the terrified child. "You have to hold real still, Ape. That ledge is none too sturdy, but it should hold as long as you don't move around. Pretend you're an Indian princess, stranded by an evil medicine man. I'm the warrior who's coming to save you."

Trace made a slipknot at the end of the rope, fashioning a kind of noose. Then he grasped the section of rope nearest the gelding in his right hand and deftly twisted the length beneath his buttocks and caught the rope with his other hand, down low by his hip, fashioning a makeshift seat.

"Annie, I'm gonna rappel my way down to her. Slow, real slow. When I get to her, I'm gonna have her put the noose under her armpits. I'll tighten it, then put my arms around her and signal to you. When I signal, you have to make Cochise pull us up."

"But you won't be tied on. If you slip you could fall to the bottom."

"I'm the crazy man, remember? Mr. Live on the Edge. I do this stuff for the hell of it." He was trying to ease her terror. Annie knew it. But all she could think of was her baby down there, her arm possibly broken, a tiny ledge the only thing standing between April and death. All Annie could think of was Trace—hurt, betrayed by Annie's own words—willing to risk his life for the child stranded down below.

Trace, reckless, brave, wild Trace McKenna, rappelling down a cliff face to reach his terrified daughter.

"Hey, Ape, you ever watch McGyver?" Trace called down.

"S-sometimes," the child sniffled, "when my stupid homework is all done."

"Great, well, you and I are gonna give him a run for his money this time, sweetheart. I'm coming down after you."

"Mommy? Mommy, don't let him! It's too far. He's too heavy. The ledge'll break."

"Don't worry, April. Trace knows what he's doing," Annie called down, praying that he did.

"I'm not gonna touch the ledge," Trace explained. "Cochise is gonna hold my weight. But you have to be real brave, April. You have to do exactly what I tell you, even if you're so scared your teeth are chattering out of your mouth. You understand, baby?"

"Y-yes."

"Stay real still, April—"

April whimpered, scooting back on the ledge in her terror. A screech pierced her lips as a portion of the ledge crumbled, raining dirt clods and stones down onto the cliff's floor.

"Don't move!" Trace roared. April froze.

"Trace, what if you get down there and I—I can't make the horse..."

"You *can,* Brown-Eyes. I know you can. Grab him by the bit and say *back.* Press the bit toward him firmly. He'll do what you tell him if you don't let him know you're afraid."

"I'm scared out of my mind," Annie choked out.

"Me, too." Trace's gaze caught hers for a moment, filled with a hundred emotions too consuming to name. Steeling herself with Trace's confidence in her, Annie grasped Cochise's reins by the bit.

The animal seemed monstrously huge, terrifyingly powerful. And Annie could tell the instant the spirited gelding knew she was the one who had hold of his reins. Cochise snorted, danced on his massive hooves.

"Easy, Cochise. Please. April, your daddy's coming down to get you," Annie said, her heart seeming to slam to a halt in her chest as Trace poised himself at the edge of the cliff. His feet flattened against the ragged line where grass disappeared into dark Colorado earth. His arms bunched, the muscles standing out against his tanned skin as he leaned back into emptiness.

Cochise stiffened at the tug on his saddlehorn as the rope took Trace's weight. The horse snorted, sidestepped, dragging Annie with him. Annie fought the huge animal, fought her own sick terror.

A thud followed by a guttural sound of pain drifted up the cliff face, the sound mingling with April's cry of alarm. Trace. If Annie didn't control the horse Trace would be beaten against the rocky surface. She braced herself against the horse's far-superior strength, her hands tightening on the reins. "Whoa, Cochise. Hold still you brainless, stubborn—"

Those moist brown eyes stared at her, another whinny coming from between awesomely big teeth. But the horse stilled, as if listening to the sound of her voice.

"That's right! You're a bullheaded, stubborn son of a..."

"Give 'im hell, Brown-Eyes." Trace's voice drifted up to her. "Hey, Ape, did you know she could cuss like that? Not bad for a mom, eh?"

He was trying to ease April's fears, trying to take everyone's mind off of the life-and-death struggle they were involved in. Annie blessed him for it when she heard April's faint voice.

"Mom yelled at some creepy man who was whacking his little boy once. She cussed good then, too."

The taut length of rope shifted, moving just a little as Trace maneuvered his weight down the cliff face. Annie discovered a new meaning of the word *hell*.

Hell was battling a horse that outweighed you by a ton. Hell was seeing Trace's rope strain and hearing April's choked sobs of terror, yet not being able to see either one of them. Both were obscured by the ledge of stone and earth, far beyond her reach. If anything happened...

"Almost there, sweetheart. Almost there," Trace said, his gaze fixed on April, balanced so precariously on the ledge, and he tried with everything in him not to focus on the narrow strip that was the only thing that stood between his daughter and death. The portion underneath

April looked as if it had been gouged out with a giant spoon, the place where rocks and earth had fallen away exposing damp dirt, embedded roots. Trace gritted his teeth, knowing in his gut that there wasn't much time.

Gripping the rope, he lowered himself within six feet of the little girl. April started to scramble to her feet, one hand stretching out to reach him.

"No!" Trace ordered her. "Stay where you are. Sit right there, sweetie. I'll bring the noose right over to you." Pushing off with his booted feet, Trace edged to the right, toward the little girl, the loop of rope dangling just out of her reach.

"Gotta get me lower, Annie! Just a... little... *there!*" Trace felt the jarring sensation of the gelding coming to a stop. "Come on, Ape, you can get it," Trace urged, trying to keep the loop still, trying to get it into her hands.

"Can't," April choked out. "It hurts."

"I know, darlin'. But you can do it. I know you can. C'mon, baby. Just reach out and grab the rope."

Trace's breath froze in his chest as April strained her fingers toward the rough noose of hemp. It bobbled out of her reach, then waved closer. She grabbed it with a sob, more dirt falling away beneath her.

She screamed, shrank back against the cliff face, but she held on to the rope.

"That's my girl," Trace said. "Now, pull the noose down until it's under your arms."

"But my arm hurts," April quavered. "I'm scared to move it."

"I know it hurts, baby. But you have to do this. That's a girl. I know you can."

Trace's heart was in his throat as he watched her maneuver herself into the noose, struggling. She'd just pulled it beneath her arms when the ledge crumbled. He heard Annie's desperate cry as she heard the stones and earth clods tumbling down the cliff, April's shriek of terror doubtlessly feeding the worst of Annie's fears.

Lightning fast, Trace let go of the rope with his left hand, catching hold of April as she swung out into nothingness.

Annie cried out, desperate. "Trace? April? My God—" Barely managing to cling to the rope himself, Trace gripped April's good hand, lowering her slowly down, putting pressure on the noose until it was anchored tight around April's chest.

"It's okay, Brown-Eyes. The fall took up the slack. We've got one dirty kid here, hanging at the end of the rope."

Trace glanced down to where April dangled, clutching his fingers in a death grip with her good hand; her other arm was turned at an angle that made Trace's stomach churn.

"I'm s-scared... Mommy?"

"I'm right here, angel." Annie's voice, still ragged with anxiety.

"I d-didn't know I hurt you by getting born, Mommy. I'm sorry."

"You're the most beautiful thing in my life, April Rose. You and your daddy. I love you both so much."

Trace's throat constricted, the words so beautiful, so unexpected. That single moment, dangling over the edge of a cliff, a rope length away from death, held out the promise of a future more beautiful than Trace McKenna had ever dreamed.

"Keep talking, Brown-Eyes," he urged. "I'm gonna get underneath her."

"No!" April cried. "Don't let go!"

"Shh, it's gonna be all right, darlin'. I'm gonna get underneath you, give you a big hug the whole way up. Would that make you feel better?"

"I g-g-guess so."

Using the cliff side for balance, Trace moved until he had the little girl encircled in his arms, his hands clamped on the rope just above the noose. April was warm, trembling so hard Trace could feel her fear inside him. The thought that he might have lost this little girl forever was the most terrifying thing he'd ever faced.

"Well, guys, the hard part is over," Trace assured them. "What do you think, Ape? Want to hang around for a while, or have you had enough of this spectacular view?"

"Think I'm a d-dummy? I want up."

"Put 'im in reverse, Mom!"

Trace heard the gelding snort, heard Annie's voice, murmuring words that would've scandalized the Ladies Aid at St. Mary's church. But after a moment, the rope jerked, swayed, the gelding dragging them up, up toward the cliff's beckoning edge.

Trace held them away from the rocky surface, bracing his feet, bouncing away, then landing several feet higher time and again. He cradled April against him, his heart still hammering wildly in his chest. His adrenaline had been pumping at warp speed. But this was a far different sensation from his usual highs. This was grinding, gritty, sanity-engulfing terror, the kind even a crazy man would never want to experience again.

"Hey, kid," Trace said, fearful April would go into shock, check-out if he didn't keep talking to her. "I bet you're gonna get one terrific cast on that arm of yours. Y'know, you can get them in all different colors now. Neon pink, green, purple. They even have some with team logos on 'em. Bet you could get one with the Sox—"

Trace broke off the sentence, his gaze fixed on the place where the rope was bent over a rock embedded in the cliff... a rock that was sharp-edged, sawing at the straining rope. Over half of the strands of rope twist had snapped, exposing the wheat-gold center.

"Annie! Top speed! Kick 'im in the butt!" Trace shouted. He felt the lurch, heard Annie bellowing at the horse, fighting with it, raw panic in her voice.

April was sobbing again, petrified.

Trace stared in horror as another strand snapped. His blood turned to ice in his veins.

The rope'll never hold you both, a voice warned inside him. *There's only one way April will have a chance....*

Trace McKenna hadn't given a damn about living until he'd found Annie again, looked into April's eyes.

Now, when everything he loved was in reach, he had to let it go.

"I love you, April. Don't ever forget it." He choked out the words. "Tell your mommy I love her, too."

"Trace?" April keened. "Trace, what—"

His sweat-slickened fingers loosened on the rope, released it.

The terrified shrieks of April and Annie were the last sound he heard before he slammed into the ground.

Chapter 14

Pain. Rasping against bones, screwing steely tentacles into every muscle, torturing ragged nerves until Trace felt like crying out if there had been anyone to hear him.

But there wasn't anyone. There never had been. Not for Trace McKenna.

For him there was only darkness. Relentless. Filled with the acrid stench of despair. It jeered at Trace, withdrawing for mere seconds like the curtain on some macabre stage to mock him with images as fantastical, as impossible, as any surrealistic painting every created.

Annie... as always, just beyond his reach. But not the sixteen-year-old, shy waif who had stolen Trace's heart when he'd been too awkward, too careless not to destroy her. Rather, it was an Annie who was strong, compassionate. A woman who didn't need him to shield her from the world. A woman as tough in her quiet way, and as fiercely independent as he was. A woman who held him, touched him, wrapped him in silken passion that exploded into diamond-bright flashes of ecstasy, joy such as Trace had never known.

And beyond the miracle that was Annie, the shadow child raced through waving grass. The baby that never existed except in the reaches of Trace's mind.

But she wasn't a baby this time. She was a little girl. Laughing, braids flying, arms reaching out... Most breathtakingly wondrous of all... reaching out to him.

Trace groaned at the beauty of it, trying to banish the poisonous demons that hacked at the dream, mercilessly driving blades of reality into what little reason Trace still clung to.

There was no child.

And Annie was gone.

For years he had felt the yawning hole inside him, the place his love for Annie had filled. Time and again, when pain had grown too fierce, night had grown too bleak, he had dredged memory upon memory from the deepest places hidden in his soul. Carnival lights and Ferris-wheel rides, first kisses that had made him shake and want and need so badly, he couldn't stop himself from touching, taking...

Why did the place Annie held inside him feel so much deeper, more ragged than ever before?

Why did Trace keep groping for something... someone he knew wasn't there.

So many times as he drifted in this half world, he wanted to let go. Wanted release. Death, if that was the only escape from the emptiness.

And this time, Trace was certain he only had to stretch out his fingers to the light, let the brilliant rays lead him away from heartache and guilt.

He should have run to embrace peace. He should have delighted in it. Exulted in it.

But to do that, he'd have to let go of the honey-curled angel with wide green eyes and a smile that was gentle, strong...a mouth that whispered deep where his heart could hear it.

I love you...I believe in you...Trace, don't leave me....

Annie, it hurts too much, he pleaded inside. *I can't have you. Can never have you...*

He dashed an arm that seemed weighted with lead over his burning eyes, and tried to stifle a moan of pain, hopelessness.

No matter what torment he had to face, he couldn't turn his back on this vision, this Annie. He couldn't leave her.

Damn. He wanted to rage, wanted to swear, wanted to rip his fingers like talons through the hazy images, drive them away. He wanted to gather the images like fireflies a child puts in a jar, to save forever. But he wasn't a boy anymore, with a boy's sense of wonder. Dreams, imprisoned, died like the bright glowing bugs, and the sense of wonder they inspired.

Dreams.

Annie.

Forever.

Trace groped for something to anchor himself. Anger. Bitterness. The sharp bite of betrayal. But those safe emotions were swept away, ripped out of his hands and replaced by the sensation of falling, plummeting into emptiness rocking through him time and again. An emptiness that wanted to suck him down into places as dark as a lost man's soul.

Something cool, damp, smoothed away the ugliness, something warm, gentle, untangled the snarls of panic and fear and hopelessness in his mind.

But he didn't want to be held back. He wanted it to be over. The pain. The loss. Over.

Trace struck out, his right hand smacking into something cool and tubular and metal.

A hospital bed rail. So familiar.

Trace let his hand sag to the mattress and stifled a choked sob that rose in his chest—rage at the emptiness. Rage at the cruel God who tormented him with those astonishing dreams. The God who would force him to waken, to confront a life without Annie. Without his child...

But they seemed so real...pigtails and baseballs, stuffed animals and long dark hair, a hairbrush sliding through it...

Voices...

So soft. Like angels.

"Trace? Trace come back to me. I need you. April needs you."

April...the month he'd loved her. Enchantment. Flowers opening, skies heavenly blue...and Annie...

The ring. He'd sold the gold watch his grandfather had given him. He'd sold his stereo, hell, anything he could get money for to buy Annie the ring that would make her his wife.

A diamond in his pocket. A ring to say things he couldn't get past the lump in his throat.

But she hadn't worn it. Never put it on...

Hot, wet tears ran from his closed eyelids, burning paths down his temples, to dampen the pillow. A tortured sound broke ragged from his throat.

"Annie...oh, God, Annie...."

Even imprisoned in his private hell, Trace felt it. The first touch, like butterflies' wings. Something small and warm and gentle closing over his groping fingers, cradling them.

Annie's touch.

God, hadn't he endured enough in these hellish dreams? Felt the loss of her again and again?

He closed his own fingers around that tormentingly beautiful touch, meaning to shove it away, force it to release him. But at that instant, his palm collided with something hard, something encircling one long, slender finger.

Metal warmed by silken skin, a stone—small as hell—feeling like polished glass against his palm.

A ring.

The reality drove into Trace with the force of a broadsword, lashing him into consciousness, making him fight with all that was in him to open his eyes.

It hurt as he peeled them open, lash by lash, his surroundings swinging in lazy circles.

Circles of honey-gold and green, a pale oval face, drawn with exhaustion.

"Annie?" He breathed her name with the awe of a penitent seeing the face of an angel. He felt something hot and wet splash his knuckles, felt his hand dragged up to be blessed with silky-moist lips, lips that were trembling with joy.

"Trace! Thank God!" Her voice, laughing, crying at the same time. She was trembling, so beautiful.

"Y-you're real," he whispered in astonishment, straining to lift his other hand, ghosting it over her dainty cheekbone, her silky hair. "I can't believe . . . you're real. Dreaming. Strangest dream . . . You were here, with me."

"It wasn't a dream. I haven't left your side for two weeks."

"Weeks? How . . . where . . . the blazes . . ."

"You're in the hospital in Denver. It seems you're a pretty steady customer here, Mr. McKenna. There's been a whole squadron of nurses coming to renew your acquaintance. I don't mind the woman with blue hair and a mustache, but that gorgeous redhead—"

"Annie . . . what happened?"

"You fell down the cliff. An emergency team airlifted you out."

The cliff.

Trace felt a jolt of blinding terror rocket through him, the scene at the cliff crashing into focus. April—his daughter, dangling above the cliff by a rope, the strands cut by the stone. He couldn't remember anything except her screams. Anguish welled inside him, and he forced himself to speak. "April...hurt. Please, God...tell me..."

"April is fine. You saved her life, Trace. But the cost to you...you could have been killed. When I saw the rope was frayed—"

"Did April tell you...what I said?"

"Yes. She..." Annie's cheeks were pink, her eyes misty, lips trembling. "She said that you wanted her to tell me that you...loved me."

"I do, you know. Never loved...anyone but you. Couldn't...stop...no matter how far...I ran...where I tried to...hide."

Trace pushed against the mattress, trying to lever himself to a sitting position. Annie helped him, looping an arm around his back, cradling him against her.

"You risked so much for April and me. You saved April's life. And mine."

"Y-yours?"

"I'd cut myself off, wrapped myself in responsibilities, work, obligations. You made me stop, realize how much I wanted someone to laugh with, to watch April grow with. You made me face the fact that I'd never stopped loving you."

He reached a trembling hand to her face, gathering the precious dampness of her tears. "Don't cry...Brown-Eyes."

"I can't help it. When I think of all the years we lost...April lost. Nine years, Trace. I can never give them back to either of you."

In spite of the pain, the dizziness, Trace caught her face between his hands, cupping it with tender worship.

"You want the truth, Annie? I wanted...to think I could...take care of you. Would have tried with every-thing...in me. But you...were right. Truth is, I was... seventeen-year-old kid who wanted to fly...Hardest thing of all...to admit was that I wasn't ready to be...husband to you, father to April. I would've found a way to blow it. Like I blew pitching. School."

She stroked his hair back from his forehead. "I didn't want to run away from you. I wanted to stay. I loved you so much, Trace. But I wouldn't change anything. Because if I hadn't felt all that pain, I wouldn't know how miracu-lous this joy is."

"Mommy?" The voice at the door was tentative, soft. "Mommy, you still talking to—"

"Come in, sweetheart. Trace, there's someone who wants to see you."

Trace hadn't believed he could endure one more drop of happiness, had believed he'd touched the pinnacle few mortals ever reach. But as he turned to see the little girl framed in the doorway, his heart burst, washing away the last remnants of bitterness.

She was real. His child. There were no words to describe what he felt in that single moment. He said nothing, just devoured her with his eyes like a starving man. She was wearing his old dive-shop shirt. A cast with the Sox logo adorned her left arm. She looked so uncertain, standing there. So shy. Indescribably beautiful as she scuffed the toe of her worn sneaker against the hospital tiles.

"April." Her name. Whisper-soft.

"You're—you're sitting up," the little girl said. "We were real scared. Even Grandpa was when the helicopter came and got you. The doctor said you would die, but I told him . . . I told him I just found you. That you promised you'd teach me to throw a knuckleball and that we could be . . . a family." Her small fingers toyed with the Pegasus that dangled from a mended chain around her throat. "But maybe you don't want me anymore since I was bad an' ran away, an' you almost got . . . dead." Two huge tears welled in her eyes.

"April . . . I want you. Forever."

"For keeps, Tra—I mean, Daddy?"

Daddy.

Trace savored the beautiful weight of that word. Wrapped it up in dream mist and tucked it away in his heart. The first time April had called him by that name . . .

Trace smiled, and didn't give a damn that it made a tender spot on one cheek ache. He patted the bed beside him. The little girl ran over, climbing on the bed like a little monkey.

"I'm going to tell you a story," Trace began, cuddling April close, Annie pressed against his other side. "About a very bad boy and a very good girl who lost each other until an angel in pigtails brought them back together. The boy and girl met in springtime, the most beautiful spring you can ever imagine. The very bad boy walked into the library. There, at the table, was a girl so beautiful he couldn't believe his eyes—"

He looked at Annie, her face soft, smiling, tears welling on her lashes. "He didn't know it, but in that very instant, the bad boy fell in love—"

"So did the very good girl," Annie said, smiling through her tears.

The bleak winter of Trace McKenna's existence was over. The promise of that long-ago springtime had blossomed into a love more beautiful than anything he'd ever known.

*   *   *   *   *

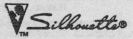

Take 4 bestselling love stories FREE

Plus get a FREE surprise gift!

SILHOUETTE® *Desire®*

They're sexy, they're determined, they're trouble with a capital *T!*

Meet six of the steamiest, most stubborn heroes you'd ever want to know, and learn *everything* about them....

August's *Man of the Month*, Quinn Donovan, in
FUSION by Cait London

Mr. Bad Timing, Dan Kingman, in
DREAMS AND SCHEMES by Merline Lovelace

Mr. Marriage-phobic, Connor Devlin, in
WHAT ARE FRIENDS FOR? by Naomi Horton

Mr. Sensible, Lucas McCall, in **HOT PROPERTY**
by Rita Rainville

Mr. Know-it-all, Thomas Kane, in **NIGHTFIRE**
by Barbara McCauley

Mr. Macho, Jake Powers, in **LOVE POWER**
by Susan Carroll

Look for them on the covers so you can see just how handsome and irresistible they are!

Coming in August only from Silhouette Desire!

HE'S AN

AMERICAN HERO

Men of mettle. Men of integrity. Real men who know the real meaning of love. Each month, Intimate Moments salutes these true American Heroes.

For July: THAT SAME OLD FEELING,
by Judith Duncan.
Chase McCall had come home a new man. Yet old lover Devon Manyfeathers soon stirred familiar feelings—and renewed desire.

For August: MICHAEL'S GIFT,
by Marilyn Pappano.
Michael Bennett knew his visions prophesied certain death. Yet he would move the high heavens to change beautiful Valery Navarre's fate.

For September: DEFENDER,
by Kathleen Eagle.
Gideon Defender had reformed his bad-boy ways to become a leader among his people. Yet one habit—loving Raina McKenny—had never died, especially after Gideon learned she'd returned home.

AMERICAN HEROES: Men who give all they've got for their country, their work—the women they love.

Only from

INTIMATE MOMENTS®
Silhouette®

IMHER09